PENGUIN BOOKS

MY AMERICAN SISTER

Born and raised in Singapore, Judy's love for reading and writing began as a child when she was introduced to children's storybooks written by authors such as Enid Blyton. During moments of inspiration, she would hunker down in a corner of her living room, writing stories of children going off on an adventure while the rest of the family members watched television. The decision to dedicate her time to writing came during her university years. After graduating from the National University of Singapore, she started writing for magazines while exploring other career opportunities. In 2017, she co-authored a book on branding titled *Are You Brand Dead?*. She currently lives in Singapore, where she also lectures at local tertiary institutions. *My American Sister* is her debut novel.

My American Sister

Judy Tham

PENGUIN BOOKS

An imprint of Penguin Random House

PENGUIN BOOKS

USA | Canada | UK | Ireland | Australia
New Zealand | India | South Africa | China | Southeast Asia

Penguin Books is part of the Penguin Random House group of companies
whose addresses can be found at global.penguinrandomhouse.com

Published by Penguin Random House SEA Pte Ltd
9, Changi South Street 3, Level 08-01,
Singapore 486361

Penguin
Random House
SEA

First published in Penguin Books by Penguin Random House SEA 2022

Copyright © Judy Tham 2022

All rights reserved

10 9 8 7 6 5 4 3 2 1

ISBN 9789815017953

Typeset in Garamond by MAP Systems, Bangalore, India

www.penguin.sg

Contents

Contents

Chapter 1

YAN

It was happening too fast, and sooner than Yan had expected.

The police arrived just when she caught a glimpse of her younger sister, Ying, through the apartment window. For the first time, it was Ying—not Yan—who lurked in the shadow, hiding in the dilapidated building's fire exit stairway landing. Even through the grimy and broken glass pane, Yan could see her clearly, confounded and distressed like a lost kitten, unaware of being watched. Her perfect face was stained with guilty tears, and her swollen eyes fixated on the fire exit window, watching the swirling lights of police cars as they screeched to a halt. Charlie stood supportively behind Ying, embracing her in his warm, tender arms and whispering comforting words into her frosty ears.

The high-pitched sirens, crackling feedback from the walkie-talkies, and shouting of homeland security officers drifted in. Yan turned around and found her father cowering under the bed like a beaten-up schoolboy, his face drained of blood and life. His small, bony body looked skinnier than ever. His large, ape-like hands clasped together, praying like a man beset with madness.

'Tell them to go away. I don't want to go back to China . . . please . . . ' he whimpered, barely audibly.

1

Yan had seen her father in many, many pathetic states, but she had never taken pity on him. Until now.

The stomping on the creaking wooden stairs came to a halt. Then the terrifying, persistent banging on the door began.

'This is the police. OPEN THE DOOR RIGHT NOW!'

They had not the nerve to even breathe. Silence ensued for a moment before the policemen pounded on the door again, only this time, harder and more intimidating than the first.

'Sir, I need you to open this door IMMEDIATELY, or we'll break in!'

Yan was as frightened as her father, too terrified to answer the door even if she had wanted to. Though she was crying as hard as Ying, there was no consoling arm or soothing words to calm her.

Because she was alone, with her father.

She sat under the window, leant her back against the bare wall, and stared at the dirty floor littered with a chaotic mess of empty cartons of Chinese takeaways, cheap beer bottles, cigarette butts, and discarded wrappers while the hammering on the door continued.

Ultra-fine with extra lube for heightened sensitivity boasted a slogan on a wrapper. It was the condom she had bought for her father just last week. Yan was disgusted, not by the ripped condom wrapper, but by the filthiness of their rented apartment.

Why didn't I clean up the place? What would the police think of us? That was the only thought Yan had.

A whiff of pungent, ammoniac odour jolted her back to reality. She turned and looked at her father to confirm her suspicion. Indeed, he had peed his pants.

The pounding on the door, the racket outside the apartment and the nasty stink of her father's fresh pee made her nauseated, and she badly wanted to puke. Crouching in his pool of urine, Yan's father pleaded with her for help again. She ignored him and went back to staring at the floor, waiting for the imminent arrest.

It was too late. There was nothing she could do. Besides, she wanted it all to end. She was done with America.

* * *

'What's taking so long?' the officer-in-charge asked testily. 'These are just illegal immigrants, not terrorists, right? So what's the problem? Do you need me to tell you how to nab illegal immigrants?'

'No, Sir. Permission to break in, Sir?' one of the guys barked.

'Who're you waiting for? The Pope? Do it now!'

Before Yan could see it coming, the apartment's flimsy, lousy excuse for a door was smashed like origami in a single attempt. A towering African-American officer with arms like Arnold Schwarzenegger bawled commands incomprehensible to Yan and waved his colleagues in. More shouting, cries, and cursing, followed by a dozen officers flooding into the small apartment. The fretful neighbours, mostly Chinese and Vietnamese cooks and waiters working in San Francisco's Chinatown, legally or otherwise, peeked through peepholes and tiny cracks of their doors, thanking their gods under their breath that it wasn't happening to them, at least not this time.

Yan was dragged on to her feet and handcuffed by Black Arnie as he scanned the room.

'Damn! Look at the condition these people live in! I wouldn't even let my dog live here,' he said.

These people. Right.

'Oh, man! This guy's sitting in his urine. It's disgusting, man! Who are these people?' another officer said.

These people . . .

'This shithole stinks! C'mon, speed things up and let's get the hell outta here,' the officer-in-charge wrinkled his nose.

He looked at Yan's father and spoke directly to him for the first time. 'Sir, we have reasons to suspect that you have overstayed in the United States of America. May I see your travel document?'

Yan's father refused to acknowledge the officer. He remained crouching under the bed, spitting at anyone who approached him. Not that the officers were keen to get him out, for his soiled trousers reeked so terribly that no one had attempted to arrest him.

The chief tried again, this time with Yan.

'Ma'am, can you speak English? May I see your passport?'

No answer from her either. She could understand him well enough, but she knew better than to acknowledge that.

'Found the passports in the drawer, Sir,' said an officer who had been searching the apartment. 'The visas have expired.'

'Okay guys, wrap it up. Take them back to the station. And look for an interpreter, pronto!'

Yan stole another glance at Ying as she was escorted out, handcuffed. Ying was still in the dark stairway landing. She was sobbing, seemingly inconsolable, even though she had her beautiful boyfriend by her side. Yan felt nothing but hatred for her sister, but she was glad Ying had made the call. It was the only way to make a clean break. It was the only way they could be free.

Stepping out of the building into one of Chinatown's foulest back alleys, Yan's father, frightened but indignant, began yelling the few broken English phrases he knew. 'I'm Li Fu. I famous father—found—lost—daughter—in America. My daughter American. My daughter Faye Williams!'

An officer looked at him for a long time, and finally recognizing him, exclaimed, 'Hey, I know you! I've seen you on TV . . . the news. You're the guy who searched for his daughter for . . . for what? Seventeen, eighteen years? Didn't you find her a year ago? Where is she? Want me to call her for you?'

Li couldn't understand him, but since he was the only person who was willing to listen, he desperately repeated his broken phrases. The officer tried again, this time slowly and deliberately as if Li would miraculously comprehend the content if he slowed down. 'Where is your daughter? Do you want me to call your daughter?'

The officer's attempt was futile, and he soon lost interest in his altruistic endeavour. He shrugged and shoved Li and Yan into a police car.

Pondering, he asked the chief, 'Hey boss, how did we find them?'

'Tip-off.'

'Who called?'

'Dunno. Some girl. Left the address and hung up.'

'Yeah? Maybe it was his American daughter who got tired of her old man,' the officer made a feeble joke.

* * *

How could she forget something so momentous, so defining, even though it occurred seventeen years ago, even though she was only four.

Yan was home with her mother Mei, who had just given birth to her second daughter. Mei was nursing the baby while preparing dinner simultaneously. According to the Chinese customs, she was still within the month of *zuo yue zi*, literally 'resting through the first month of child birthing'. During this period of convalescence, the mother is supposed to stay indoors to recover from the intense physical act of childbirth. She is not expected to do any housework, including cooking. Outside help, in the form of a hired hand, or more often, her mother or mother-in-law, is usually sought to help with the baby and the housework.

For Yan's parents, hired help was a luxury beyond their imagination. And Yan's grandmother, who was slaving away on a family farm in the impoverished province of Gansu, would have neither the time nor the means to travel to Beijing to look after her daughter. So Mei could only rely on the generosity of a neighbour, Mrs Zhou, who would occasionally prepare a meal or two for them and help with the groceries. Mrs Zhou, a superstitious woman in her sixties and an experienced midwife of forty years, had delivered Mei's baby. She was a disapproving and reluctant help, who believed that her good deeds would contribute to her 'karma bank' and hence, a better next life. Consequently, she often exaggerated her 'charitable' acts to Yan's family or anyone else who cared to listen.

Yan's father didn't like Mrs Zhou. He often complained about her condescending attitude towards his family and hinted that the only reason she bothered to come around at all was to show off her wealth. Mei suffered his complaints in silence. She didn't like being looked down upon either, but it was better than having no help at all.

Mei had given birth at home. For women like her, having a baby in a public hospital was simply out of the question. While maternal healthcare was available to all local women in Beijing with approved pregnancies at minimal or no cost, unapproved births were a different matter altogether.

Yes, there was such a thing as an unapproved birth.

Yan's parents didn't want a second child. They barely made enough for a family of three, and couldn't possibly bear the cost of obstetric care and the substantial penalty that would be imposed on them for flouting the One-Child Policy. It was the result of a stupid, drunken night of unprotected sex. Li, a farmer with no relevant skills for city jobs, had been frustrated with his constant state of unemployment and the difficulty in making ends meet since moving to the capital. So, he had turned to the bottle for solace, spinning the vicious cycle of depression, more frustration, and financial instability. One night, drunk as a skunk, he had forced himself upon his wife without a condom before she was fully awake. It was his way of reassuring himself that he was still the man of the family.

One small ego of a man, one giant mistake for the family.

Li had named his two daughters after birds, for no reason other than it being a widespread practice at that time. It was the swallow for Yan, and the eagle, Ying, for the baby girl. Ying is not exactly a girl's name but Li had wanted a boy so badly that when Mei was pregnant, he had picked a boy's name, hoping that it would usher a name bearer for the family. When a girl instead of a boy was born, he couldn't think of another name, so Ying it was.

Despite the initial disappointment, Li had fallen in love with the baby and felt that a positive transformation of his life had begun upon her arrival. This was something he hadn't expected or experienced with Yan—this natural bond, this special love. He had heard from older people with multiple children that they loved them all equally. That was bullshit. Li had a child whom he loved more than the other. It couldn't be helped even if he tried. For Yan, it was a father's obligation. For Ying, it was unconditional love.

The fact that Li's financial condition improved right after Ying was born cemented his beliefs further. Ying had brought him luck, and that had helped him secure a job as a construction worker.

'She'll bring wealth to the family. I can feel it. You'll see, things will be different from now on,' he had proudly prophesied.

With a newborn, a four-year-old, and hardly any help, Mei was exhausted and sleep-deprived on that particular day. She longed to catch a wink but her husband would be home from work soon, and he wouldn't be happy to see her lying down. The baby had fallen asleep after being breastfed, so Mei put her down on the only bed in their one-bedroom apartment and swaddled her in a thick, worn blanket, another donation from Mrs Zhou. The apartment had no heating facility, and Mei noticed that Ying had a running nose. Pneumonia was common in those days, and if you had no money, there was no cure. She wiped away the mucus on the baby's upper lips before pausing to admire the cherubic face of her child.

Unlike Yan, who had Li's northern Chinese features of a flat forehead and narrow lips, Ying looked nothing like her parents. When Mei had first set eyes on her, she couldn't believe she could produce such a beautiful child. Contrary to the meaning of her name, which is 'beautiful' in Chinese, Mei was neither pretty nor attractive. She had typical Chinese features—a flat face, flat nose, square jaw, and small slanted eyes. But unlike most Chinese, Mei had a dark and coarse complexion, a big turn-off for a race that covets fair, delicate skin. Dark and coarse skin belonged to peasants, farmers, and hard labourers. In other words, the lower class, the undesirables, the unwanted. At twenty-four, Mei already looked much older than her age, owing to the hard life she had led so far. Her acquaintances addressed her as *da sao*, or aunty, a respectful term reserved for middle-aged women. Ying, on the other hand, had fair, luminous skin, striking features, and large, dark, soulful eyes. She looked like a high-born rather than the daughter of boorish peasants. Mei had prayed that with Ying's beauty, her daughter could one day land herself a rich husband who could provide her with a good life.

Not that Mei had ever known one—a good life. As the firstborn of a large family of farmers in rural China, the only memories of her childhood were that of constant hunger and gruelling labour in the fields. During drought years, starvation could last for months, sometimes even years. She didn't know what meat tasted like until the age of seven, when a young fellow who had returned to his ancestral home from the city, boasting of the great fortunes he had made there, had given her a piece of beef jerky. It was dry, cold and old, and smelt of gasoline from the beat-up truck he had driven in. It was also the most heavenly food Mei had ever tasted. At the age of seventeen, she was sold as a bride to Li Fu because her family could no longer afford to keep her. She thought she might fare better as a young bride. But any tiny hope of a better future with Li was crushed on their wedding night when her brand new husband lumbered into their bedroom—one of the two rooms in her in-laws' mud-brick farmhouse—after a raucous wedding dinner and without looking at her face, fumbled clumsily for her pants, ripped her panties apart and thrust his hardened penis into her dry, unprepared vagina. It was shattered further into a thousand shards when she was given a sickle and shown to her husband's field the next day.

Mei returned to the kitchen, scooped three bowls of rice, and placed them on the dining table, the only table in the sparsely furnished living room. Earlier that day, Mrs Zhou had left them with some vegetables and fish, sodden and heavily seasoned with soya sauce to mask the slightly rancid smell. They were leftovers from the restaurant where her son worked as a dishwasher and as good a meal as they could hope for. Just when dinner was set, Li stepped through the door.

'Papa!' Yan squealed.

She had been daddy's girl right till Ying was born, and even though his attention had somewhat shifted to the new baby, she hadn't noticed. She dashed towards him and hugged both his legs, squeezing them so hard he couldn't move.

'Papa, Papa, guess what? Ying threw up all over herself today. Eeeewwww!'

Li patted her head absent-mindedly and frowned, his eyes already pointed to the bed.

'Is something wrong with Ying?' he asked Mei, concerned.

'She's fine. She drank a little too quickly, that's all,' she replied. 'Dinner's ready.'

Li grunted and approached the bed, on which his beautiful baby slept. As he looked lovingly at Ying, his tired, sun-beaten face lit up. A smile manifested miraculously, and at once he seemed gentle and benevolent in his worn, ill-fitting clothes. He couldn't resist the urge to hold her, and so he picked her up, startling her from a deep slumber and making her scream in protest.

'You shouldn't have done that . . . she'll get very cranky later,' Mei grumbled timidly.

Li ignored her and cradled Ying gently. She quieted down shortly and settled comfortably in his arms, sucking her thumb as he cuddled her with an ancient lullaby.

Mei averted her cheerless face and went back into the kitchen. It wasn't customary for a woman to show her emotions to her husband, especially if it was a jealous type of love. Mei didn't like Li's over-attentiveness towards the baby; she thought it was a little too obsessive. She would rather he spent more time with Yan, perhaps tutoring her a little since they couldn't afford to send her to a kindergarten. Undeniably, Ying held a special place in her husband's heart. When they were together, they were in a world of their own, a world without others, and they seemed perfectly happy.

Yan stood next to her father, holding on to the hem of his coat, waiting patiently for him to turn around so that she could tell him what she had for lunch and the cartoon she had watched on their neighbour's TV.

'Food's getting cold,' Mei murmured, this time with a tinge of annoyance in her voice.

Li looked cross. Vexed at her impudent behaviour, he deliberately avoided eye contact with his wife and continued singing softly to the baby. Without a word, Mei sat down and started dinner alone, a silent act of defiance. Yan was hungry and longed to join her mother, but she wanted more to tell her father about her day.

As the little family drama played out in the tiny apartment, a brazen knock on the door startled everyone. With hardly any friends in the city, they seldom, if ever, had company. Relatives had also stopped visiting, as previous encounters had inevitably ended with loans that would never be repaid. Puzzled by the evening intrusion, Li and Mei finally looked at each other.

'It could be Mrs Zhou. She must've forgotten something,' Mei offered as she put down her bowl of rice and chopsticks and got up to open the door.

But it wasn't Mrs Zhou. Standing outside the apartment were two men dressed in thick grey coats, each carrying a black hard-shell briefcase. They looked like important people on official business, but with eyes that were cold and hard and no longer penetrable. They walked right into the apartment without being invited.

'Mr and Mrs Li?' the older, pudgy man with a military crew cut and black-rimmed turtle-shell spectacles demanded curtly as he pushed their meagre dinner aside, planted his briefcase on the table, and snapped open the metal push clasp.

'Yes, I'm Li Fu,' Li answered apprehensively, with Ying still in his arms. 'To what do I owe this honour?'

'And you're Mei? Good, this is not a wasted trip then,' continued the man without replying to Li.

'Who are you?' Li asked again, this time a little more aggressively. He hated being ignored. He felt disrespected when people ignored him.

'We're from the Family Planning Bureau. We understand you just had a second daughter without proper authorization from the Party.'

'You're mistaken, Sir . . . this is not our baby. We're just helping a friend to take care of her daughter—' Mei lied.

'Don't take us for fools, Mrs Li. We know everything. We've been keeping track of your family for months.'

'We . . . we don't know anything about policies or the laws here. We're farmers from Gansu—'

'Shut up, Mei! Let the gentleman speak!' Li snapped at her.

'Under the One-Child Policy, your second child is considered an unapproved birth, and thus, you've committed an unlawful act. The central government is imposing a penalty on your family,' the man recited the document he had retrieved from his briefcase monotonously and handed it to Li when he had finished.

Li took the papers from the man and started reading. Barely educated, it took him some time to get through the entire document.

Once he had fully understood the content, he looked up in despair and exclaimed, 'Impossible! The penalty is five times my annual income. A friend of mine only paid a quarter of this sum!'

'Also, your second daughter can't be registered officially here in Beijing as a resident, and she's not entitled to the State's healthcare and education system,' he continued impassively without acknowledging Li's protestation. 'Please pay your fine promptly.'

He shut the briefcase with a bang, swung it by his heel, and headed for the door once again. The other official, who hadn't spoken a word since entering the apartment, reached for the doorknob.

Li looked as if he had been stabbed with a knife. He knew they had to bear the consequence of not aborting the second child. They had hoped for a boy . . . but at this price?

'Sir, wait a minute. Look at us, look at this place. Do you think we have that kind of money? Besides, it's unfair to impose such a heavy penalty for a small offence like this. I can't afford to pay a single cent!' Li said as his terror began to turn into indignation.

'Sorry, comrade. It's the law,' the man said with strained politeness.

'Well, the law just has to put me away then!'

The man looked with undisguised contempt at Li, and then at Mei. His eyes remained cold and authoritative as his lips curled up into a smile.

'You know, I've seen so many of your kind of people—stupid, ignorant cattle from the countryside who have no idea who and what they're dealing with. You think you're a hero, eh? Let me give you a piece of advice—don't be one. Pay the fine, or you'll be sorry!'

'You've no right to speak to me like that in my home! Get out!' Li flew into a rage before Mei could stop him. Li wasn't a man who could control his temper well, especially when provoked. Mei had told him his anger would get them into trouble someday. This was the day.

'We're very sorry, Sir,' Mei quickly intervened. 'Please pardon my husband. Sometimes, he doesn't know what he's talking about. I apologize on his behalf. I beg you to reconsider our case because he only managed to get a job at the construction site a few days ago—'

'Don't you dare apologize on my behalf!' Li's face turned crimson.

'It's no problem, Mrs Li. But I do suggest that your husband thinks before he opens his mouth in the future. I'm not easily offended, but if another Central Community Party official were to be here today, it could be a different matter altogether,' said the man sarcastically. The angrier Li was, the politer the party official was determined to be.

'Since you've broken the law, you'll have to pay for your mistake. There're no two ways about it,' he added.

'What're you going to do if I don't? Beat me up? Throw me in jail? Come and get me. I'm not afraid,' Li said as he spat at them. The moment his saliva hit the party official, Li's bridge was burnt forever. There was no turning back.

The man took a piece of clothing from Li's pile of clean laundry placed near the front door and wiped away the spit that had landed on his shoe. His lips, however, remained upturned.

'All right, then. You asked for it, Li. I'll make sure you regret this for the rest of your life. By the time I'm done with you, you will wish you were dead!' The officer spoke through his teeth, eyes gleaming like scalpels. Without another word, he stomped out of the apartment with his colleague following closely behind. Li slammed the door behind him.

The moment the men were gone, Mei began to cry. She knew her husband disliked Communist Party officials and often criticized them for their corrupted ways, but he had gone too far this time. No one had ever spoken to the Communist Party officials this way and got away with it, at least not ordinary, penniless folks like them. She felt trouble was heading their way.

'Why do you have to react like that?' she sobbed. 'We can't offend these people. You don't know what they'll do to us.'

'What do you want me to say to those bloodsucking swines?' he yelled. The baby, who had been undisturbed by the racket, now woke up with a jolt and started to cry.

'Sometimes you just have to suck up to them a little, whether you like to or not. You have a wife, two daughters, and no money. You can't afford to behave the way you did! Why can't you spare a thought for your family for once? Why can't you control that terrible temper of yours?'

Mei had every reason to be worried about the situation, and while Li was already regretting his outburst, he was too proud to admit his mistake. 'It doesn't make any difference. I don't have the money to pay them off anyway. They'll come after us either way,' he mumbled as he tried to soothe the baby back to sleep.

Yan started to cry too because everyone was upset and that made her upset. But her parents were too preoccupied with their own thoughts to comfort her.

* * *

It was a few days after the visit by the Family Planning Bureau officials that the actual abduction happened.

Li Fu was at work at a construction site. The workers were taking their morning break, and Li was boasting to his colleagues about what had happened the other night.

'Those dirty scoundrels who called themselves party officials dared to pay me a visit and ask for money,' he scoffed as he described the incident, exaggerating his boldness and making the visitors sound like cowards to the point of absurdity.

The workers laughed. Some even praised Li for standing up for his family.

'I'd be more careful if I were you,' a middle-aged worker, who had been listening quietly to Li's story, cautioned. 'I've heard that these people hire underground syndicates to do dirty jobs for them. They're unscrupulous, and they'll do anything to people like us for money.'

'What dirty jobs?' asked Li.

'There's a rumour going around that they take children away from couples that can't afford the second-child penalty and sell them to orphanages.'

'Nah . . . that's ludicrous!' Li replied.

'Believe the story, don't believe the story, it's up to you, but they're up there, we're down here. If anything happens, what can people like us do?'

Just when Li decided to dismiss the rumour, he heard someone call for him.

'Li, there's a phone call for you. Go to the office and look for our supervisor,' Old Chow, another fellow worker, yelled over the din of the men's chatters and pointed at the temporary office.

Li gazed towards where Old Chow stood and held up his right thumb. He got up and walked towards the office. Puzzled by the phone call—no one had ever called him at work before—he picked up his pace.

The 'office' was essentially a couple of shipping containers converted into a makeshift office parked at the entrance of the construction site. No worker was allowed to enter it unless the supervisor had explicitly asked for him. Li had only been inside once when he was being interviewed for this job. As far as he remembered, worn-out desks, dusty files, architectural plans, building material samples, spare safety helmets, and equipment cluttered the tiny, unpleasant space. The floor was littered with cigarette butts, and the air was thick with stale cigarette smoke and male body odour.

Li knocked on the door before entering. A grim, disgruntled supervisor in a grimy navy-blue parka, propping a hand-rolled cigarette between his fingers, beckoned Li with his other hand without bothering to look up.

'It's your wife. I'll make an exception this time but tell her not to call here any more. This line is meant for business and emergency only, do you understand?' The supervisor berated him with great annoyance. The old man enjoyed his solitary morning tea break in the office, away from the sweaty, smelly workers and the dust and noise of construction, and he did not appreciate this unwelcomed intrusion in his momentary tranquillity by a lowly hire.

Li nodded with obeisance.

The supervisor handed the handset to Li grudgingly and walked out to enjoy the rest of his cigarette but kept the door ajar to eavesdrop on the phone conversation.

There was no such thing as privacy. Not on this site; not in this country.

Placing the handset to his ear, Li whispered sternly, 'Don't ever call me here again, do you understand? I could lose my job.'

Instead of the apology he had expected from his wife, the reply he heard over the other end of the line was one of genuine fear and hysteria.

'The baby's gone! Can you hear me? THE BABY IS GONE!' Mei screamed maniacally.

'WHAT? Ying's gone? What do you mean gone?' Li felt the blood draining out of his face as those unfathomable words started to form meaning.

'Three men . . . it wasn't my fault . . . I tried to fight back . . .' Mei wailed incoherently over the line.

'Mei . . . Mei . . . listen MEI! Tell me what happened!'

'Three men barged into the apartment about ten minutes ago and took Ying away. They snatched her right from my arms . . . Oh God, help me, please!' Mei howled at last.

Li's heart turned to stone and a cold sweat broke out on his pallid face. His fingers gripped the handset so hard that his knuckles turned white.

'Did they say who they were?' Li asked, trying to sound more self-possessed but dreading the answer. Deep down, he already knew who they were.

'I . . . I don't know . . . They didn't say anything. I think they work for the Family Planning Bureau. But they didn't look like party cadres . . . They were nasty people . . . like . . . like hooligans. They said they were punishing us for having too many kids and for being disobedient.'

'HOW COULD THEY DO THIS? How could they take our baby away?' He pounded his fist repeatedly on the desk, which immediately attracted the supervisor's resentful glare through the window.

'They also said since we didn't have the money, we don't have to bother paying the penalty. They'd take the baby instead . . . Oh my God . . . Fu, what should we do? I don't know what to do. I don't know where they went. They grabbed the baby, got into a car, and left! I want my baby back! Please get my baby back!' Mei could not go on, for she was choking with tears and wailing uncontrollably over the line. He seemed to have lost her in her grief.

Tears that Li didn't know he still possessed formed a mist in his eyes and rolled carelessly down his cheeks. He couldn't offer solace to his wife, for his grief overwhelmed his entire being, so much so that he looked as though he had turned into a rock.

'What about Yan? Where is she?' he finally asked.

'She's here. She's right here with me.'

'Stay where you are. I'm coming home right now,' he said. 'Don't worry, I'll do anything, anything to get my girl back.'

Chapter 2

SOPHIA

'Isn't this scarf lovely?' Julie Davis asked. 'Sophia? SOPHIA WILLIAMS! Snap out of your daydreaming, please!'

'What? Yes, yes, it's very pretty, like the fifty other scarves you'd so admired since we came here. Haven't you bought enough scarves already? How many do you need, really?' Sophia, whose mind had wandered several times since she'd entered the weekend market, reprimanded her friend. She couldn't help it. She was bored out of her wits in the overcrowded market and couldn't wait to get out. Unlike her best friend Julie, a compulsive shopaholic, Sophia wasn't into buying stuff made for tourists. The trinkets sold in every stall looked the same after a while—Chinese handicrafts, silk scarves (or so the shopkeepers claimed), silk dresses, bags, T-shirts, etc. And the haggling! It drove Sophia crazy that prices weren't fixed in these Chinese markets: everything needed to be bargained for. Hard. She felt like a fish out of water, but looking at her friend, her only real friend whom she loved dearly, she knew that Julie was having the time of her life.

'Hey, we're here to enjoy ourselves, right? Well, this is how I enjoy myself! You know, sometimes I really don't get you. I think you're probably the only woman I know who doesn't like to shop,' said Julie, as she paid for the overpriced scarf, the ninth she had purchased on this trip.

'Let's just go. We're due to meet the lady from the adoption centre soon. I don't want to be late,' Sophia urged.

'That's like not for another three hours! And we just got here! This is my only chance to do some last-minute shopping before we go home, and trust me, I'm not even half done. Listen, why don't you go back to the hotel first to get ready? I'll meet you in the lobby at one o'clock. Okay, honey?'

'What about lunch?'

'No need for lunch for me! Can't you tell that I'm already in heaven? Shopping, alone, with no kids bugging me all the time. This is all the therapy I need! I tell you what, order some room service for yourself. It's on me!' With that, Julia hurried away, already distracted by the merchandise in the next shop.

Lunch alone. It wasn't the first time for Sophia, but it'd be her last.

She turned and headed back to the hotel, eager to leave the throng behind. She knew she couldn't save Julie, who was obsessed with the idea that everything was cheap in China, and so it would be a sin not to overspend. But at least Sophia could get herself out. She was glad that they were returning to San Francisco soon. She couldn't wait to start her new life, with a baby she could call her own.

It was the last day of Sophia and Julie's trip to Beijing. And Sophia was here for a very specific purpose—to pick up her new baby girl.

She had never been happier. She had waited for this for such a long time she thought the day would never come. Being so close to becoming a mother, Sophia felt she couldn't bear it any longer.

She had seen the baby yesterday while she and Julie visited the orphanage, and the little darling was perfect.

Less than three months old, the girl was a tiny, fragile creature and the loveliest thing Sophia had ever laid eyes on. She took her breath away immediately, and she couldn't peel her eyes off her angelic face. Her heart overflowed with so much love, a special kind of love that she hadn't experienced before.

Is this what they called a mother's love?

Several adoptive parents and orphanage employees had huddled around Sophia to look at the baby, brought out for the first time to meet her parent-to-be. Donned in a pink frock with a ribbon around her hair, the orphanage had spared no effort in ensuring the baby's gender was unambiguous. While it was too soon to tell how she would eventually turn out, several distinctive features had already formed— skin smooth and fair as alabaster; a tiny button nose; big, round eyes; and thick, jet-black hair. The baby was sleeping soundly, adorable and irresistible as a kitten, oblivious to the pandemonium and the admirers around her. A few loud gasps could be heard from the crowd that had gathered, followed by delightful heaves of 'oh . . . soooo cute!'

'Congratulations, Williams! What a beautiful baby!'

'You're so lucky! I know of many adopters on the waiting list who would trade their fortune for this moment.'

'This one's a keeper. She's definitely going to change your life! I had my first daughter three years ago. I couldn't keep my eyes off her for the first two months.'

'The baby is lucky to have a mother like you. Look at you, so completely mesmerized by her!'

'Don't worry, you'll do just fine! I've seen so many adopters come and go. I can tell who makes a good mom.'

'God bless your good heart for adopting unwanted girls like her. If it weren't for you, she might have to stay in the orphanage here in China for the rest of her life. And who knows how she would've turned out.'

'What're you waiting for, *mommy*? Go ahead and pick your daughter up!'

The baby cried and peed when Sophia held her in her arms, but according to the supervisor of the orphanage, it was a good thing.

'It's an auspicious sign, Mrs . . . err . . . Miss Williams. According to our Chinese beliefs, it means that she's pouring you a cup of "tea",' the supervisor cackled. 'She's going to be a filial child.'

Filial or otherwise, just by holding the infant in her arms, Sophia was convinced that this little darling would be someone she'd love for the rest of her life. She gently placed the baby on her chest and swayed her body rhythmically to calm it.

Like an expert.

Like a mother.

She had never had a child before, and already, Sophia seemed to know exactly what to do. Another rush of love and blissfulness overwhelmed her heart. She kissed her soon-to-be daughter on her forehead, and a waft of sweet, biscuit-like baby scent hit her, making her heart skip a beat.

'Do you know anything about her background? Are her parents still alive?' Sophia had asked the supervisor-in-charge, the one responsible for showing the babies to the adoptive parents visiting the orphanage. It was a cold, sterile stone cottage consisting of square, functional rooms, a large dining hall, and a small courtyard with two wilting trees— but in Sophia's view, not the kind of warm, loving place a child should grow up in. She was sure she was doing the right thing by putting the baby in a more nurturing environment like San Francisco, where there were plenty of parks and schools.

'The girls were all abandoned, either left on the doorstep of our orphanage or picked up and brought to us by policemen or passers-by. Their biological parents wouldn't leave any clues because they would be severely penalized by the authorities if they were found guilty of child abandonment. We don't even know the names of most of these babies.'

'That's so sad. Isn't it sad, Julie?'

'Yes, of course. You're doing the right thing, Sophia. You can offer her a better life.'

'If you could let me have the baby now, the staff from the China Centre for Adoption Affairs will officially transfer the baby to you together with all the legal paperwork tomorrow. Please be here at two in the afternoon. All the other adoptive parents will be here too, so it might get a little busy. Do be early if you can,' the supervisor had said perfunctorily as if she had done this many times before.

'Let me hold her for a while. We'll return her to you in a minute,' Julie had leant over eagerly to take the baby from Sophia. Sophia didn't want to let go, but like other moms, she was also eager to show off her daughter to her friend.

'She's so beautiful, isn't she? My perfect daughter,' Sophia had said, smiling euphorically at Julie.

'Oh yeah, she's the most gorgeous thing I've ever seen,' Julie had agreed without missing a beat. She was happy for her friend because she knew that Sophia had been waiting for this moment for a long time.

Single and alone at forty, Sophia wasn't exactly an outgoing sort of woman. In fact, she was insipid, introverted, and led a rather reclusive life. Her idea of relaxing was to spend an evening with a good book or watch television with her two somewhat territorial cats. If she went out, she would either be at the church, of which she was a devout member, or at a restaurant for an occasional meal with her colleagues at the local post office, where she worked as an assistant postmaster. Her work didn't pay much, but she'd inherited a tiny sum of money and a lovely Victorian house in the Sunset District from her late parents.

Besides, Sophia had always been the girl who wore sensible shoes. Somewhat overweight, she moved with a hefty gait, which made her look a lot older than she was. With a broad, solemn face, a growing double chin, and a rotund body, no one would deem her physically attractive. She wore her hair short, so that she didn't need to bother with brushing and styling, and would put on makeup—compact powder, eyeshadow, and lipstick were all she could manage—only on special occasions. She seldom smiled and often spoke curtly to get a conversation over and done with, which made her seem cold and unapproachable. Socially awkward and often uncomfortable in her skin, Sophia had given up trying to enjoy the company of people, especially men, and retracted to a solitary life.

While Sophia often gave the impression of being a sad and lonely person, she was nothing like that at all. Sophia *liked* being alone. Independent, self-possessing, or preferring to have the bed all to herself, she wanted things just as they were. She enjoyed talking with people—correction, intelligent people; she simply didn't care for bad conversations, which included most of the senseless small talks and shallow gossip that went around the post office. She felt they were a waste of time, and she would rather create insightful conversations in her head with interesting characters from the books she read. That made her look even more like a weirdo who lived in a world of her own. But Sophia didn't care.

Sophia's only regret was not having any children of her own. Not that she hated men, just that the opposite sex had always eluded her. She felt ill at ease with them, and she had enough sense to know that she wasn't attractive enough to the good ones. The few dates she had ever been on during her college days and, later in life, with older, dull men she had met at the church, weren't enjoyable. Sex was even less pleasant; it was awkward and uncomfortable, and she couldn't wait for it to be over.

But kids, she loved them. The one thing she had always prayed for was a child and with it, a family of her own, although she had no idea how God could make that prayer come true. After all, there was this one small inconvenient truth called the laws of biology, which required a male species to do the impregnating. And with her hermit-like existence and no suitable man in sight to provide the service for, or in her, it was impossible to make a baby. Neither could she afford the exorbitant fee of an artificial insemination procedure that other single mothers might have opted for. But God was an omnipresent Creator, and she wouldn't question His ability to perform that tiny bit of miracle for her. So, she waited.

Until she couldn't wait any longer. Whenever she saw children playing at the park, she felt that powerful tug of maternal instinct and heard her biological clock ticking so loudly that it almost physically hurt her! All she wanted was to just pick one up and take the child home. She decided God was working too slowly, and He needed help to speed things up a little. So, Sophia hit the laptop to do some research on the internet about adopting a baby. Fortunately for her, the internet was already abuzz with information, forums, self-help articles, and heart-wrenching stories on adoption.

'If you wish to adopt, why not get a third-world baby? You can be a parent and provide better opportunities for a poor child at the same time,' one expert advised.

'Ask not what your child can do for you, ask what you can do for your child,' another guru offered.

'The fastest and easiest way for an American to adopt a foreigner is to try for a Chinese baby. It wouldn't take more than a year from the day you file your application to the day you have the baby in your arms. Moreover, with the One-Child Policy in China, Chinese parents are dumping baby girls at an unprecedented rate in favour of boys, whom they believe can carry on their family name and take care of them when they grow old. The inheritance laws in China favour the males too, and land and property are usually passed on to sons. The Chinese authorities have more abandoned girls than they can handle, and they will welcome you with open arms,' claimed a seemingly legitimate US adoption agency on its website.

A Chinese baby. Imagine that, Sophia pondered. *Can a single woman like me really adopt a Chinese baby?*

Sophia combed the details over and over again to make sure she had missed nothing. But however hard she tried to find something to deny herself the pleasure of thinking that she could be a mother, she simply couldn't. She seemed eligible. And, so, she dutifully filled out the application forms, attended the endless talks, interviews, meetings, and waited patiently.

Then, at last, the call from the adoption agency came. A package had arrived, the nice lady on the line said. It was from the China Centre for Adoption Affairs, indicating that a baby girl had been identified and deemed suitable for her.

'Come in and have a look at what they sent. If you like the baby and decide to go ahead with the adoption, we'll arrange for you to fly to Beijing to meet her in person and bring her home. The next scheduled travel date is next month. We've quite a few other adoptive parents signing up for the trip, so I've limited openings available. Let me know as soon as you can.'

Sophia dropped in at the agency, took the package home, and 'had a look'. Her hands trembled with anticipation and trepidation as she opened the brown envelope. The package included a letter of introduction, a fact sheet that listed only the baby's adoption number and estimated age, two photographs that seemed to have been taken rather hastily, and a health record.

She took one look at the photographs and fell in love.

A gift from God, Sophia decided.

Quickly, Sophia picked up her phone and called one of the few friends she had, Julie—a regular customer at the post office turned best friend—and asked her if she wanted to visit Beijing with her.

Julie was an unlikely friend because she was exactly what Sophia wasn't. She was an eBay seller, a mother of three brawling pre-teen and teenage boys, a wife to a car mechanic, and a homemaker—in that order. She loved her eBay job because it allowed her to buy and sell all sorts of new and old trinkets—an excuse for shopping—but making a home? Not so much. Julia wasn't a good homemaker. Whether it was because of her dislike for homemaking that made her a bad one, or she was a lousy one to begin with, no one was exactly sure. And the goods—junk, according to her husband—that Julie brought home to sell online did not help her case either. Without a proper office in the house or a storage system for her fledgling entrepreneurial endeavour, Julie's home quickly descended into a state of constant fluid mess, with things and people being moved or moving around in the space that was cluttered with, well, more things and people.

This was something Sophia couldn't quite understand about Julie. If Sophia were to pick something in Julia's life that she could be envious of, it would have to be her family. In Sophia's opinion, Julie had three wonderful boys——Julie wouldn't necessarily agree with that—and a husband who, while a little too bossy and possessive, loved her deeply. If Sophia were in Julie's shoes, she would put her family first and make sure the house was spick and span. No question about it.

Julie's regular trips to the post office to mail items she had sold online ensured that Sophia got to know her well. Strangely, Sophia got along very well with Julie. The reason? Because Julie always disagreed with her. Julie would call bullshit whenever she saw one and never pandered to anyone's whim. She had three boys and a husband; at home, she needed to call a spade, a spade. Period. And so, when Sophia said anything that Julie thought was baloney, she made sure she was heard. Rather than being offended, Sophia appreciated her honesty because she knew it was rare these days.

Soon, they started doing stuff together outside of work, like going for morning walks—Julie and Sophia shared the same neighbourhood—and shopping at garage sales on weekends. They fit well together, with Julie chatting incessantly and Sophia able to be herself.

China, or anywhere for that matter, was a getaway Julie had been craving for long. But she couldn't afford it, for her husband had been in and out of work for the last few years, and her business was barely breaking even. Julie desperately needed a break from her family. Her boys, and at times, her husband, were driving her nuts—always demanding to be fed and having to constantly clean up after them and breaking off fights—to a point where she couldn't take it any more. She needed time to herself to think, to strategize for her business, and she couldn't do it with the constant racket and interruptions at home. Besides, Sophia needed her. And, so, with her husband's blessing, Julie finally packed her bags and joined Sophia on the trip.

As Sophia pushed her way out of the market and back to the hotel, she prayed that Julie wouldn't lose track of time and miss their appointment at the orphanage. Julie had the potential to shop to the point of being attention deficit.

Sophia reached the hotel, went straight up to her room, and packed her luggage. Julie's luggage was not packed, and her stuff was still in a mess—clothes hanging in the closet and her toiletries in the bathroom. They were leaving tonight after picking up her baby. Sighing, she wondered if Julie would have enough time to pack.

We'll worry about that later. Let's focus on the pick-up this afternoon, Sophia thought as she picked up the hotel phone and ordered room service.

At one o'clock sharp, Sophia emerged from the lift lobby. The bus that the agency had arranged to ferry the adoptive parents to the orphanage was already parked in the driveway, and several excited soon-to-be parents were boarding. Sophia looked around. No sign of Julie. She called her phone. She didn't pick up.

Looks like Julie will have to find her way there, Sophia thought.

She boarded the bus at the last possible minute and found a seat away from the chatters. She called Julie's phone again. No luck.

After about forty-five minutes of Beijing's traffic, they arrived at the orphanage on the outskirts of the city. The atmosphere immediately transformed from one of sombre silence to intense excitement, with the adoptive parents cuddling their babies, signing documents, and making plans with other parents to stay in touch.

Sophia wanted very much to join in, but she wouldn't savour the moment without her best friend. This was a momentous time of her life, and she wanted Julie here with her when she picked up the baby for the first time as a mother. And Julie was spoiling it for her by not being here!

So, instead of doing what she needed to do, Sophia lingered outside the orphanage anxiously, looking for Julie. As she waited, the crowd in the orphanage started to thin, and before she knew it, all the adoptive parents but Sophia had picked up their babies and settled comfortably on the bus, ready for a new life.

'Miss Williams? Miss Williams! We need you to fill in the adoption papers so we can officially hand over the baby to you.' Madam Wang, the manager of the China Centre for Adoption Affairs, tapped Sophia's back urgently.

'I'm sorry, but I'm waiting for my friend. Can you give me a few more minutes?' Sophia pleaded.

'But all the others have already completed the process. And the bus is leaving soon,' said Madam Wang, eager to get the last adoptive parent out of the door so that she could pack in for the day.

'That's not a problem. Let the bus leave. I'll call a taxi later.'

Madam Wang hesitated, but she decided not to offend her client. 'Okay, I'll let your agent know.'

Sophia called Julie again. It rang several times before Julie's voice came on the line, sounding excited and apologetic.

'Honey? I know, I know, I'm so sorry! I meant to call you, but I lost track of time,' Julie shouted over the deafening background noise. 'Listen, I've just met a distributor here who has an amazing range of merchandise that I could sell online. His stuff is so good and soooo cheap! I need to make arrangements with him before we leave tonight. Do you think you can manage the pick-up without me? I'm so sorry, but this is an opportunity I can't miss.'

Sophia felt a pang of anger. This moment should be hers, and she wanted her friend to be with her. But her resentment soon gave way to understanding and forgiveness, as it always had in the past. Moreover, she couldn't stay angry with Julie. She knew Julie had already spent almost all her time in Beijing being with her at this dreary orphanage instead of doing the usual shopping and sightseeing. Plus, the thought of her baby made her feel more magnanimous than ever.

'All right, you go ahead with your business. I can handle things over here. Don't you worry,' Sophia replied, trying not to sound too disappointed.

'Oh, thank you, thank you! I'll make it up to you, I promise!'

'It's nothing. I'll see you at the hotel, okay?'

With hunched shoulders, Sophia headed back into the orphanage and looked for Madam Wang, who was carrying the baby, anxiously waiting for Sophia.

'I'm so sorry for the delay, Madam Wang. I'm ready to sign the papers now,' she said.

'That's great,' Madam Wang said with an effort to sound cheerful. 'I'll be back in a moment.'

As promised, Madam Wang returned quickly with the baby in a bassinet and a stack of papers.

'Now, let's see. These legal papers are yours to keep. They're all ready; just make sure you show them to the customs at the airport. These are for the orphanage. I'm afraid there're quite a few pages to fill in, Miss Williams,' Madam Wang said as she sorted the papers quickly.

As Sophia started filling in the document, another worker at the orphanage hurried into the room and whispered fervently to Madam Wang. Instantly, Madam Wang's countenance turned from the usual solemn look into one of absolute panic and fear. She glanced furtively at Sophia and said as calmly as she could. 'I'm sorry Miss Williams, we can't do this now. You've to leave immediately.'

'What? Why?'

Madam Wang paused to consider, and continued cautiously, 'We've just been informed that the authorities will be here soon to inspect the orphanage. We need all visitors to vacate the premises now.'

'Can't we finish this? It won't take another minute.'

'There's no time. We have to move now!'

'C'mon! That's ridiculous! I can't leave without the baby!'

But Madam Wang wasn't listening any more. She was in such a frenzy mode that she practically shoved Sophia out of the room.

'I understand your concern, Miss Williams, but we can't finish the procedure today . . .'

'Forget about the procedure. Please, I don't want to miss our flight, with the baby and all. Do me a favour . . . just . . . just let me have the baby. I beg you!' Sophia's mental state began to mirror that of Madam Wang and went on an overdrive. She didn't know what was going on, but she knew she couldn't leave without the baby.

'I . . . I don't know about this . . .' Madam Wang said, looking unsure.

Sophia saw an opening and took it. She surreptitiously slipped three thousand yuan into the manager's hand and said in an assuring voice, 'Forgive me. I forgot to thank you for doing such an excellent job and going the extra mile for me.' It was the first time Sophia had offered a bribe to someone, a dirty trick she thought she'd never resort to. She had no idea how to go about doing so until that moment. But with the baby almost within reach, it came so naturally, so easily, as if she had done it all her life.

Madam Wang felt the cold, hard cash in her hands. It was a lot of money to her, more than a month of her salary. It could do a lot for her and her family. She needed the money badly. At that time, everyone in China needed money.

'Well, I suppose we can finish filling in the forms for the orphanage another day, since the papers you need are all there—' she relented.

'Yes, yes, they're all there. I can just grab them, and the baby, and leave right this minute!'

'Okay, Miss Williams, but please, don't tell anyone. And please go right now!'

'Not a single soul, I promise. Thank you, thank you so much,' Sophia said, weak with relief that the ordeal was over.

It was a promise she would keep for seventeen years.

* * *

Sophia slumped down in the backseat of the taxi and placed the bassinet next to her, her knees buckling from intense anxiety. She was still bewildered by the sudden turn of events at the orphanage several minutes before when she saw police cars speed past her taxi.

As the taxi turned the corner, she saw that the policemen were getting out of the vehicles and rushing into the orphanage.

'What's happening?' she asked the taxi driver.

'Raid, I think. Illegal babies.' That was all the driver could manage in broken English.

Sophia was shocked beyond words. 'Illegal babies? What do you mean illegal babies? The orphanage is legal, and I've right here all the papers from the China Centre for Adoption Affairs, a state agency!'

'You don't understand China,' replied the driver. 'Don't worry, if you've the legal papers, you and the baby are safe.'

It would be a few days before Sophia could connect all the dots. Still shaking, she looked down at the baby. For the first time, she noticed a baby coat with two Chinese characters sewn on the right lapel in the bassinet.

'What do they mean?' Sophia asked the driver, holding up the lapel in the rear-view mirror.

'Oh, I think it's the baby's name. It says Li Ying; Li is the family name and Ying, the given name. Ying means eagle in Chinese,' the driver said. 'Where are you and the baby going?'

'We're going home to San Francisco,' said Sophia, giving the baby a peck on the cheek.

Bao bao, ni yao fei qu mei guo la!'

'What did you say?'

'I told her she's flying to America. "Fei" means fly in Chinese.'

'Yes, that's right. She's flying away.'

'By the way, have you decided on an American name for the baby?'

'Faye, I'll call her Faye Williams.'

Chapter 3

YAN

Yan watched impassively as her father pissed on the street. Again. She could see him clearly from where she was squatting, even though it was already after midnight and the jaundiced light of the street lamps, few and far in between, was dim and the bulbs coated almost black with soot and carcasses of long-dead insects. She watched as he staggered to a tree and fumbled to unzip his pants, and listened to the gushing of his urine. She could imagine the familiar and disgusting odour even though she couldn't smell it—a concoction of ammonia and liquor stench that reeked of defeat and despondence. If anyone were to ask her how she felt about watching her father pee on the street, she would say that there was nothing unusual about it—that wasn't the first time and it wouldn't be his last. It was just how things had always been, and how they would be.

He was so wasted that he couldn't put his penis back into his trousers after he had finished with his business. He stood wobbling for a long time, leaning his crown against the tree trunk for support. Then, oblivious to his daughter's presence—or anyone's presence for that matter—he began to rub himself. Like a chimpanzee's visceral reaction to satisfy its urges as soon as it felt them, Yan saw her father work expertly on his penis, which soon stiffened and swelled hungrily.

No one could tell what she was thinking as she took all this in while squatting across the street. Her emaciated face was deadpan, and her sunken eyes dry and impenetrable. No one would think that a child like her could bear to watch her father descend into such a state where only the street dogs and feral cats belonged. But no one should underestimate her.

Yan could. Because she had to.

She could let him finish masturbating and then drag him away, but she wouldn't. Not that she wanted to save whatever little dignity or decency he had left; she wanted to stop him for a simple, practical reason: she didn't want him to soil his trousers again. It was his only clean pair, and they hadn't done laundry for a while.

It might sound insane to most people, but in Yan's world, the line between insanity and normality had never been clear.

Yan stood up, walked across the empty street to her father, and shoved him hard on his back. He stumbled and knocked his head hard against the tree trunk, abruptly ending his act of pleasuring himself. He swirled around shakily, fists raised feebly to his chest level, ready for a fight against some invisible enemies. But when he saw that it was Yan, reality dawned upon him. He looked ashamed and tried to reclaim a tiny bit of dignity by straightening his shirt, although he had forgotten that his now limp penis was still hanging outside his trousers.

'Let's go home,' he mumbled, averting his eyes as he steadied himself.

He tried to walk without Yan's help, but he couldn't make it beyond the corner of the street, passing out on the sidewalk after a few steps. Yan didn't know the way home. It didn't matter because even if she did, the ten-year-old wasn't strong enough to carry her father all the way back. She neither had any money to hire a taxi nor knew anyone to call for help. So, like many other nights, they'd spend this one on the streets. Yan was grateful that it wasn't at least raining or too cold because she'd lost her only cardigan, which she'd picked up from the Red Cross. It was a good cardigan, and she'd felt an ache in her heart when she'd dropped it while running away from the police. She obviously couldn't go back to retrieve it. Her father and she, together with his friends, had been picketing at Tiananmen Square the day before when the police had arrived with batons and tear gas. She liked the cardigan; it didn't have holes in it.

She tried to roll her father to a patch of grass along the sidewalk so that he'd sleep on softer ground, but his dead weight wouldn't budge.

We'll have to deal with his aches tomorrow, Yan thought helplessly.

She removed the haversack on her back, lifted his head gently, and placed the soft bag underneath his neck. Hopefully, it'd prevent him from getting a stiff neck tomorrow.

While shifting her father around, a photograph of baby Ying fell out of his breast pocket. It was the only good picture of her, although over time, the image had faded slightly and the corners had become dog-eared. Ying was only about a month old in the photograph, and Yan was sure her little sister looked nothing like the baby in the photo now. But her father guarded the photo like a knight protecting the Holy Grail. When he showed it to strangers, which he would do numerous times each day, he wouldn't let them touch it. He wouldn't even allow Yan to touch it. But he was dead drunk now, so Yan could do anything she pleased. She wanted to spit and trample on it, rip it into tiny pieces, and then shit on it. She wanted to burn it and throw the ashes into the Yangtze River. She wanted to bury it six feet under—no, further down to the eighteenth level of hell. Instead, she wiped away the dirt off the photograph with her not-so-clean sleeve and carefully placed it back into her father's pocket.

Then, she settled next to her father, snuggled closer to his vomit-and-liquor-marinated body to keep him warm with her body heat, and watched vigilantly over him.

* * *

Yan and her father started a nomadic sort of life after Ying's disappearance about six years ago. Not immediately, perhaps a year or two afterwards, because papa and mama had a lot of blaming and fighting to do before everything eventually fell apart.

Yan had once seen a big-shot clever psychiatrist on television, who said that sad people go through five stages of grief—denial, anger, bargaining, depression, and acceptance. She was deeply suspicious that this was exactly what her father experienced, except that he never got to the acceptance part.

Yan remembered distinctly when her father had first learnt about his younger daughter's abduction. He had told his wife that it was a mistake on the part of the Family Planning Bureau and that he would have it sorted out as soon as possible. He said he would eat his humble pie, ask for forgiveness and beg, borrow or steal whatever amount the Bureau wanted to get Ying back. He called the Bureau and asked to speak to the officers who had come to his apartment. But he soon realized that he didn't even know who to ask for because he had neither got their names nor asked to see any identifications.

But Yan knew her father wasn't someone who let up easily. He went to the Bureau daily—daughter alongside the father—and lurked outside the building, hoping to catch hold of one of the two guys who had visited. It took them two full weeks to finally spot one of them—the pudgy one with the black-rimmed shell spectacles—while the party cadre was leaving his office one evening. However, Yan didn't see her father eat any damn humble pie as he had promised. Instead, she watched him silently as he pounded on the Bureau officer like a hound ready to draw blood. It went something like this—

'Where the fuck is my daughter? Give me back my daughter, or I'll feed you to the dogs!' Yan's father bawled as he seized the officer by the throat.

Perhaps the officer was used to this sort of pounding and threatening. Or, perhaps the officer was a magnificent thespian who could put on a composed front when faced with imminent danger. Or, he simply didn't give a damn because Yan's father was just one of the hundreds of cases he had processed over the past months. There were many people from the rural areas flooding into Beijing at that time, and consequently, many unlawful births to prosecute.

Either way, the pudgy officer, cool as a watermelon, grabbed the father's hand and peeled it off his throat, one finger at a time. He was surprisingly strong for his age, and as he gripped the fingers, he bent two of them so far back that they almost reached the back of his assaulter's wrist. Yan's father collapsed on to the ground in agony, fingers still locked in the officer's hand.

'First of all, I don't know what you're talking about. Secondly, touch me again, and I'll break every damn finger of yours. Do you understand me?' the officer whispered gently into Yan's father's ear, his lips forming a disturbing smile.

All Yan's father could muster was a slight nod, which was enough to earn him his unbroken fingers back. Without another word, the officer walked away, not bothering even to look back.

So much for sorting things out.

Even though Yan's father realized that it wasn't possible to 'sort it out as soon as possible', he still believed he would get his daughter back. Eventually. A matter of time. In fact, that would be what he would still say six years later, albeit a little less convincingly. He insisted that people couldn't simply disappear without a trace. There had to be a way, a link to somewhere, or a clue from someone to get his daughter back.

Unfortunately, he hadn't got a damn clue.

Next came the anger. It was fast and mighty furious. Like a deadly tsunami, destroying everything in its path and washing away the tenuous comfort that the family had painstakingly created in their tiny home.

Yan knew that when her father got angry, he liked to nurse that foul-smelling, nasty-tasting drink from a special bottle that only he was allowed to touch. As time passed, he hit the bottle more frequently. And when he drank enough of that foul drink, he would get angrier and take it out on her mother.

At first, Yan's mother would fight back, but her husband knew how to wear her down. He hit where it hurt most—her heart. After all, the baby was snatched from her arms, he would insinuate. If she had held her tighter or fought the men harder, Ying wouldn't have been abducted.

After a while, Yan's mother started to believe that it was true. And gradually, the fighting stopped and only the beating remained. Yan watched her mother take the beating like how Chinese women at that time did—silently and without resistance. The berating, the blows, and the forced sex—the poor woman let it happen because she let herself believe that she was to be blamed.

Yan hated the violence, but she knew her father wouldn't stop simply because she asked him to do so. In her young head, she began to come up with ways to approach her father so that he would listen. She would employ words that the adults around her often used in their speech. She'd tell her father that the beating was counter-productive, or that their family should focus on 'smashing the four olds' instead of smashing each other, although she had no idea what the four olds were. But whenever Yan tried to engage her father, she got tongue-tied, lost her nerve, and was unable to articulate the words that she had so carefully formed in her mind.

Paranoia soon set in on Mei. She never lost sight of Yan, the only daughter she had now left. She was reluctant to let Yan leave home. If they had to, she wouldn't let go of Yan's hand or allow anyone to so much as glance at her. Her protectiveness got to a point where she refused to let Yan go to school, and when the teacher called enquiring about Yan's absence, she'd make up excuses. When Mei couldn't do so any more, for her husband soon found out, she'd go to school with Yan and wait outside her classroom.

During this time, Yan became the sole purpose of her mother's existence. When she was alone with her daughter, Mei wouldn't mention her second daughter or even acknowledge her existence. She would pretend that the abduction—or, for that matter, the pregnancy of her second child—never occurred. When she needed to have a conversation with strangers about her family, she would say that she only had one daughter.

Even though they had very little, Yan felt like a princess, albeit a caged one. She was in want of nothing, and every penny that her mother had was spent on her, saving nothing at the end of the month, which inevitably aroused the wrath of her father.

As the violence got more frequent, Yan noticed that her mother became more forgetful about things. Little things, like fixing dinner or fetching Yan to school. That begot more beating, and soon, Yan experienced first-hand what a vicious cycle was. Even as a child, watching her mother's descent from a normal, healthy woman to a lunatic tormented by self-loathing and heartbreak was excruciating for Yan.

Mei endured her husband's anger for a long time until she couldn't endure it any more. One day, she simply ran away, leaving Yan behind with her father. It wasn't like she had planned it or anything. Yan would undoubtedly have noticed it because she spent every waking hour with her mother. Mei just took off; walked out on them with a pot of porridge still brewing on the stove, without taking a single personal item with her. It was as if a switch in her had been turned off, the switch that connected her to her family. Mei switched it off and walked away.

Despite being left behind, at some level, Yan admired her mother's courage to leave her father, until she realized that it wasn't courage that compelled her mother to do so. It was fear. Her husband's rage had got so terrifying that Mei, paranoid or otherwise, knew he would kill her one day if she hadn't left.

So, Yan suffered yet another loss, this time much more devastating than the first. Her mother, the only person whom she could wrap her arms around and talk to about anything in the world, was gone. But her loss seemed to be lost on her father. Instead of consoling his only daughter, he declared that Mei had walked out on them because she got tired of looking after Yan, exactly how he had blamed his wife for losing their second daughter. And when Yan asked him why her mother wouldn't tell her so, he simply looked at her in contempt.

Perhaps the reason was too complicated for a child like me to understand. Yan cried in desperation. Without her mother, she had to lull herself to sleep by sobbing silently under the old, worn-out blanket every night for the rest of the year.

Three months later, a relative spotted Mei wandering in the clandestine red-light district of Tianjin, a city about one hundred and forty kilometres from Beijing, hustling for customers.

'She's a prostitute now; I saw it with my own eyes! And a cheap one too. Fifty yuan for a . . . a transaction,' the relative swore. At that time, Yan didn't know what a prostitute was. She simply presumed her mother had found a new profession of poultry-retailing—she took the literal meaning of 'transaction' and the word 'prostitute', which in Chinese sounds like 'chicken girl'. And so, Yan couldn't understand why her father got so mad at her mother for working so hard for a living.

On the other hand, her father was too embarrassed to even ask what the relative had been doing in Tianjin's red-light district. He supposed every man had his demon to fight.

He thought that Mei would rather be a prostitute—a cheap one—and be fucked by hundreds of other men than return to her husband! But that was how afraid she was of her husband, or how much she loathed him. No one would ever know the truth.

With his wife bringing shame to his family name, Yan's father swore he couldn't call himself a man if he didn't do something about it. With the seven-year-old Yan, he took a train to Tianjin with the intent of persuading his wife to return home. Perhaps persuade is too kind a word. He was determined to bring her home no matter what it took, even if it meant smashing her to a pulp and lugging her battered and likely gonorrhoea-infected body to the train.

It didn't take them long to find Mei, for their relative was very specific about the location. There she was, sitting on a stool outside a seedy karaoke bar along the Wei Jin canal, back hunched and chin jutted out and smoking a Lucky Strike. Other than the cigarette and the thick layer of makeup she had painted on her face, Mei surprisingly didn't look that different, except that there was a sort of emptiness in her gaunt eyes that the make-up failed to hide. They made her look dazed and melancholic. Perhaps she wasn't just smoking Lucky Strike.

Yan had never seen her mother in clothes like that before—a shining blue sequin dress with an unflattering tight skirt that accentuated her protruding belly. It was so short that the hem rode right up to her panties when she sat down. They could tell her business wasn't exactly thriving: the karaoke bar was booming with male customers who were accompanied by younger, prettier escorts. The only other available prostitute sitting next to Mei was a woman who looked as old as a grandmother.

Yan and her father stood across the street and looked at Mei for a long time. Yan wanted to run to her mother, hug her and pull her skirt down a little so that it could cover her panties, but her father stopped her in time, his fingers locked firmly around her wrist. She began to cry, her free hand flailing desperately and the arrested hand yanking her father's as hard as she could. Her father stood rooted and stoic, unable to move, unable to approach his wife. His plan to drag her by her hair and slap her repeatedly at first sight faltered.

Then, Mei saw them.

Yan thought her mother would flee or cry in shame or pretend that she didn't know them; by now, she understood what a prostitute was, a bitter pill for a seven-year-old to swallow. But that didn't happen. Mei simply stared back at her husband. And smiled. A bitter, bitter smile. A smile that said she had found another form of punishment. A smile that said she deserved every ounce of her prostitution. A smile that said she wasn't going back, no matter what.

Never once did she look at Yan. She could stare at her husband the whole night, but not her daughter. She was too ashamed to.

At that point, Yan's father walked away, leaving his wife alone. Somehow, Yan felt that it was the kindest thing he had ever done for her mother.

In the following years, Yan saw her mother twice. The first time was a year after the Tianjin encounter. As suddenly as she had gone, Mei reappeared one afternoon when Yan had returned home alone from school. Her father was at work. Mei had somehow let herself into the apartment and put on a pot of porridge—the same meal she had been preparing when she had walked out. As Yan entered the door, her mother turned around and smiled at her. As if nothing had happened. She was no longer wearing the 'chicken girl' garb or the ugly make-up but had put on her old clothes that Yan had carefully folded and put away in the wardrobe. She told Yan to change and clean up while she laid the table. When Yan returned to the dining room, Mei had once again disappeared.

A year later, while Yan was playing in the courtyard at her school, she saw her mother again from far away, this time in a 'chicken girl' custom. Their eyes locked, and Mei waved sadly at her daughter.

Immediately, Yan ran towards her. But when she reached the spot where her mother had stood, she was nowhere to be found.

After her mother's departure, Yan took it upon herself to take care of her father. To her, it was an implied responsibility because deep down, she knew her mother wasn't coming back. It never occurred to her that it should be the other way round.

Soon, her father lost his job. The same way he had lost his daughter and his wife: he couldn't sort it out. Even as a nine-year-old, Yan could see it coming. With money drying out and the heavy drinking, it was no surprise that her father couldn't pay the rent and subsequently, they were evicted from their apartment.

With nothing left to his name, Yan and her father's lives crumbled before them. They lived off handouts and charity of friends and relatives, staying in their apartments, sleeping in living rooms, kitchens, or courtyards, depending on what was offered. When their friends and relatives no longer welcomed them, they lived on the streets.

Gradually and subconsciously, their clothes became shabbier, their bodies dirtier, their hair more unkempt, and their meals less regular. People on the streets averted their glances and avoided them. Friends and relatives stopped returning their phone calls.

As Yan was the only family left in her father's world, he began to take his anger out on her. No, he didn't beat her. He knew better than to hit his daughter. He tried to be a good father to her, in a weird sort of way, although he still maintained that her mother had run away because she got tired of taking care of her. That was the story, and he was sticking to it. But rant he did, day in and day out, incessantly.

'Ying was the special one. Why did they have to take away my special girl?'

'Your mother's a useless bitch, you hear? The baby would be safe and sound if it weren't for her. Never trust a bloody woman!'

'Remember this, Yan, if you were born again, make sure you pick a rich family. Don't pick a worthless father like me. Look at what I've got you into—'

'If I ever see that son-of-a-bitch officer again, I'll rip his head off!'

At first, Yan thought it was her duty to reply to her father, so she'd asked questions like 'what's a son-of-a-bitch?' But her childish responses were met with more indignation and resentment. She soon realized that the best way to deal with his rhetorical tirades was to keep quiet. So, the more he ranted, the less she spoke. Eventually, she stopped talking altogether.

By now, it had been five years since the fateful day. Yan was nine years old and had been in and out of school, partly because of her father's erratic income and partly their nomadic life. And she didn't have a single friend in the world.

That was how far his anger had got them.

Then came the bargaining part of his grief-coping mechanism. It began after he realized that he was no closer to getting his daughter back despite years of prideful denial and futile ranting. So, he decided to bury the only thing that had never left him, his ego, and return to the Family Planning Bureau. It was difficult for him, to say the least, for he was a proud man. But he loved his daughter more than he loved himself.

The next day, he went to the Bureau with Yan by his side and vowed not to leave until he could determine Ying's whereabouts. He went from desk to desk, officer to officer, clerk to clerk, and even to the janitors, showing them the only good photo of Ying that had been taken years ago and pleading for any scrap of information. Of course, none of them entertained him, and all of them vehemently denied his accusation. Some even jokingly claimed—out of earshot of the officers, naturally—that the Bureau didn't need to be involved in any baby-snatching business because they made more money simply by penalizing couples with multiple children. He begged, cajoled, threatened, bribed, and bargained, but got himself nowhere except thrown out of the Bureau's building numerous times a day.

By now, one would have dismissed Yan's father as a useless imbecile. But Yan knew that there were two things about her father that most people probably overlooked: that he loved his youngest daughter to a fault and that he was tenacious. As the Chinese like to say, 'One does not stop until one reaches the Huanghe River.' Yan's father wouldn't let up. He wouldn't let up because he didn't know how to. Like a quixotic fool, he believed he could fight the entire Communist Party. In fact, the more resistance he faced from the authorities, the more he wanted to fight, to a point where he couldn't tell whether he was fighting for his daughter or himself.

For a long time, despite ritually getting himself piss drunk at night, he'd get up at dawn, drag Yan from her warm bed, take the first public bus and arrive at the Bureau. They'd loiter outside the building—the Bureau wouldn't allow him inside any more—and show Ying's photos to anyone entering or leaving the premises. He'd talk at length to anyone who bothered to listen to him about his abducted daughter. Sometimes, he'd make banners or placards and make Yan hold them up at the entrance. 'Look pitiful. Cry if you can,' he would instruct Yan.

Eventually, he became kind of famous, or rather, infamous, locally. He even inspired a few other parents who faced similar circumstances to stand in the picket line with him. The people at the Bureau despised him immensely and had him arrested several times, during which Yan would be brought to some temporary shelters. But upon his release, he would simply pick Yan up and return to his spot in the picket line.

Perhaps Buddha took pity on them because his tenacity paid off and a lead was thrown his way, although it didn't come from the Bureau, at least not directly. After all, if there was anything the Chinese Communist Party wouldn't do, it was admit their wrongdoings.

It happened one night at the watering hole that Yan's father patronized regularly. This was not a fancy bar. It was, in fact, the opposite—a shithole serving moonshine and cheap, highly lethal local liquor, and cheaper, more lethal prostitutes. It was crawling with lousy low lives—the rejects, the poor, and the scum of Beijing. In other words, the likes of Yan's father. The bar's house rules, if there were any, were so slack that they allowed Yan to come in with her father. If he were to order an alcoholic drink for Yan, they'd have served it to her, no question asked. Yan's father was such a regular that if he didn't come in for the night, the bartender would assume that he'd been arrested again.

Yan's father was nursing his Er-Guo-Tou in the bar when a burly, hard-bitten man walked in. The man's clean, expensive-looking parka, shaven face and sober eyes gave him away at once. He was not one of them; he didn't belong here.

It was true the man didn't belong, for he was here on a mission.

He walked around, eyes scouring for someone, a face he hadn't met but would recognize. His gaze rested on Yan's father. He hesitated. He sat down next to him at their table. Without looking at him, he said in a low and sombre voice, 'I'll tell you what happened to your daughter if you promise never to return to the Bureau again for as long as you live.'

Yan saw her father freeze. He had waited so long for this moment, but when it finally happened, he found himself unprepared. The man looked at Yan, and then said condescendingly to her father, 'You shouldn't bring your daughter to a place like this.'

Yan's father looked sorry for a moment, but retorted instead, 'Where she goes is none of your business. Who're you?'

'You're indeed an obnoxious bastard like everyone said you were.'

'Who are you?' Yan's father repeated, breathing heavily.

'That's also none of your business,' the man replied.

'You're one of the Bureau's dogs, aren't you? Trying to shut me up?'

'You're causing the Bureau a lot of embarrassment. Promise you'll leave them alone, and I'll tell you about your daughter,' said the man.

'Is that how the Bureau gets rid of people like me now? Sending in a dog?' Yan's father said tersely.

The man suppressed his anger and said nothing. He was a patient man, and he knew the man sitting next to him desperately wanted the information he had brought with him, but he needed him to play the game his way.

'Tell me what you know,' Yan's father said at last.

'No. You've to agree to my terms first.'

'Look here, you shithead. Do you think I like going to the Bureau? You think I enjoy being looked down, shoved around, spat on, and cursed by those motherfuckers every day? You know damned well

I wouldn't go back to that fucking place so full of liars if I knew where my daughter was. I'd be too busy looking for her, wouldn't I?' Yan's father took a big gulp of his drink and murmured, 'Moron!'

'Thanks for the colourful tirade. It's goodbye then!' the man scoffed as he got up to leave.

'Okay, okay,' Yan's father stopped him. Yan could tell he knew full well that this was his only opportunity. He couldn't afford to blow it.

'So, what's it gonna be?' the man was losing his patience.

'You're right, I'm sorry. I promise. Please tell me what you know about my daughter.'

'What do you promise?'

'What the fuck?'

'What do you promise?'

'I promise not to go back to the Bureau ever again. Happy?'

The man relented, sat down, and lit a cigarette with deliberate languid casualness, relishing his small victory. Yan could tell that her father strained every fibre of his muscles to stop himself from beating the shit out of the man.

'Your daughter had been taken to an orphanage and put up for adoption five years ago.'

'Did the Bureau do that?' asked Yan's father, trying to sound measured in his tone.

'That's not important.'

'Not important? It's fucking important to me! They abducted my child and sold her to an orphanage!' Yan's father raised his voice. 'God damn it! Those sons-of-bitches! Did the orphanage pay for her?'

'Look, you can't ask questions, okay? Just listen. Do you want the rest of the story or not?'

Yan's father looked as if he was ready to burst. Instead, he simply nodded and let the man talk.

'Having you been following the news?'

'Well, my HD TV and fancy radio just broke down, so I haven't had the time to catch up,' he replied sarcastically.

'Listen to this. This news bit was recorded from a Taiwanese radio station this afternoon,' said the man. He took out a portable recorder from his parka's pocket and switched it on. As he adjusted the volume, a female reporter's voice with a nasal Taiwanese accent blasted from the small device.

'Chinese authorities announced in a press conference today that the leader of one of the largest child-trafficking syndicates in China's recent history, who was arrested five years ago, was found guilty of all charges in court. Here's the story from our correspondent in Beijing, Xu Wenjing.

'Five years ago, an international child-trafficking syndicate here in Beijing was busted by the Chinese authorities and several ringleaders were arrested, one of whom was a high-ranking Chinese Community Party official. The syndicate, led by the party official, had a broad network that spanned the entire country. It allegedly seized babies by force from poor families that were unable to pay the steep fines for having more than one child per family. Under the One-Child Policy, the Chinese law forbids married, urban couples to have more than one child to curb its burgeoning population. Fines, abortions, and even forced sterilization usually accompanied second or subsequent pregnancies. Sources said that these traffickers targeted impoverished, poorly educated couples, often menial workers or farmers who came from rural areas to the city to look for jobs and had little or no social connections here. With no means to pay the hefty penalty, they were often the subjects of abuse. Some families were told that the child would only be temporarily confiscated until the fines were paid up.

'Unfortunately, once the child was taken, they'd be sold to orphanages or welfare agencies, where they'd be registered as "abandoned" and their names would be removed from the registry, making it virtually impossible to trace their biological parents. These babies would then be adopted by overseas parents for a profit. Sources said that each baby could net up to USD 5,000. A director of an orphanage from Henan Province confessed that the demand for babies had been strong and rising, especially from Western countries, and they were always in need of more babies.

'China, which implemented its Adoption Law in 1992, was fast becoming the world's largest provider of children to adoptive families in developed countries.

'The syndicate leaders were arrested in one of the orphanages on the outskirts of Beijing five years ago. Apparently, twelve "fresh" babies, all "supplied" by the syndicate, had just been adopted by American adoptive families, that were said to be completely unaware of the situation.

'The news shocked the world at that time, and in response to pressures from the international children's welfare organizations, the official involved was quickly condemned by the Chinese Community Party as a traitor. The Party had also issued a statement promising a thorough investigation of the case and assuring the victims that justice would be served swiftly and fairly. It also pledged to help affected families to find their abducted children.

'After five years of investigation and numerous court sessions, the court finally pronounced the party official guilty of all charges this afternoon. He'll be sentenced tomorrow.'

That was the end of the news. The man switched off the recorder and put it back in his pocket.

'The audacity of the Bureau! Sent a dog to tell me the crime of their own people!' Yan's father murmured, barely audibly. 'It said this happened five years ago, but I didn't know about it at all. How do I know if you've made it up?' Yan's father decided to ask finally.

'The Chinese media would never report this kind of news here in this country. Although the Party could suppress the story here, they couldn't control what was being reported overseas. As I've said, what you've just heard was from a Taiwanese station.'

The man paused and took a sip from his drink. 'The party official will be given a death sentence in court tomorrow. The case will soon be blown over, and the Party will bury this story as quickly as possible. Now that you know, you should accept the fact that justice has been served.'

'How do you know the man will be hanged?' asked Yan's father, still trying to process the plethora of information in his Er-Guo-Tou-infused brain.

The man gave a mirthless laugh and said, 'I didn't expect you to ask such a stupid question.'

'Who's the official who led the syndicate? What's his name?'

'You really don't know anything, do you? That man's just a scapegoat. Do you really believe the syndicate is led by just one man?' the man blurted. Realizing that he had said too much, he stood up quickly.

'Who sent you?' Yan's father tried again, holding firmly on to the sleeve of the man's parka. He might be a semi-literate drunk peasant, but Yan knew that her father wasn't stupid. She could tell that he already knew who sent this man and what their intentions were. He knew that they wanted to warn him to stop pestering them or else . . . *They* wanted him to know that *they* were above the law. *They* wanted him to know that *they* couldn't be touched. But he wanted to hear it from this man.

'I think you already know,' said the man as he walked briskly out of the bar.

Chapter 4

YAN

It took Yan's father three epiphanies to get to America.

The first came after the encounter with the burly man at the bar.

Yan's father didn't return to the Family Planning Bureau after that night. Not because he got the 'message' but because he had a different plan. He realized two things from his contact with the man: that the days of standing in the picket line outside the Bureau were over. He had already achieved what he set out to do—he had driven the Bureau into giving him information. More importantly, he knew that his little girl was still alive. Yan's father was no longer interested in the Bureau.

His primary concern now was the whereabouts of Ying. He needed to start somewhere, and his first stops were the most logical places: orphanages.

By that time, Yan and her father had moved back to the old apartment, the one from where Ying had been forcefully taken. A generous relative who was tired of taking them in and putting up with Li's drunken antics had given them some money to live on their own, at least for a while. It was probably one of the most 'normal' periods of their lives, especially for Yan, who could even go back to school.

Without her mother, the onus of taking care of the apartment and her father was on her. She cooked, washed, cleaned, paid the bills, bought groceries, while learning to read and write. It was tough for a little girl, but anything was a vast improvement from living on the streets.

Yan saw a drastically different father since the encounter with the man. She caught a cautious glimpse of hope as her father, with a new mission at hand, cleaned up his act: he stopped drinking—well, stopped drinking heavily—and even started a small part-time plumbing business to take care of the bills. As for the rest of his time, he spent it all at orphanages.

It turned out that Yan's father was a stellar planner and organizer. He devised a methodological approach to categorizing the orphanages in and around Beijing and visited each of them systemically, starting with the ones Ying would most likely have been sold to.

Many of the orphanages had been shut down, especially during the witch-hunting years following the arrest and scandal. The news had been covered extensively by the international media, and the Party wanted scapegoats to show the world that it would not stand for such decadent and corrupt practices among its officials. Some orphanages had managed to escape the persecution and continued operating, albeit in a low-key and small-scale way.

Whenever he identified an orphanage or someone who had worked in one before, Yan's father would figure out the most economical way to get there—walking if it took less than three hours, hitching a ride or using the public transportation system if the orphanage was farther. Almost all the time, he'd return empty-handed: the orphanage would either be closed or taken over by new management, with all old records either destroyed—a mysterious fire or collapsed roof—or missing. Many people whom he tried to interview either refused to talk to him or chased him out the door. If someone was kind enough to offer clues or open records for him, he couldn't find anything about Ying or any useful information that would lead him closer to her.

It was gruelling work and soul-wrenching for Yan to see her father fail, repeatedly. He often returned home looking defeated and depressed, but for the first time for as long as Yan could remember, he didn't complain, curse, or blame anyone.

Yan also noticed that meeting the man that night had given him an impetus. Ying was undoubtedly still on his mind all the time, but his determination seemed to be driven further by a different force. Call it the force of vengeance, the force of justice, the force of defiance, or whatever else. The stakes were raised. It was no longer just about getting his daughter back; it was more than that. Yan knew his father wanted to show *those people* that he wouldn't be beaten, that the more they wanted him to fail, the more he would stand tall and firm.

She just wasn't sure whether it was driving him forward or driving him crazy.

This went on for three years before he got to Madam Wang.

It was a Friday winter morning, freezing and windy. Yan's father had decided to take Yan with him to an orphanage just outside Beijing, instead of dropping her off at school. It was an unusual decision because he preferred to visit orphanages alone to save on bus fares. Yan had later asked her father why he had taken her with him that day. He said he didn't know why, but he had a hunch that he would discover something important there and that he needed someone who could read better than he could.

The orphanage looked like all the others, except that it was bigger, possibly one of the largest in the vicinity. The signage outside the compound indicated that it was a state-owned orphanage, dating back at least sixty years—a fact that lifted Yan's father's hope higher than usual.

When Yan and her father arrived at the orphanage, they headed straight to the administration office and found only a tired-looking bespectacled man in his fifties, on all fours cleaning up vomit on the ground. He looked too tidy and scholarly to be a janitor.

'How're you? May I know where I can find the manager of this place?' Yan's father asked courteously. Yan was pleasantly surprised by her father's politeness. Since she seldom accompanied him on these trips to orphanages, she'd never heard him use his rehearsed conversation with what he referred to as 'the upper echelons of our community'. Nevertheless, her old man seemed to have changed for the better, and in her heart, she almost wanted to thank the burly man at the bar for it.

The man looked up from his cleaning, his glasses dangling precariously on the tip of his greasy nose. He used his forearm to push it back on to the ridge of his nose, took a good look at them, and said pleasantly, 'I'm the manager. How can I help you?'

'Nice to meet you, Mister—' Yan's father offered his hands to the crouching manager. Yan's heart leapt with joy at her father's civility.

The manager stood up, wiped his wet hands vigorously on the back of his pants, and took it. 'Song, I'm Song Zhiwen. Are you here for someone?'

'Well, yes, actually we're looking for someone,' Yan's father replied, taking Ying's photograph out of his shirt's front pocket. He began explaining the purpose of his visit and the backstory of Ying's abduction.

'I'm sorry to hear about your misfortune. The thing is, I've only been here for a couple of months. This place was shut down for several years after the . . . the scandal. I was transferred from Henan to Beijing to reopen the place. You see, they can't keep these orphanages closed forever because of the overwhelming need. As long as the One-Child Policy is in place, they need orphanages,' said Mr Song, pushing his slipping glasses back up.

'As you can see, we're very short-handed here,' he pointed at the vomit on the floor embarrassedly. 'I can't afford the time to help you check the records, but you can go through them yourself and see if you can find anything useful.'

It was more than what Yan's father could bargain for. After thanking Mr Song profusely, they found themselves in a dark, dusty room filled with shelves and file cabinets stuffed with crumbling sheets of old records. The only sources of light in the room were from a small window with frosted panes and a naked tungsten light bulb with exposed wiring that hung precariously in the middle of the room.

Yan looked at the mountains of papers in dismay while her father's eyes gleamed with delight.

* * *

It took them days to go through the records. Yan had to cut classes to accompany her father to the orphanage every morning, staying in the stark, stuffy record room the entire day and leaving the compound only after lights-out. She hated every minute of it. She thought it was futile and foolish to spend so much time looking for a needle in a haystack. Time was better spent in her classroom, which she missed terribly, learning something new. Time was also better spent getting more plumbing jobs so that both of them could eat a little better.

But like always, she said nothing. Dutifully, she followed her father to the orphanage, looking through stacks and stacks of old documents.

Long, tedious days ensued.

It was Yan who stumbled upon Ying's papers. Her cold, ungloved hands trembled and her heart fell through her chest as she stared at the name and the photo that was glued on the admission form. The same luminous skin and large, soulful eyes. Yan had looked at Ying's picture so frequently over the years that she had imprinted every feature, every curve, and every shade of her face into her hippocampus.

Her first instinct was to hide the paper before her father could see it. She closed the file and placed it on the pile of papers marked 'rejected'—yet another manifestation of Li's stellar organizational ability—trying to appear as nonchalant as possible. Unfortunately, her nervous hands knocked the file off the pile, spilling the content on to the floor. She leapt from her chair quickly to pick up the papers, but it was too late. Her father's eyes caught a glimpse of the half-revealed photo.

'Wait!' he cried, snatching the admission form off the floor. 'Isn't this Ying? Isn't it? My goodness! Yes, it's her. It's her! Look at the name; the characters say "Li Ying", don't they?'

Yan cast her eyes down and said nothing.

'Don't they?' her father repeated tersely, his wild, desperate eyes upon her.

'Yes, they do,' she finally said as a flush of blood rushed to her cheeks. 'Look, we've found her records!' She feigned a cheerless smile.

'What's wrong with you? You almost placed it on the rejected pile, you idiot!' he said reproachfully but grinning all the same. 'It's HER! Didn't I tell you I'll find her?'

Elated though her father was, his happiness was short-lived. The records showed that Ying had been adopted by a person named Sophia Williams, but nothing else was filed. No personal information, no address, not even a country of origin.

'The records in this file are incomplete. Look, the files of the other orphans who had been adopted come with details like the date of adoption, country, and address of the adoptive parents, but Ying's file contains only the name of the adopter. All other information is missing. Why's that so?' Yan's father shoved the files into Mr Song's hands and looked at him expectedly for an answer.

Mr Song took his time to examine the papers, shaking his head intermittently and avoiding his interrogator's stinging gaze. Finally, he said with a shrug, 'The paperwork is dated almost ten years back. I've no idea what happened. It could've been a mistake made by a clerk or something—there's no way of knowing. I'm sorry.'

Yan looked at her father as Mr Song spoke and thought she had just witnessed her father being evicted from heaven and thrown into hell all within a short span of an hour. She felt that if the gods existed, they must be like some teenage bullies who enjoyed nothing more than knocking a smaller boy around and having a good laugh at it. Fortunately, this time, help came, albeit in the human form of Mr Song.

'Wait a minute,' Mr Song exclaimed as he scrutinized the papers again. 'There's someone who might be able to help you . . . It says here that Madam Wang handled the case. I know where she is.'

Madam Wang. The manager of the China Centre for Adoption Affairs. The official who pocketed three thousand yuan and allowed Sophia to take Ying away without completing the adoption papers right before the police raid, thus altering the course of the girl's life forever.

As it turned out, Madam Wang's life had also changed drastically after the raid. As one of the Party officials who had been indicted after the syndicate was busted, she was branded indefinitely as a fallen cadre. Although the authorities couldn't find sufficient evidence to convict her, and thus, she was eventually released from jail, she was no longer a desirable member of the Party. People who knew her didn't want to talk about her or even acknowledge that they had known her. Shamed and ostracized, she left Beijing and found work as a kindergarten teacher in a small and insignificant village in Liaoning province, earning a meagre wage to support her equally meagre living. Her husband had long divorced her and forbidden the children to contact their mother. Destitute, alone and cast away, the only thing she felt thankful for was that she had escaped prison time.

It was time to visit Madam Wang.

That meant a seven-hour bus ride for Yan and her father to the city of Liaoning and finding other modes of transportation to Madam Wang's village. It took Yan's father almost a month of planning, including locating the village on the map, finding the cheapest bus fares available, and borrowing more money for the trip.

Finally, he was ready.

But not Yan. Nor was she willing. She wanted to go back to school. She wanted to continue living their current, comparably peaceful lives. She wanted to erase the part where they had discovered Ying's record. But she'd rather lose an arm than tell her father what she wanted.

Thus, to Liaoning it was.

Life in a farming village had cost Madam Wang much of her youth and health. She was no longer the sharp, intelligent, and promising Chinese Communist Party official she once was. Not even a shadow of her former self. What was left was a bitter, beaten old woman who didn't seem to care about anything or anyone any more.

When they arrived at her small, dilapidated hut off the dusty main road, she was sitting on her veranda in the cold, looking shrunk and morose.

'What do you want?' she barked as they approached. 'I don't need hired hands. I don't have a farm. Go away.'

'That's not what we're here for, Madam,' Yan's father replied gingerly.

She took a look at Yan and said apathetically before he could go on. 'She's too old to be in a kindergarten. If she can't read by now, there's nothing I can do.'

She got up slowly, shivered in the cold, and started towards the door.

'You're Madam Wang, aren't you?' Yan's father asked hurriedly.

She froze. She hadn't used that name for a long time. Without turning around, she asked, 'Who wants to know?'

'I'm here to ask you about an adoption case you'd handled about ten years ago. I want to know where Li Ying is.'

His words provoked an immediate, intense reaction from her. The slow, hefty steps that she had taken were replaced with swift strides as she turned around and charged at them.

'What agency are you from?' she asked in a low voice, walking right up to Yan's father, inches from his face with eyes like a cornered she-wolf. 'You don't look like you're from the Party. Are you here to extort me? I've nothing left. Besides, I was cleared of all charges. There's nothing more to say about the case. Can't you people leave me alone?'

'I'm the father of Li Ying. I just want to know where she was taken to,' he said in a measured tone, careful not to reel off into anger. 'Please, we won't take up too much of your time.'

Madam Wang took a step back and sized him up again, deciding if he was to be trusted.

'Please, you're my only hope of ever finding my daughter—'

Madam Wang thought for a while, cleared her throat, and said, 'Three thousand.'

'What?'

'Three thousand yuan for the information. No bargaining . . . and . . . and promise of anonymity,' she said.

Even at a tender age, Yan thought this woman must either be the dumbest person in the world or the craziest. If they had three thousand yuan, they wouldn't be standing in the middle of her dirty yard, begging her for information in mended trousers and worn-out shoes.

But like every Chinese in the world, Yan's father understood that everything came with a price tag. And true to his roots, he started to haggle with her and eventually got the price down to five hundred yuan. Looked like Madam Wang was desperate for cash, as she was ten years ago.

'I remember this case distinctly because it was my last case before I was wrongly arrested,' she said, insisting upon her innocence. 'Anyway, an American lady named Sophia Williams took your daughter away. She was about to sign the adoption papers before we were interrupted by the police's . . . visit. My heart was filled with compassion for her. I couldn't bear to separate her from the baby, whom she had taken to very quickly, so I simply let her leave with it. If my memory hasn't failed me, she said she was returning to San Francisco. That's all I know,' she said as she carefully counted the five hundred yuan in her hands.

'Do you have the address in San Francisco?'

'I said that's all. Now, leave me alone and don't ever come back here again, you hear me?'

* * *

Theoretically speaking, it was Yan who gave her father his second epiphany.

Since their visit to Madam Wang, all he talked about was going to San Francisco, except that it was impossible, given their circumstance. Mounted with debts and armed only with a part-time plumbing business, he hardly had enough to pay for their food and rent. It would take a year's earnings, maybe more, just for the airfare. And, even if they did have the money, they had no idea where exactly Ying was. They soon found out that San Francisco was bigger than they had imagined. Without an address, they couldn't even write her a letter.

They had a clue that had led them to a dead end.

Though Yan's father knew Ying was very likely alive and living somewhere in San Francisco, he had to wait. He had to come up with a plan. But he had no idea what the plan was, at least not yet.

It was one of those rare nights when he stayed in. Business had been slow, and there was no money left to visit the watering hole. Bored and frustrated, he paced the room, searching every nook and cranny, hoping to find a half-empty bottle of beer or leftover liquor, while Yan did her homework. She was reading an abridged version of *Romance of the Three Kingdoms*, a legendary story in Chinese literature. It told the story of a battle between three kingdoms in ancient China. The story's protagonists are villainous and heroic emperors and sages, each trying to out-manoeuvre the others at war with their strategies.

Yan tried hard to ignore the racket that her father was making in the tiny apartment and concentrate on her work, and subconsciously read aloud one of the most famous quotes from Suan Quan, an emperor in *Romance*.

'If you manipulate the power of the masses, you're invincible; if you employ their wisdom, you're as fearless as a sage,' she recited.

Yan's father stopped and turned to Yan. 'What did you just say? Can you read that again?'

Yan coloured up. He barely paid her any attention when she read. In fact, he barely paid her any attention ever. Not when she had wet her bed almost every night after her mom left. Not when she had socked that skinny scoundrel at school who had called her a weirdo because she wouldn't speak in class. Not even when she had tried to burn her bed sheet that was stained with her first menstrual blood. But to this, he paid attention. She was nervous and stammered badly as she reread the quote.

'Explain to me what it means,' he demanded after she was done.

So, Yan awkwardly explained the meaning of the quote as best as a thirteen-year-old could. When she'd finished, he sunk into the worn, rattan chair, and stayed pensive for a long time.

'The power of the mass...,' he murmured to himself. 'Do you know how many children have gone missing each year in this country?'

Yan didn't answer.

'Tens . . . maybe hundreds of thousands,' her father answered himself. 'And do you know how many parents are out there looking for their missing kids?'

Again, Yan didn't answer. She knew he wasn't expecting her to.

'If only we can gather them together, pull our resources together . . . manipulate the power of the masses as you said. If only we can unite, fight the system, and show them that we can't be bullied. Imagine what we can achieve with such a force! Some of us could even get our children back!

Yan wanted to say that it was Suan Quan, not her, who said it. But she knew it didn't matter.

'I can start a movement. I can lead the mass. I'll show the Bureau what we're made of—'

There it was. The second epiphany.

And this was precisely what he went on to do—manipulate the power of the masses and show the Bureau what he was made of. He turned his attention to the parents of other missing children. He focused his energy on getting their voices heard, on making sure that others knew the tragic stories of his people.

Almost overnight, he transformed himself into a crusader, and in Yan's eyes, a hero—albeit a middle-aged, potbellied, balding hero with a greasy comb-over. But who says heroes always come with great hair?

For several years, Yan's father channelled all his energies into the cause. He recruited parents, organized meetings, sought donations, and staged protest rallies, demonstrations, sit-ins, and picket lines. And with seventy thousand children missing every year, there was no lack of volunteers. Soon, the group organized itself into an underground syndicate, sniffing out clues from all corners of the country. They recovered children who had been abducted and reunited them with their parents. Every reunion gave hope to the other parents, including Yan's father, even though he knew that he could only find his daughter in America.

Perhaps not many people gave him enough credit for what he had achieved because he wasn't the most reliable leader of them all, often showing up late, showing up drunk, or not showing up at all.

His quick temper and bullheadedness offended many, so much so that his leadership was questioned and subsequently removed. But Yan, who worked alongside him all the while, knew how hard he had worked and how many sacrifices he had made. A semi-illiterate, under-employed peasant with no contacts, no money, or resources tirelessly gathering thousands of parents together, helping each of them find their children. She couldn't help but admire this new version of her father, even though Father 2.0 was losing sight of what he was trying to achieve.

To what end was he doing this? What personal benefit could he get out of this crusade of his? Perhaps even Li Fu himself couldn't answer this, but Yan knew that he did this because he had to do something—anything—to redeem himself. For losing his daughter and his wife. For his failure in finding his daughter, despite all these years of searching. For being robbed of a life they could've had. For being bullied, terrorized, and oppressed. He'd been told by Big Brother that they could do whatever they wanted to him, and there wasn't a thing Li Fu could do to get back at them. He wanted to prove them wrong.

Of course, no local media would cover their cause. Mouthpieces of the Party and the state-owned press shunned all activities and publicity by the group. As a result, little about their predicament was known by the country's vast population, let alone the world. Demonstrations and campaigns were quickly shut down by the police, who were a lot more efficient in breaking up rallies than in finding missing children.

Then came Liu Gang, the key to Yan's father's final epiphany.

* * *

When Liu Gang bumped into Yan's father, literally, the collusion sparked an idea. It happened during a demonstration Yan's father had helped organize in Dongguan, Guangdong Province, to call for the authorities to take action in finding the country's hundreds of thousands of missing children.

Liu, a Beijing resident, was in Dongguan for a job interview that hadn't gone well. Frustrated by the lack of job prospects and the intense competition for every IT position in Beijing, he had used the last penny of his savings to come here, hoping to find something, anything, that could make use of his skills. Either he would get the job, or he would be officially broke.

Pale, emaciated, and bespectacled, Liu was a pragmatist and an idealist, in that order. Being both wasn't an oxymoron, not to Liu, who believed that one must first be practical and secure a decent living before pursuing ideals. Such reasoning could only come from the mind of an engineer, to be specific, a computer engineering graduate of a local university in Heilongjiang, the far-flung province in the north-eastern tip of China. Similar to the fate of his many contemporaries, he had been in and out of work for the last two years, since he had moved to Tangjialing, an area on the outskirt of Beijing, densely populated by university graduates with little income. In Beijing, graduates were a dime a dozen—the result of millions of them from all over the country flooding into the city seeking fortune and some more. Numerous remained unemployed or underemployed. Others resorted to menial work to make ends meet.

Liu's last job was at a local computer software development start-up headed by a twenty-something who claimed to have worked in Silicon Valley and have 'awesome connections' to international venture capitalists—not just any venture capitalist but venture capitalists who had invested in Google, Facebook and Tesla—and Peter Thiel and Elon Musk. Having made a name for himself as 'one of the pioneering technopreneurs in China,' Liu's boss had hired hundreds of computer engineers, promising them rapid expansion into global markets, opportunities to work in Europe and America, and lucrative stock options, only to lay them off half a year later, offering pittance as their severance package when the millions of investment dollars failed to materialize.

Despite everything that unfolded, life went on, although Liu had no idea how. Burdened by his predicament, Liu watched the demonstration with disinterest on that fateful day. He had stepped aside into an alley to let the demonstrators march by as they chanted rally cries. Much to Liu's surprise, it didn't take long for the local police to arrive and begin dispersing the crowd and arresting demonstrators. Soon, the scene turned chaotic, with people screaming and scattering away frantically. Fights broke out as soon as the police started clubbing demonstrators.

Yan and her father took flight as soon as the authorities arrived, but two policemen saw and chased them closely. They dodged into a narrow alley, through which the march had just passed, and before they knew it, a pair of arms reached out and pulled them into a small internet café.

'If you run, the police will know you're running from them,' Liu whispered. 'Stay and pretend that you're not part of the demonstration. Here, wear my jacket.'

'Thank you,' Yan's father said, trying to control his panting as he kept an eye on the glass door and windows. Soon, the two policemen ran past the café and turned the corner into another alley. Yan's father let out a soft, nervous laugh before showering Liu with gratitude.

'I don't know how to thank you enough. Please, let me buy you a drink.'

'It's a small matter. Don't worry about it,' Liu Gang said in his gentle voice.

'No, I insist. You just saved me at least a month of jail time.'

They chose a table in a corner and ordered some coffee while they waited for the chaos outside the café to clear.

'By the way, what are you demonstrating for? Sorry, I'm afraid I was distracted by my thoughts and wasn't paying much attention,' Liu said.

Yan's father spent the next half an hour explaining his tragic story as Liu listened quietly, nodding or shaking his head at the appropriate moments to show his empathy.

When Yan's father finished his story, Liu said pensively, 'I may not know enough about this, but I think staging rallies isn't the solution to your problem. You're embarrassing the authorities, so why would they help you out? Look at how they reacted to your demonstration today. How often do you see them taking action so swiftly? I say find your kid on your own.'

'What the hell are you talking about? Were you not listening to my story? That's what I've been doing for the past sixteen years! I've literally travelled the entire country searching for her,' Li Fu said, sounding rather vexed.

'I'm not saying you aren't trying hard enough. I'm saying you're not doing it right. The world has changed. You need to use the right tools to get the best results.'

'What do you mean?'

And so began Liu's scheme. He explained how they could harness the power of the internet to reach out to more people, specifically an international audience who would be more sympathetic to Li's situation. 'The power and wisdom lie not in the people, but in technology, my friend.'

'We Chinese are too jaded when it comes to tragedies; I mean, *we* invented tragedies! You'll have limited success in our country. Look beyond, look towards the world,' he said.

His words resonated like Beethoven's Fifth Symphony in the ears of Yan's father.

'First things first. You need donations. You need to build a fund to finance your operations.'

Yan's father felt as if his prayers were being finally answered. It seemed like a Bodhisattva, albeit in the form of a pale, skinny, young man with sophisticated intelligence, had descended on Dongguan to help him. This Bodhisattva, however, came with a price.

'Twenty per cent of all your donations,' Liu proposed.

'TWENTY PER CENT? What are you, a pimp?'

'I'm telling you, it's worth it,' Liu replied without showing the slightest hint of being offended. 'The amount of money you'll collect will be so huge you won't stop thanking me later!'

Chapter 5

FAYE

Faye could hear the television in the kitchen from her bedroom upstairs, but she was sure Sophia wasn't watching it. Her mom was never comfortable with silence in the house and would always leave the radio or television on as background noise, a habit that annoyed the hell out of Faye since she was a little girl. Sophia had left the coffee machine on too—the aroma of freshly brewed coffee had permeated Faye's bedroom, lifting the remaining fogginess of sleep off her head. The sound of her mom fussing around the kitchen preparing breakfast and going through the same morning routine for the past seventeen years cued Faye to get ready.

'Faye, hurry up! I need to get to work as early as possible today,' Sophia yelled, her timing as regular as clockwork.

'Why are you so eager to get to work? Is it because of the new cute guy you talked so much about last night?' Faye popped her pretty little head with her jet-black tousled hair into the kitchen, dressed only in a black bra and mini skirt.

'Don't be silly! That guy's way too young for me. It's the post inspector; he's coming in today. Didn't I tell you last night that the headquarters is sending someone down today to do a post-office inspection? I was sure you weren't listening, and I was right. You used to hang on to my every word. Nowadays, you don't even listen when you're supposed to . . .' Sophia rumbled on without turning, as Faye made a face.

'Anyway, I need to sort out the parcels in the backroom before the inspector arrives. I'm telling you I don't know what people are sending these days, but those boxes are getting much heavier than they used to . . .' she continued. Faye knew her mom was already regretting mentioning the new guy to her. She never missed a chance to get her mother on a date, and Sophia was tired of it.

'Maybe the problem isn't with the parcels; the problem is you. You're getting old, and you're no longer as strong as you used to be. You should get an easier job, or better still, get a man, retire, and travel the world with him. But then again, I can't think of an easier job than working at the post office.'

'Hey, that's not nice! My job isn't as easy as it looks. Besides, it puts food on the table for both of us, okay?' Sophia turned and saw with horror what Faye was wearing—or not wearing. 'Jesus! Cover yourself with something, young lady!' she chided.

Faye returned to her room to get dressed. She could hear Sophia turn up the volume of the television to listen to the morning news.

Coming up, a heart-wrenching story of a Chinese father looking for . . .

She hurriedly put on a brown halter top and shoved her books into her bag, deliberately leaving the Chinese textbook half-buried on her desk. Just when she was leaving her bedroom, she heard her mom's voice shouting over the morning news.

'Don't forget your Chinese book, dear. You've a class with Madam Ip after school today.'

'Fuck!' Faye cursed under her breath.

There was no getting away with it because Faye knew that Sophia had already memorized her schedule by heart. As intelligent as she was at most things, Faye was terrible at skiving, and the few tricks she had up her sleeve almost made her a laughing stock to any mother. Forgetting to bring her books was one of several that Faye liked to pull. While Sophia might cut her daughter some slack occasionally,

Faye knew that she would never allow her to miss any of her Chinese classes. Faye hated her Chinese classes, and while she got excellent grades in all her academic subjects, she never seemed to be able to pick up the language despite the many years of coaching.

So, Faye would try to come up with fresh excuses each time they argued about this.

'It's just too difficult a language for me!'

'Do you know that bilingualism can potentially harm academic growth?'

'You can't browbeat me into learning something I don't want to learn!'

'That's a new one—browbeat!' Sophia would laugh.

'Why, Mom? Why is it so important for me to learn Chinese? It's not like we speak it regularly here,' Faye would plead when her indignation didn't work. 'Besides, I don't know anything about being Chinese. I'm ethnically Chinese—yes, I'm born with the Chinese genes, but I'm American, you're American. We're all Americans!'

But no matter what Faye had to say about this, Sophia would insist on getting her daughter to learn about her roots and disregard her increasingly loud protests.

'I brought you out of China. The least I could do is to try to make you learn something about the place you were born in, whether you cared for it or not,' she would reply patiently.

At least mom was right about one thing: Faye didn't care about her past because she believed a person shouldn't be valued based on their roots but rather, where they were going. Faye had a very clear idea of where she wanted to go. She would finish college and then spend a couple of years travelling around the world. Mom had never enjoyed travelling—the only place they had ever visited was the Grand Canyon, which Faye didn't count as "real travel" because it was a local trip. She wanted to visit historically significant and exciting places like Europe, Asia, and the Middle East, and she would write stories about them and sell them to news agencies or websites or maybe even publish a book. Then, she would return and look for a job at a newspaper or publishing firm as a journalist. She wasn't thinking of the cliché

American dream—she preferred 2.5 dogs to children—but believed she would marry if she found the right guy.

These were the things she cared about, not wasting her time learning Chinese from a second-rate tutor in Chinatown. But in order not to break her mother's heart, Faye would drag herself to the Veronica Ip Chinese Learning Centre in San Francisco's Chinatown twice a week for her lessons.

Faye heaved a sigh, picked up the Chinese textbook, dropped it into her bag, and went downstairs for breakfast, trying to look despondent. Before Sophia turned around, she already sensed her daughter's bad mood.

'C'mon, don't be such a pain. It isn't that bad. Madam Ip told me just last week that you were making good progress. I think this personal coaching thing is working,' Sophia cajoled.

'That's exactly what she wants you to think so that she can continue hoodwinking you into paying her for those useless lessons,' Faye retorted. Not only did she hate the lessons, but she also disliked Madam Ip just as much. She didn't care for the tutor's condescending criticisms of the 'bourgeois, consumerist ways of the Americans' even as she appraised everyone and everything solely in monetary terms.

'At least you can write simple Chinese sentences now. And your daily conversations are good.' Sophia tried to be encouraging.

'Yeah, like that's a real accomplishment. I'm sure you're so damn proud of me.'

Sarcasm was Faye's choice of a defence mechanism against her mom because she loved her too much to get into a real fight with her. People often say that one can't choose family. Faye certainly didn't choose her second family, but she thought someone out there had made an excellent choice on her behalf. While she didn't necessarily agree with her mom on everything—for one, Faye refused to go to church lately—she thought Sophia was as good an adoptive mother as anyone could hope for.

Nobody loved Faye as her mom did and Faye knew this fact. And it wasn't one of those I-want-to-nurture-you-to-be-the-best-so-that-I-can-show-you-off kinds of love. It was gentle, compassionate, and omnipresent. Sophia would do anything for Faye. Anything.

Take a bullet? Easy-peasy. Need one of my kidneys? Take it! If Faye had wanted a father, Sophia would marry a man in a heartbeat, just for her sake. But Faye had always said that she didn't need a father because her mom was already giving her twice the amount of love she needed.

Faye grew up knowing that she was loved. Perhaps that was the formula for parenting success because Faye turned out to be balanced, conscientious, and intelligent. In addition, she was also pretty, cheerful, and sociable, which made her a dream girlfriend for many boys at school.

As she gobbled down her cereal, Faye braced for a reprimand from Sophia for swearing at the table, but it never came. Somehow, Faye had lost Sophia's attention. Her mom was listening intently to the morning news and ignoring her completely. Faye let her mind wander; her seventeen-year-old mind wasn't too concerned about what was happening around the world. She was thinking about her date with Charlie tonight.

For about a year, Faye had been going out with Charles Murray, who attended the same high school as Faye. She didn't like him at first; she had thought he was a bit of an arrogant prick. When he had first asked her out, she had the suspicion that she was the target of a nefarious trick conjured by him and some other popular boys at school, so had turned him down curtly. But he didn't stop asking her out for the next three months. He would ask her out every time they bumped into each other in the hallway, which was suspiciously frequent enough for her to think that he had been stalking her! Surely, he and the boys would have found the idea old by the third month? When she finally said yes, just for curiosity's sake, nothing terrible happened to her. He was simply infatuated with her. He had dreamily said he had never seen any girl smarter, prettier, or more exotic than her. She wasn't sure if she should take the word 'exotic' as a compliment, an insult, or a red flag for an 'Asian chick' fetish. But by that time, the foetus of their romance had begun to grow steadily, and the more she got to know him, the more was enamoured with him.

It turned out that Charles came from a very wealthy family—old money—and thus, some 'residual aristocratic blood' still flowed in him, manifesting itself in the form of an 'arrogant prick' from time to time. But, she soon learnt not to judge him because of his family's wealth just as she wouldn't judge anyone by their background, race, or gender preference. As she looked inside the real Charlie, she realized that other than being brazenly handsome and unbelievably rich, he could also be the most caring and sweet guy if he chose to. Still an arrogant prick at times, and more than a little self-centred, nevertheless, he was almost too good to be true. Because he was rich and handsome, he had always been popular at school and treated like a rock star by the other students; even the teachers couldn't help themselves. He could get any girl he wanted, so Faye didn't know why he had picked her as his girlfriend. Lots of girls would commit murder or perform any kind of salacious act to be with him, and he had dated quite a handful before her. On the other hand, Faye had insulted, ridiculed, and intellectually challenged him from the get-go but he had remained loyal to her. She could never truly understand why—she liked to think that he was attracted to her wit, athletic abilities, free-spirited personality, and her hatred for anything hypocritical and phoney, but whenever she asked him, he would shrug and quip, 'What can I say? You're a forbidden fruit from the mysterious Orient—exotic and exciting. Don't you know guys lust for anything mysterious?'

Back in the kitchen, Faye thought about what to do after dinner. Maybe a comedy or an action film. Her mom would be at the church, as usual, for Bible study, which meant she could spend the entire evening alone with Charlie, something she very much looked forward to. She hurriedly finished breakfast and put the bowl and cup in the dishwasher while her mom, eyes still glued to the TV, hadn't touched her cereal. Rather odd behaviour, for mom would usually be waiting at the door by now, jingling her car key and hastening Faye to leave for school.

'Mom . . . MOM! It's time to go. I thought you said you needed to be early at work?' Faye tapped Sophia's shoulder impatiently.

Sophia peeled her eyes off the TV and looked at Faye, eyes glazed, face drained of life. Within a matter of minutes, Sophia seemed to have aged ten years, resembling a terror-stricken old woman lost in Dante's inferno world.

'Oh, yes, that's right . . . uh . . . dinner tonight, sweetie?' Sophia struggled for a reply.

'No, Mom! I've a date with Charlie tonight, remember? And it's Bible study night for you. Are you okay? You look so pale. Are you sick or something?' Faye studied Sophia's face with grave concern.

'Yes, I mean, no, I'm fine. Sorry, I forgot about your date. It's fine. Listen, why don't you run along? I forgot I need to do a thing. I need to call someone before I get to work.'

'Are you sure? 'Cos you don't look so good to me. Maybe I should stay home with you or take you to the doctor or something.'

'No, no, I'm fine . . . really. You go ahead, sweetie. I don't want you to be late for school,' Sophia insisted.

'Okay then,' Faye relented, a little unsure. 'Call me if you need me, okay? Bye Mom, love you!' She gave Sophia a quick peck on the cheek and left the house in a flash, like a fresh morning breeze blowing through an old and musty room.

SOPHIA

The kitchen was quiet again without Faye. Sophia waited and listened for Faye to get into her car, turn on the ignition, and back up the driveway. Then, she got up shakily, staggered to her phone, and call her friend, Julie. The phone rang twice before Julie answered.

'Hey Sophia, I was about to call you. Listen, about tonight's Bible study session, I was thinking of inviting—' Julie rattled on without giving Sophia a chance to speak.

'I'm not calling about Bible study, Julie. Something came up. I need to see you immediately,' Sophia interrupted her impatiently.

'Well, we're meeting tonight, darling. Can it wait?'

'No, it can't wait till tonight. It's bad, very bad. I need to see you now!'

'Oh dear! What is it? All right, all right, let me think . . . I've a meeting with Eric's teacher in about half an hour. My beloved son has got himself into trouble at school again! I guess the earliest I can catch you would be at lunch. Is that okay with you?' said Julie.

'Okay, I'll see you at the Irish bar next to my post office at noon. Please be there. It's very important.'

'Are you okay, honey? You don't sound right—'

'Just be there at noon. This is serious.'

Sophia placed the phone in her bag, but she was unable to get up from the chair. She was paralysed by fear and shaken to her core by what she had just heard on the news. She wasn't sure if she could go to work in this state of mind but decided that work might shave some nerves off her, at least for a bit. Gathering all the strength she could muster, she pushed herself up from the seat, grabbed her bag, and walked unsteadily to her car.

* * *

Sophia was already waiting in the booth seats at the back of the bar when Julie walked in a few minutes past noon. Julie immediately noticed a glass of scotch, almost empty, on the table as well as Sophia's puffy red eyes and swollen cheeks as she sat down opposite her friend. She knew something diabolical was brewing.

'When did you start drinking at noon? And scotch? Really? Don't you need to get back to work after lunch? Have you been crying? What's going on?' Julie, with her insatiable appetite for answers, fired a series of questions barely after she had sat down. This wasn't like Sophia; Sophia never drank at lunch, and the strongest alcohol she could stomach was red wine, which she seldom drank more than a glass.

Sophia ignored Julie's interrogation, her mind somewhere far away, clouded by some dark, looming threat that was about to wreck her quiet, perfect life. She started speaking in a melancholic and trance-like manner.

'I think it's time Faye and I get out of town. I'm thinking of selling the house and moving away. Do you know any good realty agent?'

'Move? Why? Where to?'

'Somewhere remote, somewhere peaceful, where no one can disturb us. Maybe to a different country, like England or Australia.'

'You've never mentioned anything about relocating before. What for? Who's been disturbing your peace?'

'No one. At least, no one yet.'

'This is ridiculous! I've known you too long; you're not going anywhere. You're like a hobbit. You hate adventures, surprises, or changes of any kind. You're boring and predictable. Uprooting your family and your life to a different place? That's the last thing you want to do,' Julie ranted. She paused and then added in a concerned voice, 'Why are you talking like this? Just spare me the crazy talk and tell me what's wrong, okay?'

'What do you think of Alaska? It's admittedly a little cold, but I saw a TV documentary about how much oil they've been getting from the place. I personally think it has a lot of potential—'

'Sophia cut the crap! Tell me what happened! Is Faye in some kind of trouble? Is she pregnant?'

'Of course not! She's only seventeen, for goodness sake!'

'What is it then? Sophia, you know you can't hide anything from me. I'll find out sooner or later, so you might as well tell me now,' Julie said.

Tears flooded Sophia's eyes. She wiped them away quickly before asking, 'Did you watch the news on TV this morning?'

'No, I had to meet Eric's school teacher, remember? About the fight he got into yesterday? I told you this morning over the phone—'

'Have you heard of a man called Li Fu?' Sophia interrupted.

'Nope, doesn't ring a bell. Wait a minute, is he the Chinese Premier visiting Washington this week? No, no, that's a different name. Who is this Li guy? What's he got to do with you?'

'He was in the news this morning. He is a Chinese guy who's been looking for his long-lost daughter.'

'Here in San Francisco?'

'No, in China. Apparently, his daughter was abducted many years ago. The Chinese authorities had long given up hope of finding his daughter, but he didn't. His daughter would be seventeen this year,' Sophia said, almost breathing her words out. She couldn't look at Julie as she spoke, so she fixed her gaze on the traffic and the grey sky outside the window.

Julie looked ghastly as she listened to the story. She wanted details, but she was too afraid to ask. She waited with trepidation and braced for what was about to come.

'There's nothing unusual about this story. I mean, so many children go missing in China every year. Li Fu is just smarter and more resourceful than most of these Chinese parents with missing kids. He uses social media to spread his story. And the international media has picked it up. He even receives online donations from people all over the world to help fund the search for his daughter. He claims that he'll come to San Francisco, where he believes his daughter is, once he gets enough money. Donations are pouring in, Julie. He's not giving up, and he's coming here soon.'

'He may not be who you think he is. As you said, there're so many missing kids in China—' Julie said feebly. She loved Faye as much as Sophia did, and had been a caring and generous aunt to her all these years. She couldn't bear to face this day, the day she and Sophia had dreaded for so long.

'That was what I had hoped too, until he mentioned his daughter's name—Li Ying.'

'Oh my God!' Julie exclaimed.

'I don't know what to do, but I know I can't bear to part with my daughter. Faye's my only family and my life. Without her, I'll just be another sad, lonely, old maid. She's made everything better since the day I took her from the orphanage. I'll die if they take her away from me.'

Sophia broke down in tears again. Julie held her hands firmly across the table to offer solace and waited until Sophia was calm enough to go on. She knew that no words could comfort her old friend at this moment.

'Does Faye know about this?' Julie asked quietly.

'Not yet, but I don't think it'll take her long to find out. The story's all over the internet. That Lady Gogo or whoever even Tweeted about sending money to the guy,' Sophia managed between her sobs.

'Faye may not know the man is looking for her.'

'She knows her Chinese name. I've shown her the coat she had worn at the orphanage. You know the one with her name sewn on it?'

'Shit.'

Silence ensued between them.

'What are we going to do?' Julie asked, almost to herself.

'I don't know. That's why I wanted to talk to you so badly. You know the internet better than I do. You sell shit on it,' Sophia blurted. 'I'm sorry. I shouldn't have said that. The stuff you sell is great,' she said regretfully.

'It's okay, honey. And I'm so sorry I couldn't get here earlier. I didn't know it was so serious.'

'Julie, please help me!'

'Right, okay. Well, let's see. Right now, I don't think you have much choice here. It's either she finds out about it on her own or you tell her yourself. I think the latter is the lesser evil of the two.'

'I can't! What am I supposed to tell her? That I knew she might not have been an orphan? She won't understand!'

'It'll be a lot worse if she finds that out on her own, don't you think?'

Sophia didn't like her options. She took the half-empty glass of scotch and finished it in one big gulp. She thought for a long time, weeping and smiling now and then, like a demented woman on her deathbed experiencing flashbacks of all her moments in her life. Finally, she made her decision.

'I'll tell her. I'll tell her the truth tonight.'

'That's good. That's the right thing to do.'

Sadly, Sophia had no idea how fast news travelled on the internet. Just as she finished speaking those words, her cell phone rang. It said 'incoming call from Faye'. She sniffed, wiped her tears, and cleared her throat before answering the phone.

'Hi honey,' she chirped, trying to sound as cheerful as possible.

'Remind me, Mom. Is my Chinese name Li Ying?'

Chapter 6

YAN

Yan and her father got off the crowded public bus after a long, dusty, and uncomfortable ride. They had arrived at Tangjialing and decided to take a break at the bus stop to stretch their legs. Her father was busy trying to recall the way to their destination. Yan already knew the way by heart because they had been here before. But she knew her father wouldn't like it if she led the way. Neither would he ask for directions. So, she decided to wait for him to figure it out.

About an hour's drive—that meant a two-hour bus journey—north of downtown Beijing and close to Zhongguancun Software Park, China's answer to Silicon Valley, Tangjialing was a small, sleepy village occupied by farmers and labourers for the longest time. Recently, the area had transformed itself into a populous real estate for cheap accommodation and was now home to as many as fifty thousand lodgers. Most of the lodgers belonged to the *Yi Zu* or 'Ant Tribe', a group of young, educated, migrant white-collar workers who, armed with a diploma or a university education from rural towns, flocked to big cities searching for a better life, only to find themselves eking out a meagre living in these places. Mostly in their twenties, these 'ants' were predominantly from poor rural families, employed in temporary and low-paying jobs, and were often unemployed or underemployed. Even with a tertiary certificate, their education in ordinary universities did not provide them with sufficient skills to compete in China's cutthroat job market. There were simply too many universities and too many graduates here, and employers preferred graduates from the Chinese 'Ivy Leagues'. So, instead of landing themselves in high-paying jobs, the 'ants' found themselves scraping by on the edge of poverty and living in quarters of sub-standard, miserable conditions. Like the name given to them, they were like a colony of ants—intelligent and hardworking, yet anonymous and underpaid.

It was late morning and the village, emptied of its 'ants', was not as crowded as it would be after dark. The way to Yan and her father's destination was an unpaved but well-trodden track, but a heavy thunderstorm last night had sodden the earth. Yan's father's only pair of good shoes were soiled with mud by the time they reached the non-descript three-storey cement block, which stood among other ramshackle buildings constructed so closely one could almost reach out and touch the neighbour's window across the alley. He cursed under his breath as they walked up three floors to Liu Gang's unit.

Impatiently, Yan's father knocked loudly on the chipped and paint-peeled wooden door. It took a while before a young man answered it, opening the door suspiciously just a crack, barely enough to see his eye.

'Looking for Liu Gang,' Yan's father said gruffly. 'And hurry up, I don't have all day.'

Yan stood behind her father, dying to apologize for his ill-bred, ill-mannered behaviour and wishing she could say something nice to the young man.

I'm sorry. We're not barbarians. It's just that he isn't a nice man when he is drunk. Truth be told, he isn't a nice man when he is sober either, she wanted to say, but she remained quiet, expression unreadable.

Recognizing them, the young man swung the door wide open, turned around, and murmured, 'It's for you,' before returning to his tiny, crowded desk and burying himself in the screen of his laptop again.

It didn't take them long to find out if Liu Gang was in, for they could see the entire apartment from where they stood. It was a windowless, concrete box, barely the size of a bedroom. Nevertheless, the tenants had managed to squeeze in a wardrobe, two narrow desks, and two bunk beds with beddings that looked like they hadn't been washed for months. There was, however, hardly any walking space. A naked fluorescent bulb hung from the cracked and unpainted ceiling, and the floor was littered with cigarette butts, dirty laundry, and empty Styrofoam bowls that used to contain plastic-tasting instant noodles. Apart from the young man who had answered the door, there were two other tenants—both intelligent-looking men in their prime. One at the other desk and the other lying on the bed, reading a newspaper. The room was hot and stuffy and smelt of soured beer mixed with cigarette smoke; there was no ventilation and air-conditioning wasn't an affordable option. Only a noisy fan encrusted with a thick layer of grime at a corner of the room provided some relief for their lungs.

Liu Gang, seated at one of the desks, swivelled his chair around to see who his visitors were. He gave a slight nod of acknowledgement and waved them in before turning his attention back to his laptop. Liu was way in his twenties although he still looked like a nerdy teenager. He had been unemployed for almost half a year and was surviving on instant noodles and, for variety, ramen noodles. Together with his equally unemployed roommates, they shared the puny, cheap room for five hundred yuan a month. His project with Yan's father was his lifeline now, and hopefully, a tunnel out of this hell hole.

Yan and her father entered the apartment, ignoring the musty, sweaty smell of scarcely washed men. Now that Yan had fully blossomed into a twenty-one-year-old woman, she felt self-conscious whenever she was in the presence of men, particularly testosterone-powered, libido-driven young men. She was very aware that her body had undergone physical changes in the past few years—her breasts were fuller and spilling out of her ill-fitted four-year-old bra, and her buttocks much more voluptuous. Being ashamed of their size, she often took small, awkward steps so that they wouldn't sway or bounce too much. She was no longer a child but didn't yet know how to behave like a woman.

If her father had noticed any changes in her, he didn't show it. Maybe he didn't want to add to the awkwardness that she was already feeling about herself. Maybe he didn't want to accept that his baby girl had grown up so quickly. Or maybe, just maybe, he didn't care.

Yan's father sat down next to Liu on a rickety stool, the only unoccupied seat in the room, while Yan remained standing behind him. No one offered her a seat or even looked her way. Not that she minded. She wanted to be as inconspicuous as possible. She wanted to be left alone. So she pretended to stare blankly at the dirty cement floor while she listened to the conversation between Liu and her father, who started gloating as soon as he had settled down.

'Did you watch the news last night? Not the shitty local channels, the international news. Guess what? I was on CNN last night. CNN!'

Liu raised one of his eyebrows ever so slightly. 'You have cable TV?'

'No, no. I watched it at the bar that serves the *laowai*[1] on Wangfujing Street. Xiao Zhang works in the kitchen there and sneaked me in just to watch the segment.'

'Ah!'

'I was interviewed by the Americans!' Yan's father puffed up his chest, slapped it lightly with his hands, and grinned. He looked around hoping for a wider audience, but Liu's roommates couldn't stand his loud and obnoxious bragging. One of them left the room in annoyance. The other put on his headphones and continued working on his laptop.

Disappointed, Li's grin narrowed.

'Yes, I know,' Liu answered with an air of irritation. Yan could tell that he wasn't fond of her father and hated giving him any credit. Not when most of the ideas and work done were Liu's.

'This internet thing is so great! And you made it happen! The websites, the Facebook pages, the blogs, the YouTube videos, made for the world to see!'

'Circumventing the Great Firewall of China—' Liu couldn't help but boast a little too.

---

[1] Laowai means Westerners in Chinese.

'Yes, that too! You know, I've been dealt a bad hand by life, and I would still be heading nowhere if it weren't for you. I'm so happy, my good brother. After all these years, I'm finally making good progress,' said Yan's father, revealing a missing tooth and a few decaying ones as he flashed a broad smile across his weather-beaten, wrinkled face. He slapped Liu affably on his back, but his display of camaraderie made Liu flinch involuntarily, both from the physical force and the thought of being his 'brother'.

Yan's father waited for Liu to say something nice but was rewarded with silence instead.

'Did you know how CNN found me?' Li babbled, filling the dead air. 'They said they saw my, no, I'm sorry, OUR video on YouTube. You know the one where I held the placard that said "Help! Corrupted authorities took my daughter away!" in English at the international airport?'

Yes, I remember the video too, Yan thought as she watched her father talk incessantly. *I held the placard with you, Papa. It was your idea to go to the airport because you wanted to reach out to the laowai. 'Forget the locals; they're useless, and they don't have the balls to defy the authorities,' you said. I remember being at the airport every single day for almost a week, walking around with the placard, dodging airport security guards, and eating travellers' leftovers at the airport cafés. I was so scared all the time, but you kept pushing me to go on. We were there until we finally got thrown out by the securities. Liu was there for a day to film us, and I vividly remember he made sure he stayed at a safe distance so that he didn't look like he was one of us. Did you remember that about your 'good brother', father?*

'And you were absolutely right; we needed to do this in English. Otherwise, the Americans wouldn't understand us. But I don't know a word of English. You, on the other hand, are different. You are educated, smart, savvy. You know the new world while I'm left behind in the old one. Anyway, the people at CNN saw the video and read our Facebook posts. The reporter told me the posts had gone viral. It's global now,' he continued, still basking in his moment of glory.

'The reporter told you that?' Liu's interest was piqued.

'Through an interpreter, of course. They sent a correspondent in Beijing to interview me—a *laowai* who's been here for two years. She could speak a little Chinese, and she said she could help me do some research on my daughter—'

'Anyway, donations started flooding in right after CNN telecasted the interview last evening. I think you already have more than enough to go to San Francisco,' Liu interrupted impatiently. Yan noticed that he was a little jealous of her father's recently acquired fame and fortune. After all, it was indeed him who'd made it happen.

'How much do we have now?' Yan's father asked a little too quickly, his eyes glinting a little too brightly.

Yan saw disgust in Liu's eyes as he contemplated the greedy countenance of this person he had to call his associate, and she knew what it was about. Rather than being sympathetic to his circumstance, which in many ways were not unlike those of the Ant Tribes, Liu despised Li Fu. He despised him because he reminded him of his own poverty, that despite his education, intelligence, and hard work, he had still ended up in a state that wasn't so different from this uneducated, unskilled, boorish peasant. He felt like he belonged to a higher social stratum—the worldly, the skilled, and the employable. He belonged to the new economy, the modern China, and he ought to be allowed to prosper. Instead, he was living in a stinky hole, collaborating with this bloody country bumpkin who was polluting the very air he breathed. He detested the fact that he had to be this man's partner-in-crime in order to survive. But he hated himself more for agreeing to—no, suggesting—this association.

Yan was sure that Liu wouldn't so much as look at her father, let alone help him, had he not been so desperate for money. Heavily indebted and out of cash, he would have to pack up, return to Heilongjiang, and live off his parents—not a coveted prospect for a young man of his ambition. It would also mean having to admit failure to his family, his relatives, and possibly, the entire village back home. Besides, the employment prospect in Heilongjiang was as dim as his hope of ever returning to Beijing. No, Liu wouldn't go home. He would much rather stay in his colony on the fringe of the big city and burrow his way to success, no matter how much bullshit life threw at him.

Somehow, Yan understood Liu. She also knew that whatever contempt he might feel for her father, he had to repress and lock it deep inside him, at least until their 'project' was done.

Liu glanced at his laptop screen and said, 'As of five minutes ago, you've over eight thousand US dollars in donations. Minus one thousand dollars as internet fee and twenty per cent of my cut, as we've agreed, you've about five thousand four hundred dollars or over thirty thousand yuan. I'm sure more will come in within the next few weeks.'

Yan snorted at the mention of the internet fee but quickly turned the snort into a cough when both Liu and Li swirled around and looked at her. She gave a half-smile and looked away. She rummaged her mind for the costs she had researched on the internet.

Internet fee my foot! She thought, twisting her mouth wryly as if something distasteful had entered it. *It would've cost you less than a hundred yuan to purchase the domain name and a web hosting package, maybe a little more for a virtual private network to circumvent the firewall. My father may be a fool, but I'm not! You're ripping him off as much as you can, thinking that we'll never find out!*

Yan wanted to say something, but when she saw her father's face so filled with bliss and hope, a look she hadn't seen since the days before Ying's abduction, she decided to let him enjoy the moment. A little ripping off wouldn't hurt.

'Thirty thousand yuan!' Yan's father whispered. It was more than two years of his returns for his plumbing business, the kind of money he had never owned in his life.

'Yup, that should be enough,' said Liu with forced enthusiasm.

Close to tears, he looked at Yan and said, 'Daughter, we can finally go to America to find your little sister. We'll soon be together again.'

Rather than meeting his gaze, Yan looked away, her mind continuing to question this reality.

Should I feign enthusiasm like Liu? Should I believe that everything will be fine from now on? Should I pretend that no damage had been done to our family, and no casualties declared in the past seventeen years? I want to, Papa, for your sake. You look so happy, and you're seldom happy. How can I break your heart?

But Yan couldn't do it; she didn't know how to. So she gazed stoically at the ground and merely nodded in acknowledgement.

'You can't even manage a little smile at such fabulous news, can you? What a bore! I wish I didn't have to take you to America. When we find your sister, you better start learning from her,' he said reproachfully.

Still, Yan said nothing and kept her head down, although she couldn't hide the hurt on her face. Despite all the years of thrashings, insults, and verbal abuses from her father, his words still stung.

Liu turned around and looked at Yan's father with disdain. Yan could tell that he pitied her and disapproved of the way Yan's father treated her. He looked as if he wanted to say something to defend her but decided against it. Yan knew he didn't want to challenge her father at this point. To Liu, everything came with a price, including standing up for her, and he wasn't ready to pay for it yet, not when he was about to pocket two thousand six hundred US dollars.

Instead, he did the next best thing. He deflected.

'Hey, Li, you want me to announce on your social media platforms that you've collected enough for your trip? I can stop the donation drive right away,' Liu said. While the money was lucrative, he wanted to end his dealings with Yan's father as soon as possible.

'Stop sending money? What are you, shit-for-brains? This is the most profitable venture I . . . no, we . . . will ever have. You must be stupid or crazy to end this,' Yan's father said without a morsel of guilt.

Yan could tell that Liu was boiling with repressed rage. 'Well, in my book, it's unscrupulous to take money from people when you don't need it. These people are helping you out of their kindness, and you've taken more than enough already. Collecting more would be amounting to cheating, even fraud—'

'Fraud? Cheating? What do you know about cheating, young man? I've been cheated of a good life. I've been robbed of a beautiful family. What have I done to deserve it? Nothing! Who cared about my misfortunes? Nobody! Nobody gave a fucking shit! So don't you dare lecture me about cheating!' said Li, nostril flared. 'Now an opportunity has finally arrived, and I'm not letting it slip out of my hands without milking every single cent out of it first. In *my* book, Lady Luck doesn't come knocking often, at least not at my door.'

Realizing that he had lost his temper, he tried to regain his cool. 'You're still young. You may not think like that now, but you'll understand someday.'

Silence filled the room as his words sunk in. And like heavy stones and leaking holes in a small boat, it sank the last ounce of their honour and integrity into the ocean abyss.

'Now listen, write a new post. Say that we still need more for the trip . . .' Yan's father contemplated for a while and continued. 'We need a new story . . . say that I've just contracted tuberculosis and I need money for treatment.'

Liu looked at him with disbelief and blatant disgust.

Sensing Liu's abhorrence, Yan's father tried to mollify him. 'Look, I need just a little more to safeguard my trip, and I promise I'll stop. I don't know how long it'll take me to find my daughter, and America is a big and expensive country. I'm sure you can understand that,' he said in a gentler tone.

'Fuck it,' Liu murmured incomprehensibly.

'What did you say?' Yan's father asked.

'I said fine, I'll do this one last time, then I'm done. I don't want to have anything more to do with this whole ruse,' Liu said tersely without looking up from the laptop.

'We'll see,' Yan's father said barely audible. He turned to Yan and said, 'Now, let's book our tickets to San Francisco.'

A wide grin manifested on his face once again.

Chapter 7

FAYE

'Well? Do you have anything to say?' Faye demanded curtly.

'Is that how you speak to your mother, young lady?' Julie reprimanded.

Her comment put Faye in an even fouler mood, but Julie didn't seem to care. Faye had never shown disrespect to her mother in front of Julie before, and it seemed to Faye that Julie wasn't about to let her start.

Sophia placed her hand gently on Julie's arm, a non-verbal plea to her friend to not start a fight with her daughter. Faye knew that under normal circumstances, Sophia wouldn't have allowed such behaviour from her but she chose to let it slide today. Perhaps she felt she deserved the disrespect.

'What do you want me to tell you?' Sophia asked quietly.

'The truth, for one!' Faye snapped.

Sophia sighed.

Faye knew that sigh. It was the sound her mother made when she wanted to hide something from her. Faye knew her instinct was right; her mother hadn't been entirely truthful with her past.

'You already knew some of it—' Sophia began.

'Telling me half the story doesn't necessarily mean it's true, isn't it? It's still lying,' Faye interrupted impudently. 'Wasn't it you who taught me that?'

Faye knew Sophia couldn't deny the fact that she had taught her about half-truths. In fact, she had been meticulous in teaching Faye all the moral values she thought a good Christian girl should possess. What she didn't expect was that Faye hadn't quite turned out to be the kind of girl that embraced Christianity wholeheartedly. But now, Faye was determined to use all the moral ammunition she could gather against her mother.

'You're right. I haven't been absolutely candid with you—'

'You think?' Faye murmured sarcastically.

'Faye, that's enough!' Julie cried.

'What? Am I the one who's wrong here? Am I the one who's been lying to my child all this time? And I'm chided for being rude? Right now? Hello? A little perspective here, please?'

'Julie, maybe you can get us some coffee, that is, if you don't mind,' Sophia offered, trying to mollify the tense situation.

'Fine, if that's what you want,' Julie said indignantly, throwing her hands up as she stood up and walked towards the Starbucks' order counter.

A sense of awkward truce lingered after Julie's temporary departure. Faye's mind was whirling with questions and more questions, but she had obstinately decided to stay indomitable and would rather suffer the crushing silence than be the first to speak. Her mother, on the other hand, buckled swiftly under the burden of guilt. She spoke quietly without looking into Faye's scalpel-like eyes.

'I'm sorry, honey,' she said. 'Ask me whatever you want, and I'll answer you truthfully and unreservedly.'

'Oh trust me, I will!' Faye said defiantly.

'Okay, then.'

'Was my birth name really Li Ying?' Faye volleyed her first shot.

'I'm not a 100 per cent sure, but you had a baby coat with those Chinese characters sewn on it. The people at the orphanage told me there was no official record of your birth name, but it was very likely

Li Ying because it was a common practice for Chinese mothers to sew their children's names on their clothes.'

'I remember the jacket. You showed it to me once.'

'It's still in one of the boxes with your old baby stuff in the garage if you want to look at it again,' Sophia offered.

'Do you know who my biological parents are?'

'Not a clue. As I said, the orphanage claimed they didn't know anything about you.'

'Do you know this man—this—Li Fu?'

'No, I've never heard of him in my entire life, that is, until this morning.'

'So you don't know if he's my real father?'

'No, I don't. But he posted a picture on his blog, of his youngest daughter when she was a newborn. The resemblance between his daughter and the pictures I took of you when you were a baby is striking. Also, the age of his baby, the time she was abducted and the syndicate fit perfectly. I'll say it's the same baby.'

'So, all those stories about how you have adopted me from an orphanage in Beijing. Were they true or just a load of bullshit?'

'Well, they were true, although there was more to it . . .'

Sophia paused, trying to find the strength to go on. It was excruciating for Faye to watch her mother.

'First of all, let's be fair; I didn't know the rest of the story until I had brought you back here, and I had to piece them together, so—' Sophia continued, avoiding Faye's penetrating gaze and struggling to pull the words from her mouth.

'So it was a lie. A half-truth isn't the truth,' Faye said firmly.

Sophia's eyes were on Faye's now. Other than tears, they were filled with a concoction of shame, guilt, and agony. Faye never knew a pair of eyes could say so much.

'Just lay it all out plainly, Mom. I want the whole nine yards.'

'All right. This is what I've gathered. You're the second and youngest daughter of a married couple in China. You were considered an "unlawful birth" under the Chinese One-Child Policy—'

'Wait . . . what's the One-Child Policy?'

'Google it later. Basically, in China, a married couple is only allowed one child. Because of that, your parents were fined by the government. Your father, presumably Li Fu, was unable to pay the heavy penalty, so the authorities hired local hooligans to seize you from your family and sold you to an orphanage. Now, at that time, foreign adoption, particularly by childless couples and singles like me, was widespread. The Chinese orphanages made huge profits from the adopters by charging a thinly disguised adoption fee that could go up to five thousand dollars per child. That was considered a lot of money to the Chinese at that time. So, to meet the demand for more babies, some corrupt officials started abducting babies from poor families that had violated the Policy.'

'THE authorities? That's totally mental!'

'What can I say? They were people powerful enough to form a huge child-trafficking syndicate. I suppose some shady orphanages played a part too. Now, bear in mind that this was China. Most people there didn't want to get into trouble with the Communist Party, so those who knew turned a blind eye. Of course, we naïve Americans didn't have a clue about what was going on. We thought we were "saving" abandoned babies from a Third World Country.'

'And you were one of those naïve Americans who wanted a real-life Barbie of your own to play with. Why did you carry on with the adoption when you know that the babies weren't abandoned?'

'I didn't know until after the syndicate was busted by the police and the media here covered the story, although there was this little incident that happened at the orphanage that made me think that something wasn't quite right,' Sophia confessed.

Faye raised her eyebrows, expecting more. Right at that moment, Julie came back to the table with three cups of latte.

'You see, I was waiting for Julie at the orphanage, and she was very late. In fact, she didn't turn up, and all the other adoptive parents had already picked up their babies and left.'

'I told you why! I was negotiating with a distributor, who turned out to be a crook,' Julie chimed in.

'Anyway, when I finally got on the phone with her and knew that she wasn't coming, I decided to go ahead with the signing of the adoption papers. But before we even got to it, the manager suddenly hurried me along and told me to leave immediately because they had "police visitors". She said she couldn't finish the paperwork with me, and that I had to come back another time to get you.'

'Police visitors?'

'Let me finish the story,' said Sophia. 'I panicked, and deep down inside, I just knew that I had to get you out of there or I wouldn't ever see you again.'

'It's a mother's instinct, honey,' Julie added.

Faye glared at Julie vexingly, wishing she would go away.

'Thank you, Julie. I think I'll take it from here,' said Sophia between her teeth.

'Oh, you're very welcome, Sophia,' replied Julie, oblivious to the annoyance she had caused.

'And?' Faye prodded.

'I bribed the manager so that I could take you away without completing the adoption papers at their end. In other words, no one could have known who had adopted you because all the papers are missing. Well, no one except the manager. I believe that's why this man, this Li Fu, has never found you despite all his efforts.'

'You bribed them? You, Sophia, the pious Christian who never lies and never cheats, bribed them? You hypocritical bi . . .'

'Watch what you say, Faye. Don't say things you can't take back,' Julie interrupted her before it was too late.

Faye took a deep breath and asked her mother, 'Is that all?'

'Actually, no,' Sophia continued. 'As I was leaving the orphanage to return to the hotel, I saw the police raid in the taxi. But I didn't know what it was until I found out the next day from the news that it was *the* raid. That was when I realized you might have been abducted—'

'So you knew? You KNEW I was abducted all this time? Oh my God! I can't listen to this. I mean, how could you do this?' Faye cried, her whole body producing such a maelstrom of fury she couldn't control the trembling. She felt like she had just been betrayed by the very person whom she had trusted all her life.

Sophia's face burnt crimson with disgrace.

'Slow down, Faye. Breathe and let your mother finish the story,' Julie wrapped her arm around Faye to comfort her.

'I said you might have been. I didn't know for sure. I put two and two together, and the story did fit—the timing, the child-trafficking syndicate arrested by the Central Communist Party at the orphanage, the terror on the manager's face when she asked me to leave. But they couldn't tell which child was abducted and which was abandoned or orphaned. The director of the orphanage was the only person who knew, but he kept mum and took the secrets to his grave. I just thought there might be a chance that you had been abducted. I never found out until Li Fu and his story appeared.'

'Why not?'

'There was no way I could've found out.'

'Really? Did you try?'

'No.'

'Why not?'

Sophia paused for a long time. 'I guess I didn't want to know.'

Faye sat there, still as a China doll. Only her eyes left Sophia's and moved aimlessly to the crowd that was beginning to form in the café. She had come prepared for whatever surprises her mother might hurl at her, but she now realized she could never be prepared for this. She tried to muster some strength from her emotionally spent body but there wasn't any left. She felt every bit like what Sophia must have thought of her when she was a baby—a hapless Third World child waiting to be saved by some altruistic White woman who wanted to play mother.

Strangely, she also felt numb, and her mind couldn't focus on the situation at hand. Instead, it wandered to little things, things that shouldn't matter in a moment like this. She wondered, for example, was her outfit weather-appropriate and should she have checked her Chemistry assignment one more time before she handed it in.

Sophia reached out to embrace Faye, but Faye drew back instantly. She couldn't deal with her mother at this point. She certainly didn't want to be touched by her. She knew her reaction would break her mother's heart, but it was visceral. It simply couldn't be helped.

Fortunately, Julie saw the whole thing and came to Sophia's rescue by distracting her. 'Then how did this Li Fu know Faye's whereabouts? Does he know exactly where she lives?'

'I don't know how he found out. All that's mentioned in his postings was that he's heading to San Francisco,' Sophia said.

'Has he contacted you?' Julie asked again.

'No, not yet.'

'That's right, he's coming! Did you know that everyone who knew about his story sympathized with him? And guess what, they'll soon know the truth too, that you knew I was abducted but did nothing about it!' Faye burst out, quietly and bitterly.

'Don't say that! Your mom didn't know if you were abducted or abandoned,' Julie said.

'But she did nothing. Doing nothing is as bad as doing evil!'

'Look, your mom's already finding it hard to deal with the situation. Please don't cause her any more pain,' Julie pleaded.

'It's okay, Julie. She's right. I've no right to deprive her of her parents. I deserve everything she is saying.' Sophia turned to Faye, her eyes once again moist with tears. 'I know this is a lot for you to handle right now, and you've every right to be angry with me. But ask yourself this: have I not loved you like a biological parent? Have I not provided you with everything that you needed? Have you ever felt like you were adopted?'

Right now, Mom. Faye screamed in her head. *Right now, I feel like I'm adopted.*

Instead, Faye said nothing.

'I've devoted my entire life to you, and I've always, always thought of you only as my own daughter. Isn't that enough to redeem my one weakness?'

'No, it's not enough. You hid the truth and lived in lies. I thought I was an orphan. I've accepted that, even though it has been tough. You've robbed me of the chance to be with my real family, to lead the life I was supposed to have. You've denied me of the truth about who I really am. That's what you've done! Don't you understand how I feel? Don't you understand anything?' Faye burst out. She felt sorry for her mother, but she was more disappointed with her self-justification. Suddenly, Faye couldn't stand being with her mother for another moment.

'You know what? I can't even look at you right now. I'm done with this conversation.'

Still in tears, Faye left the café. She walked out of the only family she had ever known.

Orphaned once again.

Fearing for her safety, Julie ran clumsily after Faye, her high heels making loud click-clack noise on the tar of the parking lot outside, leaving Sophia at the table, stunned and rendered immobile by her daughter's truthful, hurtful words.

'Young lady, you stop right there!' Julie ordered Faye like she would her own sons, already panting with the physical exertion. 'Where do you think you're going?'

Faye finally stopped right before she reached her car in the parking lot. Taking a deep breath, she turned to face Julie.

'I can't be with her right now. Did you not hear what she said? I can't talk to her. I can't even look at her.'

'I know it's hard for you to deal with this now—'

'You don't know shit! And don't get me started with you. You knew about this all along, but you said nothing too. You've conspired with her against me,' Faye said in full rage, arms flailing dangerously. The moment those words got out of her mouth, she knew they had offended Julie deeply. She had gone too far.

'I'm sorry,' Faye said. 'I didn't mean to say that. I'm just very . . . very upset right now.'

'It's all right. I understand,' Julie said in a strange tone. Faye realized the damage had already been done, even though Julie didn't want to admit it. 'What are you going to do?'

'I don't know. I'm too confused right now. I think I'll crash at Charlie's place for a couple of days till I sort things out. Please let Mo . . . let her know, would you?' Faye said.

'It's probably the best thing to do for now, for both of you to cool down and work things out separately. Don't worry, I'll take care of her. I'll send some of your stuff over to Charlie's if you want,' Julie offered.

'That would be nice. Thanks.'

Faye got into her beaten-up Honda Civic, a gift from her mother, a gift that Faye knew her mother had penny-pinched for a long time to save. Suddenly, she was filled with self-loath and remorse for treating her mother the way she did. Wiping her tears away, she turned on the engine and drove recklessly away.

Away from her mother. From her troubles. From the mess.

* * *

Faye drove through the massive automated front gate into the mansion's gravel-filled driveway that was adorned with beautifully sculptured shrubs and bushes, and arrived at Charlie's home. Her boyfriend and his parents were already standing at the entrance of the house to welcome her.

Henry Murray, Jr., son of a successful businessman whose family wealth was built on a series of shrewd property investments, was a man of the world. While he had inherited a substantial amount of money from his father, who had passed away prematurely at the age of fifty due to a fatal heart attack, Henry had tripled his heritage over the last thirty years. An astute investor, he had dabbled in practically anything he could lay his hands on—stocks, property, foreign exchange, gold, commodities, derivatives, and for the last ten years, start-ups in the Valley and Bay Area—and so far had been very successful in most of his ventures. He had even earned the name 'The Alchemist', bestowed upon him by the media, for it seemed like he could turn anything he touched into gold. His only failure it seemed was his inability to interest either of his sons to take over the family business empire. Charlie's elder brother, Phillip, was, in Henry's exact words, a useless, bloodsucking, lusty bum. In reality, Phillip was a failed painter and sculptor who, after a series of self- and family-funded solo exhibitions, hadn't been able to sell a single piece of his artwork. He liked to akin himself to the tortured soul of Vincent Van Gogh and felt that his art was unappreciated and ahead of its time as the genius artist. He declared he had resigned to a similar fate—to have none of his paintings sold in his lifetime and his livelihood indefinitely sponsored by his father (a.k.a. Van Gogh's brother), which he squandered through careless and excessive consumption of drugs, alcohol, and whoring on the sun-kissed beaches of Phuket, Thailand. Phillip had found his Paradise in Phuket, where the Thai boys were so young, so beautiful, and so delicate. He loved the sweet boys of Thailand, who he claimed were 'respectful of him' and 'accepting of who he was', including his fondness for cross-dressing, his insatiable sexual appetite, and his unwanted, twisted paintings. Phillip would never trade his Paradise for America. No way would he ever return to America.

So, Henry turned to his second son, Charles, his only hope to perpetuate the family legacy. Young, dynamic, sociable, suave, and handsome, Charles possessed everything Henry had ever wanted for a successor; everything except one crucial trait, greed. Charles wasn't like his dad; Charles was easily contented and didn't like biting off more than he could chew. Charles was honest and generous, and even as a child, he would give up anything for his elder brother as long as it made him happy. No doubt his good-natured personality was admired by all and made him popular among his peers, but Henry knew Charles wouldn't survive the cutthroat, dog-eat-dog world of business. Not that Charles was interested. He had no intention of taking over his father's business, for the world of term sheets, returns on investment, and initial public offerings held no meaning to Charles. He belonged to a different dimension—a 2D, pictorial dimension of photography. Charles didn't just dabble in photography. He ate, slept, and dreamt of taking pictures. In fact, all he wanted to do was take pictures. As cliché as it might sound, he knew he would one day be a photographer like his hero Steve McCurry. He would trot around the globe and enter the treacherous war zones of Afghanistan, Pakistan, and other parts of the Middle East—he hadn't figured out the rest of the countries in that region yet—and explore the hidden worlds of North Korea, Tibet, and Xinjiang to capture untold stories of the meek, the oppressed, and the tortured. He would find his 'Afghan Girl', photograph the perfect image, and put it up on the cover of the *National Geographic* magazine for the world to see.

So, even though Henry owned everything he could possibly want in this and the next lifetime, he wasn't an entirely happy man. He knew if he didn't do anything soon, the legacy he had so painstakingly built up would crumble into pieces once his children laid him six feet under.

Henry was genuinely glad to see Faye when she drove up to his front door. Charlie might not have made many wise choices in his young, charmed life, but to Henry, Faye was one of them. Henry loved her like his own daughter and felt she possessed great potential in the business world. She was sharp, smart, gutsy, a natural leader, and she wasn't afraid to make bold decisions. While he knew they were too young to even consider it, he secretly hoped that they would get married one day. Perhaps, having a daughter-in-law take over his business wasn't too bad an idea. Turning to his wife, Claudia, whose face had already lit up when she saw Faye, he knew that she, too, would agree with him.

Charlie leapt forward, bouncing down the stairs two steps at a time to greet his girlfriend and squeezing her tightly as she stepped out of the car. They kissed briefly before she murmured through their interlocked lips, 'I hope your parents won't mind me staying here for a few days.'

'Are you kidding? They love you! Besides, they're aware of your situation, and they'll do anything to help you,' Charlie said.

As they ascended the steps to the front door, Charlie behaved more caringly than usual, insisting on carrying Faye's school bag, the only possession she had with her, and not letting go of her hand. It was as if overnight, she had become disabled simply because of a terrible thing that had happened to her.

'Faye, sweetie! I'm so sorry about what happened. Charlie told me everything. Don't worry about a thing. You're most welcome to stay here for as long as you like. Let us know if you need anything, anything at all.' Claudia came forward to embrace Faye warmly. Faye felt welcomed immediately.

'Yes, and if you need any resources to sort out your troubles, just let me know. We're all here for you,' Henry added, resting his huge, fatherly hand on Faye's shoulder.

'Thank you,' she said in a hoarse, all-cried-out voice, tired but grateful for a friendly resting place in this maelstrom.

'We've prepared a guest room for you. Charlie, why don't you show Faye to her room and make sure she's comfortable? Is there anything you need, my dear?' Claudia fussed about.

'No, I'm fine. Thanks again, Mrs Murray,' replied Faye politely.

'Mom, just leave her alone! She's exhausted. I think we should all give her some space to breathe,' Charlie jumped in. While he was probably not the most sensitive guy in the world, Faye was glad that he noticed her red, puffy eyes and despondent tone.

'You're right. Anyway, your dad and I need to attend a dinner party, so you'll have the house entirely to yourselves,' Claudia said quickly. 'Oh, and we've left some dinner in the oven for both of you.' She took Faye's hands and squeezed them warmly. 'Make yourself at home, my dear.'

Although Faye loved Charlie's parents and didn't mind spending time with them, she was glad to see them leave. She didn't want anyone's company tonight but Charlie's. With tremendous relief, she exchanged good nights and watched them drive away in their sparkling new BMW. Once they were gone, Charlie took her hand tenderly and led her to the guest room.

Compared to Faye's tiny, cluttered room, which was decorated with a strange collection of mismatched furniture, garage-sale embellishments, and posters of pop icons from the sixties—a 'style' Faye insisted on calling 'eclectic'—the guest room was a real estate heaven and an interior designer's wet dream come true. Like its owners, it was lavish, over-the-top, and overly ambitious. The en-suite bedroom was made in a Victorian-style design with matching furniture. Rose-pink and teal wallpapers and thick, intricately patterned carpets covered almost every inch of the room's surface. A pair of heavy silk damask curtains guarded the windows regally. Faye hadn't been in the guest room before. Whenever she visited, she usually went straight to Charlie's bedroom. If Faye were her usual self, she would have a lot to say about how people's desire for ostentatious display of wealth was ruining the country—Charlie's parents had subconsciously chosen this opulent Victorian style of decorating. But she was not her usual self today and wasn't in a mood to comment on the aesthetics of the space she'd be occupying for the next few days. In fact, she barely noticed it.

'So how bad was it, the fight with your mom?' Charlie asked as he watched her sink wearily into an ornately carved chaise lounge. She stared blankly at the antique Tiffany lamp hanging from the ceiling.

'Bad enough,' Faye replied without elaborating. She felt too tired to talk.

Charlie decided not to press on. He moved around the room listlessly, fiddling with the furniture, not knowing what to say or do. His stomach growled aloud. Faye knew that when Charlie was hungry, all he could think of was food but he was afraid to suggest dinner. He knew he was supposed to listen to his girlfriend's troubles right now.

'Sophia told me that she knew I might have been abducted from my real family all along, but chose not to do anything about it,' Faye couldn't keep it in her any more. She began to recount what Sophia had said at the café. Charlie listened without interrupting, nodding now and then.

'Who does she think she is, Mother Teresa? That she has saved me from godlessness, hopelessness, and poverty? You should see the self-pitying, self-gratifying, and self-righteous look on her face!' Faye said with such vex that Charlie was a little taken aback.

'Well, did she?' he asked as he finally stopped moving around. He sat down heavily on the bed and began bouncing lightly on the mattress.

'Did she what?'

'Did she save you from hopelessness, poverty and, wait, what was the other thing? Oh yeah, godlessness,' Charlie said with a smirk.

'Well, that's not the point,' she said after a long pause.

'What's the point then?'

'The point is, she shouldn't have lied about it. Like, she should have told me the truth right from the start.'

'Would that have made a difference?'

'I don't know, but it would be nice to know who I really was and where I came from.'

'Now that you know, has it changed anything? Are you going to leave Sophia for your real family?'

'I don't know,' she said honestly, a little confused. 'I just feel like I shouldn't have to make such a difficult decision, you know? I mean, at least not right now! I don't even know what my real family is like. How do I know what's good for me?'

Charlie did not answer her. Instead, he lay supine on the perfectly-made bed and listened to the growls made by his untamed stomach.

Silence ensued.

'What do you think I should do, Charlie?' she finally asked.

'I can't tell you what to do. You have to make your own decision.'

'Yeah, thanks. That's really helpful, Mr Genius!'

'Listen, it's a critical decision that'll have lots of consequences, right? I think you shouldn't rush into it. Just give yourself as much time as you need to think it over in the next few days. Keep an open mind and go with what you feel is right. Don't fight it,' he offered.

That was typical Charlie—deconstructing complex issues into simple steps, and going with the flow. Faye wouldn't go with the flow; she would overthink her problems and listen to her head rather than her heart.

They were quiet again, each absorbed in their thoughts. Faye was sure Charlie was hatching a plan to get her out of that comfortable chaise lounge to dinner downstairs. Apparently, a brilliant plot struck him.

'Is your biological father really coming here?' he asked. 'He said in his last post that he didn't have enough money yet.'

'I don't know. I haven't read anything since this morning,' she replied, taking her iPhone out from her pocket. 'Let's check.'

'Your phone's battery is almost dead. You can use the iPad in the kitchen. Let's go downstairs. I'll get dinner out of the oven while you read the latest update,' Charlie said quickly with a grin on his face. Faye was sure he was thinking how subtle and ingenious his plan was.

'I'm not hungry, Charlie. I'm so tired!' Faye groaned. 'Besides, I brought my charger with me. It's right over there in my bag.'

Her reply wiped Charlie's grin off his face. He thought for a while, and then came up with the cheesiest lines ever.

'But you must eat something. You can't afford to fall sick right now. And . . . and you need your strength to get through this.'

Faye surrendered. He had to be really hungry to resort to B-grade movie lines to get her to the kitchen. She hauled herself up and went downstairs with Charlie to the Murrays' gorgeous kitchen, which was as well-equipped and well-stocked as Nigella Lawson's film studio. The helper had already left for the day, but she had carefully wrapped their dinner in the oven to keep it warm. The wonderful aroma of roast chicken and potatoes finally roused Faye's appetite. She realized she hadn't eaten anything since this morning.

Faye turned on Charlie's iPad. While Charlie wolfed down his dinner, she picked at her plate and read the latest post.

'Well?' Charlie asked with his mouth full of shredded meat.

'It says here that Li Fu has tuberculosis,' she said faintly as she looked up in disbelief. 'Also, he has received enough donations. He's coming.'

* * *

Faye was waiting for Charlie after class in front of the school building when she saw Sophia standing across the road. It wasn't a pretty sight: her mother looked like an old gypsy in a train wreck. Sophia had probably slept very little in the past few days. Her insomniac nights were haunting her makeup-less face, revealing deep wrinkles as labyrinthine as the New York subway, winding their ways out from the edge of her lips and the corners of her eyes, baggy and red from restlessness and the constant stings of salty tears. And, Sophia seemed to have grown squalid in her grooming, a sharp contrast to the past where she wouldn't allow herself to look less than decent even to take the garbage out. Her wiry hair, which had turned grey overnight, was dishevelled and in need of a good shampooing and conditioning. Her clothes were in disarray; on closer inspection, they looked like the same pair of grey pants and white collarless blouse she had worn five days ago.

Faye tried to think of the best way to talk to Sophia without admitting defeat. She missed her dearly, and the pathetic sight of the woman across the street who was supposed to be her mother stung her heart. But she wasn't sure if she had forgiven her mother and was even less sure about what she was going to do about the Li Fu situation.

Sophia's eyes met hers, but she kept her distance. Faye looked away and started to walk away, still feeling her mother's pleading eyes on her.

No, she hadn't forgiven Sophia.

Just then, Charlie pranced out of the building like a Jack Russell Terrier on steroids and ran towards Faye, panting heavily as he put his arms amorously around Faye's waist. When she didn't respond with her usual lovely smile and a peck on his cheek, he followed his girlfriend's stolen glances to Sophia.

Whether Charlie had forgotten about the saga that had happened between the mother and daughter or he wanted them to talk again, Faye would never know. Nevertheless, he did them a huge favour. He waved enthusiastically at Sophia and shouted, 'Hey Sophia, come on over!'

For the first time, Sophia smiled a hopeful smile. She crossed the road without even looking and lumbered briskly towards them.

'What're you doing, you dumb dumb——? Look what you've done; she's coming over now,' Faye whispered between her teeth.

'She's your mother, Faye. Whatever happened, happened. Talk to her, okay?' Charlie said.

Faye knew he hated it when she was miserable, and she had been miserable the whole week. It wasn't fun for Charlie. And, according to him, life without fun wasn't a life worth living.

'How're you doing, Sophia?' Charlie asked. Then, realizing what a stupid question it was, he scratched his head embarrassedly. He had always called Sophia by her first name because he couldn't add a 'Mrs' to her family name, and it was weird to address her as Miss Williams. To make things less awkward for him, Sophia had told him fondly that Sophia was fine by her.

'Not very well, Charlie, but thanks for asking,' Sophia replied, her gaze fixed on Faye all the time. While she didn't mean to be sarcastic, it somehow came out sounding like one.

'Sorry to hear that, Ma'am,' Charlie said, colouring up a little.

An awkward silence followed.

'Listen, I need to do some editing for the photos I took for the school yearbook, so I'll probably be in the computer lab for a while. Sophia, do you mind giving Faye a ride back to my place? She came with me in my car to school this morning, so—' Charlie fumbled. A white lie. He had all the software he'd ever need in his super-expensive, ultra-high-end computer at home to do whatever editing he needed to do, but he was sensitive enough to know when to leave the two of them alone.

'Yes, yes, I can do that. Is that okay, Faye?' Sophia pleaded, holding her breath while she awaited her daughter's reply.

'Yeah, whatever,' Faye said without looking up.

They walked towards her car without exchanging a word. As they got into the car, Sophia attempted some small talk.

'How's that English essay of yours coming along?'

'Fine.'

'Do you need more clothes? I can pack some more and drop them off later.'

'No, I'm fine.'

'Are you comfortable at the Murrays'? Do they have any room for you?'

'You know they have a house big enough to accommodate all the hobos in San Francisco.'

'They are nice people, aren't they? I like the Murrays.'

'Yeah.' Faye decided it was safer to give monosyllabic answers. She didn't want to start another fight with her mom. She was too tired for it.

'When are you coming home?'

'I don't know.'

'Well, you can't stay with the Murrays forever.'

There was another uncomfortable silence in the car. The only sound to fill it was the music from the radio turned down to a soft buzz in the background. Sophia deliberately drove at a crawling speed, trying as much as possible to prolong her time with her daughter.

'I'm sorry,' Sophia said after a while.

'I know.'

'Will you ever forgive me?'

Faye paused. 'Maybe. I don't know yet.'

'What can I do to make it right again? I'll do whatever it takes, sweetie,' Sophia begged.

'You can't undo what you've done. Do you honestly believe that things could go back to where it was? I'm sorry, but I can't pretend that it never happened,' Faye said, embittered.

'But we can move on . . . we have to move on—'

Faye didn't answer her.

'Another chance, that's all I ask for. I'll support your decision, whatever it is. I'll not stop you from meeting your real family. In fact, I'll facilitate it. I'll fly to China now and beg Li Fu for forgiveness if that's what you want me to do,' said Sophia. Unable to hold her tears any longer, she let them roll freely down her cheeks, blurring her vision as fresh tears flooded her eyes again. She pulled over to the side of the road and waited for her fits of sobbing to stop.

Bitter as Faye was, it was too much to watch her mother descend into such a ruinous state. Her mother had been her pillar, her superhero on a pedestal, and the bearer of all nasty things in her adolescent life. Not this devastated middle-aged humanoid creature who had crumbled into utter hopelessness. At this point, Faye pitied her. But for the first time, she also realized that she had become bigger, stronger, and better than her mother. She no longer needed her mother; it was her mother who needed her.

Faye had never felt lonelier in her life.

In her grief, Sophia reached over to hug Faye. And to Faye's surprise, she found herself not resisting it. She missed her mother—her smile; her warm embrace; and her unfaltering, eternal love. She needed to savour the feeling of being mothered one last time before she fled from her.

So, instead of being comforted, Faye comforted her mother. She no longer had any tears left, but she let her sadness flow. Faye held her mother until she was sufficiently calm. Then she whispered to her, like the way she used to do so as a child, revealing her little secrets to her mommy because she couldn't keep them in her any longer.

'I want to find out who I am.'

Sophia sniffed, wiped her tears away, and said, 'Okay, let's meet your father.'

Chapter 8

YAN

Dear Mr Li

My name is Faye Williams, but I think I was named Li Ying when I was born. My mother, Sophia Williams, adopted me in Beijing when I was a baby seventeen years ago. Not much was known about my past, except that the name Li Ying was sewn on to the jacket I wore when I was given to the orphanage. I think I am your biological daughter.

Yan looked up from the bus seat and caught her father reading the letter again, mouthing every word silently like a child learning to read and pausing to scrutinize the words he thought he had missed earlier. When he finished, he carefully folded the letter twice before putting it back into his pants' side pocket. A moment later, he took it out, smoothened the crease on the paper, and slid it into his shirt's front pocket. He would then pat the letter gently every once in a while as if to assure himself that it was still sitting safely in his pocket.

Liu Gang had called and told him about the letter the night before. Yan's father was so mad with excitement that he almost broke the phone. He would have probably gone to Liu's apartment immediately if it hadn't been so late and the buses were no longer running at those hours. So, he spent a sleepless night agonizing over the letter, tossing and turning in the bunk bed he and his daughter shared. Yan had heard him murmuring to himself on the lower bunk every once in a while. Whenever he got up to check on her on the top bunk, she would pretend to be fast asleep because if she hadn't, she knew he would suggest something crazy like walking to Liu's apartment or stealing a motorbike to get there sooner.

They had boarded the first bus at the crack of dawn and arrived at Liu's apartment so early that neither Liu nor his roommates were up. Liu didn't look happy, to say the least, to be woken up at such early hours. He made them wait outside the apartment in the cold and took a long time—deliberately—to print the letter before shoving it roughly into the frozen hands of Yan's father, slamming the door and crawling back into his warm blanket. Liu had shut them out before Yan's father had a chance to say a word to him.

On their journey back, the bus was packed with workers commuting to the city. The passengers jostled for as much room as possible for their rides to be more tolerable. With all the seats already occupied by dozing office workers nodding in synchronization with the gentle rocking of the bus—this meant that no one was getting off the bus until it entered downtown Beijing—Yan and her father had no choice but to stand in the moving bus for the whole hour. Yan's legs were tired, and she was getting increasingly uncomfortable with a dirty old man who stood next to her. He had been staring at her breasts and bumping a little too hard and too often into her whenever the antiquated bus jerked to a stop. She hated these bus rides to Liu's apartment, and since her father had forgone breakfast, it was particularly rough for her this morning. Luckily, a passenger on a seat right in front of her stood up to get off the bus. Relieved, she immediately sat down before anyone else had a chance and craned her neck to look for her father. She spotted him a few commuters away.

'Papa, I've found a seat. Come over here,' she shouted.

Nobody on the bus bothered to look up or even bat an eyelid. After all, it was China, where people had to fight for every tiny bit of resources on a daily basis, even something as insignificant as a bus seat.

Yan's father pushed and shoved through the pillar of passengers, almost knocking over an elderly woman along the way. She cursed at him. He cursed her back. When he finally reached Yan, she gave up the precious seat for her father. He almost sat down before he noticed the old man.

'No, you sit. There are lots of rotten hounds around,' he thundered, his every word intending to be heard. He hovered protectively over Yan while keeping an eye on the old man. The old man gave him a dirty look, snorted, and mumbled defensively, 'Who cares about this tramp? Smells like a wet dog. Keep her if you want.'

Without turning back, the old man pressed the bell and got off at the next stop.

'You can't have scumbags like him copping a feel for free. Nobody would want you any more if you let that happen,' he said loud enough for a few young women on the bus to turn around and glare at him for making such a ludicrous remark. Instead of feeling embarrassed by her father's display of bigotry—which wasn't possible as Yan had reached the point where there was nothing her father could do to embarrass her any more—she felt good. In this seemingly foolish remark, her father showed care, maybe even love, for her, in a twisted sort of way.

The bus became quiet again. Yan's father fished out the letter carefully and started rereading it. Yan had read the letter too. She had taken it from her father, who had almost slipped into a state of comatose from its startling revelation after he had read it for the first time at the bus station. Even by her low academic standard, Yan could tell that the letter, which was written in Chinese, wasn't well composed. It used the simplest vocabulary, strung together in almost childlike sentence structures, and was dotted with miswritten characters. But all in all, they got the gist of what it tried to convey: the writer claimed to be Ying and that she would like to meet them if they came to San Francisco. The letter had arrived in the form of a message in the Facebook account that Liu Gang had set up for her father. Liu had checked that the letter wasn't a hoax: he assured them that Ying's Facebook account looked authentic—the five hundred friends listed in her account genuinely looked to be American high-school kids with dozens of daily posts, with each of them having five hundred more friends of their own.

Of course, there was no way of telling if she was his real biological daughter. While he had his doubts, the details mentioned in the letter did match the facts of Ying's early life; the names (Ying and Sophia) were right, the time of the adoption was spot on, and most importantly, Ying did wear a pink jacket with her name sewn on to it when she had been taken away. A hoaxer couldn't possibly have known this because Yan's father had never mentioned it in any of his posts or videos. They had received letters from hoaxers before and they, including Liu Gang, could always tell if the letters were genuine from the details they had provided. But this was different. All the details were accurate, and the sender of the letter didn't seem to be hiding anything from him.

'She's the one. I just know it. No one could possibly know so much about Ying. I think this trip to America is going to be very fruitful,' he mumbled aloud as he reread the letter, losing himself in his own world, a world that included Yan a moment ago but was now racing towards Ying.

* * *

Yan was in the bedroom packing her father's luggage when she heard a knock on the apartment door. She stopped and peeked through the bedroom door that was ajar. Her father was in the living room going through the travel documents. He had heard the knock but ignored it because he hated to be interrupted when he worked. Yan knew that perfectly well. She slipped out of the bedroom immediately to answer the door.

Liu Gang was standing outside the door with a brown envelope tucked tightly under his armpit.

'Hello, Yan! Is your father in there?' he asked. He seemed more cheerful than the last time they had met. Yan guessed that it was because his business with her father was coming to an end soon.

Yan blushed feverishly. It was rare that people acknowledged her, least of all talked to her. Liu was one of the few who bothered to say a few words to her now and then. She cherished the scraps of attention thrown to her, but it also made her uneasy. She nodded, smiled shyly, and ushered Liu in.

'Hello *Lao Li*[2], I've brought you the donations,' Liu said, patting the envelope under his armpit. 'Cash!'

'Good, good. The timing's perfect. I've just booked the flight, and I need the money to pay for the tickets. Come, sit down and have some tea,' said Yan's father, waving Liu to the rattan chair next to him and ordering Yan to make tea.

Liu sat down and placed the envelope on the coffee table in front of him. 'Here you go, more than eight grands. American dollars! You lucky bastard, that's more money than I've ever seen in my life. Go on, take a look. Count them if you want.'

'I've never seen so much money in my life either,' Yan's father replied. Nervously, he reached for the package, hands trembling a little from the anticipation. He opened it slowly and carefully, and as his hand reached inside and pulled out the piles of cash, his face glowed.

Yan returned with their tea. Like everyone in the room, her eyes were on the bills too, for she too wanted to know what eight thousand American dollars looked like. Liu's eyes cast on her, and she saw pity oozing from them.

'You know, well . . . this is just a suggestion . . . since there's more than enough money here for your trip, why don't you set some aside for Yan? She can use it to further her education or something . . .' Liu said, moistening his lips. Yan could tell he was uncomfortable in bringing up the matter, but something—perhaps pity, perhaps compassion or sympathy—made him say it.

'Education? What are you talking about? She already had an education,' Yan's father said, looking up from his money and raising his voice defensively. 'She doesn't need any more of that, I can tell you that much! What good would that do? Look at her! Does she look like a professor to you? No, no, that would just be money down the drain. I'll be lucky if someone's willing to take her as a wife. You know, take her off my hands. Ying, on the other hand, is different. She has a Western education and a future ahead of her. I'm betting on Ying.'

---

[2] Lao means 'old' in Chinese. Older friends are usually referred to as 'Lao', followed by their family name.

He then looked at Liu and whispered lewdly, 'You lonely? Do you want Yan? Is that it? I've seen the way you looked at her and talked to her. You can have her cheap. I promise I won't ask for too big a dowry.'

Liu looked at him incredulously. 'What? No! That's not what I meant. Besides, I can barely feed myself. The last thing I want is a wife!'

'Well, a man has his needs, so I thought . . .'

'That's not the point. All the things you've done over the years . . . isn't it about finding Ying and knowing that she's well and alive? What's this "betting on Ying" thing about?'

'Of course, it's about finding Ying! But now that I know she's not only well and alive but doing amazingly well in San Francisco, there's . . . well, there might be an angle to it.'

'Angle?'

'I don't know yet. We'll see—' Yan's father hesitated and said no more. He turned his attention from the conversation to the pile of cash and started counting them while Liu and Yan looked on awkwardly.

'It's all there,' Liu said sorely. The whole conservation had made him very uncomfortable, and he wanted to leave the apartment as soon as possible.

Yan's father ignored him and continued counting to the last dollar. When he'd finally finished, he sat back and grinned satisfactorily. 'Yes, there's enough money here to last me for a while.'

'Spend it wisely. America is an expensive country. You can't be too sure,' Liu advised.

Yan's father didn't like what was said, but he didn't want to let Liu spoil his moment of triumph. He took a deep breath and waited for his anger to subside. Then, he changed the trajectory of the conversation.

'Tell me, what kind of adoptive parents do you think Ying has? Do you think they're wealthy? What kind of income are we looking at?'

'Parent. The lady who adopted your daughter is single. You knew that, didn't you? Ying has explained it in the letter,' Liu replied as he finished up his tea hurriedly.

'Yes, yes . . . that's right. Imagine that—a woman who isn't married adopting a child. These *laowai* certainly have very bizarre ideas! I mean, what would other people think of her? I bet she's rich and has nowhere else to spend her money.'

Liu looked uncertain and seemed as if he wanted to correct Yan's father, but he decided against contradicting him and starting another argument. He stood up, murmured some excuse, and said goodbye. Yan's father held up his hand and shook Liu's fervently. He looked Liu in the eyes and said with deep gratitude, 'Thank you, my brother! I could never have got this far without you. I'll never forget what you've done for me, and I'm forever indebted to you.'

Liu was taken by surprise at this display of appreciation and affection by Yan's father, for he didn't think the old man was capable of such emotions.

Standing in a corner of the room, Yan took all this in, including Liu's astonished look, without so much of a twitch of a muscle. But in her racing mind, she issued a silent warning to Liu.

Run, Liu. Run, she screamed in her head. *I like you; you're a nice man, but don't fall for this. You see, that's what my old man does. Just when you least expect it, this diabolical monster who seems incapable of having any human empathy will offer you the sincerest smile, the deepest concern for the slightest things. But if you let down your guard just a bit, he'll get you like the same vulgar fiend you once knew. Yes, that's my father, Liu. He's all of it, Liu. He's the embodiment of the good and the bad, the pure and the corrupted, the kind and the cruel. He's all of it, although the world only chooses to see the bad, the corrupted, and the cruel.*

But like always, the words stayed lock Yan's head, hidden forever, ignored altogether.

Perhaps the Goddess of Mercy decided to bless the young, unlucky man because right at that moment, Liu's phone rang, breaking the spell that Yan's father was casting on him. He hastily said his goodbyes again and disappeared through the door, vanishing from Yan's life.

After Liu's departure, Yan's father remained in the living room, smoking his Lucky Strike and sipping the supermarket-grade Chinese tea. He sat there for a long time, contemplating. Plotting. He was still in a pensive mood when Yan finished packing and emerged from the bedroom. She was on her way to the kitchen to fix lunch when he said, 'Yan, come here. I've something important to discuss with you.'

Yan was bewildered and more than a little wary. Her father never 'discussed' things with her; he simply ordered her around to get things done. The word wasn't part of his lexicon, nor of most Chinese fathers. She sat down gingerly beside him, trying not to look too frightened or excited.

'How do you feel about staying in America?' he began.

'Isn't that what we're doing? Going to America and getting Ying back?' Yan asked.

'No, I mean living there forever—'

'Live there? Why?' Yan was caught by surprise this time, so much so that she let it show.

'I'll let you in on a secret. I don't intend on returning to China once I leave for America. Everyone's been telling me the bloody place is a land of opportunities. I'm thinking of making something out of this trip. If everything works out the way I planned, I'll stay there with Ying. But we have to decide what to do with you. I know you can't speak English well, but you understand a little, right?'

'Just the basic stuff.'

He nodded. 'All right, then. Maybe you can work in a kitchen at a Chinese restaurant or something—'

Thanks, Papa! Thanks for telling me about your fabulous plan now, at the eleventh hour. And how kind of you to let me in on your little secret and this little 'discussion' on 'what to do with me'!

'It's illegal. We would be illegal immigrants. It'd never work,' Yan said guardedly.

'Stop being so negative, will you? America is a big country. They'll never find us if we're smart enough. If I can outsmart those fucking dirty cops here, I'm sure I can outsmart any cops anywhere. I've heard so many stories of people like us making it in America. Some of them even became millionaires overnight!'

Right . . . stories told by a bunch of low-lives and losers in shitty bars. They're hardly the go-to sources to authenticate millionaire biographies.

'I mean, I'm done with this place. There's nothing left for us here. This is a chance of a lifetime for us to start afresh in a new place,' he continued, sounding genuinely hopeful.

'But what can we do over there?' she asked, her stomach sickening as their conversation, in her opinion, deteriorated further.

'We could start a small business,' he said. 'Maybe behind closed doors at first until we get our green cards. I'm sure Ying's adoptive parents, I mean, parent, will compensate us for the losses we've suffered all these years. We could use that sum of money to do something—maybe buy us a couple of green cards, open our restaurant or a small mah-jong den or something. I know of a friend who could hook us up with his friends over there—'

We're going to be illegal immigrants AND gambling criminals. Yan's thoughts turned from apprehension to terror. *I'll be locked up forever and never see the light of day again!*

'I've thought about it a lot. I think it's the best move for all of us, for our family. I'm pretty sure Ying wouldn't want to live here, and I won't blame her. Who would? So, why not go live with her over there instead? That's what we wanted all these years, right? Reunited as a family?'

Ying wouldn't want to live here. How convenient! What a perfect excuse! Yan couldn't stop screaming in her head. *But have you forgotten someone, Papa?*

'I know what you're thinking . . . "What about Mamma?" Am I right?' he said in perfect timing.

'We can't say we're a whole family if she's not there,' Yan said cautiously.

'Well, we'll have to make do with just the three of us until we figure out a way to get her to America. That is, if she wants to go.' He paused. The mention of Yan's mother made him both irate and melancholic at the same time. He cleared his throat and mumbled. 'I mean, we're not even sure where she is now. Even if we knew, are you sure you want that whore to live with us?'

'But . . .'

'No more buts! Why do you want to ruin a perfect opportunity to have our family back together again? Plus, it'll be a better life for you! Do you seriously want to continue living like this? My God! Sometimes I don't know how that tiny brain of yours works!'

A better life for me? Working in some greasy Chinese restaurant sixteen hours a day? Yan's thoughts switched from terror to bitterness.

'Look, I'm not dumping your mother, okay? Don't forget, she's the one who walked out on us first. She left us without so much as a goodbye. And how are we going to explain her "occupation" to Ying and her adoptive mother? It's not so simple, can you understand that?'

Sounds to me like you've already made up your mind, Papa, Yan thought sullenly.

'What? Don't you have anything to say? After all the effort I've put in to come up with a perfect plan for us, you're not even grateful? Look at it this way, America is our future, our only hope for a better life, and I've already made up my mind to have a fresh start there. You can either come with me or stay back. But if you stay here, you're on your own. Do you understand me?' he said with palpable frustration. He was disappointed with Yan's lack of enthusiasm in his search for utopia.

So much for a conversation, thought Yan as she nodded and rose, heading for the kitchen to make lunch.

* * *

Yan was awoken at very early hours the next morning by a slight sound and movement made by her father. She had always been a light sleeper—a survival skill acquired through years of sleeping on the streets next to a drunken parent. This was a fact she had never made known to her father. From the soft rustling of his clothes and the careful jimmying of the often-jammed locked cabinet drawer where he kept his newly obtained money, she could tell that her father wanted to slip out of the apartment unnoticed.

Without her.

She remained on her bed, pretending to be asleep, wondering what he was up to. There was nothing left to do except wait for their flight the next day—the visas had been approved, the tickets had been paid for and collected, and all the things they needed for the trip had been purchased and packed neatly in the luggage and bags. So when her father finally left the apartment, Yan couldn't resist the urge to find out where he was going. She sprang from her bunk bed, threw some clothes on, and surreptitiously followed him.

While she kept a safe distance from her father, Yan could tell that his mind seemed unusually heavy and preoccupied, so much so that he was oblivious to his surroundings. She was more afraid than curious that he would do something stupid, like gambling his money away the day before they were to leave for their promised land. But he did nothing of that sort. Instead, he boarded bus 618: the final destination of the route was Changping District. Yan got on the same bus with several passengers behind him. Fortunately for her, the bus was crowded and the passengers who stood between her and her father were tall, large men who would have obstructed her father's view if he happened to look her way. But he was so immersed in his thoughts that he didn't look up, even once.

Yan was puzzled now. They didn't know anyone in Changping District. Even if they did, with the massive borrowing and the handouts given in the past, no friends or relatives would want to have anything to do with them any more, not even to say goodbye.

At the Huilongguan stop, Yan's father got off the bus and headed towards the Huilongguan Hospital.

A mental institute? Why is he going to a mental hospital? Yan's bewildering thoughts burgeoned.

He entered the hospital from the main entrance and greeted the receptionist in the lobby. They chatted for a short while before he continued his way along the long corridors that led to the wards. He seemed to know his way as if he had been here before. Yan waited until the receptionist turned around before she sneaked in and ran in the direction her father was headed. Unfortunately, her delay had caused her to lose him. She wandered along the corridors searching desperately, carefully avoiding the gaze of the hospital staff.

Eventually, she found him in the courtyard.

Correction. She found *them*. Father and mother.

Mother.

Her father was pushing her in a wheelchair as he wiped his face repeatedly. Even from afar, Yan could tell her mother's health had deteriorated a great deal physically and mentally since she had last seen her outside her school. She looked used up, depleted—as if there is only so much life one could have in a lifetime, and if it is used up before one dies, one would be left with an empty, decrepit shell of a human. Skin and bones with a vacant soul—that was what was left of Yan's mother, so frail and spent that her whole body had sunk into the wheelchair, hardly breathing, hardly alive.

As Yan looked closely, she realized why her father had been wiping his face; he was weeping the whole time and talking to his wife as she stared emptily into space. Yan had never seen her father cry like that before. In fact, she couldn't remember ever seeing him cry. But here at the hospital with his wife, he wept openly, unreservedly.

Yan's father pushed the wheelchair to a corner of the courtyard while Yan crept closer to listen to the one-way conversation.

'I've no other choice, Mei. You'll have to stay here for a little longer,' he said gently as he took out a comb and started tidying up his wife's nest of wild, grey tress. 'At least we've found our daughter as I promised. She's turned into a lovely young lady, and she has an American name. I've seen pictures of her; she looks so beautiful, just like her mamma.'

He paused, attempting to control his tears.

'Yan and I are leaving tomorrow to find a way to live there. Now, don't you worry, I'll come back for you as soon as I figure out a way. That's a promise. And you know I keep my promises.'

How Mei ended up in the mental hospital would forever remain a mystery to Yan, but it didn't take a genius to figure out how a woman like Mei could lose her mind. What surprised Yan was that her father chose not to tell anyone, including her, about it. Perhaps he didn't want anyone to know. Perhaps he didn't think it necessary to tell Yan. Perhaps he felt it was his sole duty to take care of his wife. No matter the reason, she could finally feel the love her father had for her mother.

Yan felt that she had no business being there and that she should leave them alone. As quietly as she had come, Yan left the hospital.

Now, she was ready to go to America with her father.

Chapter 9

YAN

They had no idea how the media had come to know of their arrival in America.

Perhaps Liu had sold the story to someone, or Ying or her adoptive mother had been talking to the press. They would never know. It wasn't that they wanted to keep it a secret or anything, but the magnitude and level of attention were far beyond what they had expected or could ever be prepared for.

The moment Yan and her father stepped out of the customs into the airport's arrival hall, they were blinded by unceasing camera flashes and overwhelmed by a sea of reporters, who shoved microphones, recorders, and smartphones in their faces and asked all kinds of questions—some appropriate, some not. Not that they understood a word of what the journalists were saying. They shouted their questions with such urgency and in such strange accents that what little English Yan understood was rendered utterly useless. But even without any coherent response from Yan or her father, the media continued to follow them doggedly. As the father and daughter tried to break through the thick, impenetrable human wall, every little movement and every word they occasionally uttered to each other were carefully scrutinized and recorded.

It confounded Yan—this media frenzy and obsession with them. She didn't understand why their story was interesting to anyone other than themselves. To her, they were the plainest, dullest folks, unlike the beautiful, exotic people she had seen on television. Shouldn't the media be focusing their attention on other more important stories, like a scientific breakthrough or a natural disaster, or even the lives of political figures?

'A human-interest story, that was why your family story was so appealing,' someone told Yan later. 'People need to hear the ebb and the flow of their own kind to make them feel good or bad about themselves. Call it the other theory of relativity.'

Yan had found the argument rather silly. No one would ever find it humane or interesting if they had lived her story.

While Yan was bewildered by this whole media circus, her father seemed to enjoy every moment of it. He basked in their attention and quickly became a master at manipulating the reporters, smiling at them one moment, and shaking his head and refusing to answer anything the next. He was thriving. For the first time, the *laowai* were lapping up every word he said. He was no longer the low-life who was always sponging off someone. Rather, they were coming to him and eating out of his hands. This role reversal had a profoundly positive effect on him, and he glowed with pride and confidence as he walked into the airport as the 'man of the hour'.

Ying and her adoptive mother were supposed to meet them at the arrival hall, but as it had turned into a hall of pandemonium, it was impossible to penetrate through the throng of journalists and onlookers. Fortunately, a Chinese interpreter from a well-known news network stepped forward to help Yan and her father understand what was going on.

'It would help the situation and calm the people down if you could say a few words to our reporters and answer a few questions. The people in America are very keen to know about you and your plans,' the interpreter offered in a gentle voice. 'I'll be most happy to be your interpreter.'

The idea seemed to bode well with Yan's father, and with a sense of importance, he began speaking to the journalists through the interpreter.

'I've suffered terribly through the years. I've endured poverty, hunger, cold, humiliation, and many, many rejections. I've been shamed, blamed, jailed, threatened, and beaten. But I've never given up because the idea of abandoning my daughter was inconceivable.'

As if someone had pressed the mute button, the entire hall fell into complete silence the moment Yan's father spoke; his sad, compassionate voice pitching at a baritone range. He was now a broken, melancholic man, and everyone present was lapping up every bit of his performance, feeling the same melancholy he felt, experiencing the same pain that hurt him most.

'I believed in my heart that someday I would find my daughter. I believed it because it was all I had. I was willing to sacrifice anything, everything in exchange for any information about her. The only wish of a devoted father is for his daughter's happiness and safety. And I was willing to give up my life for that . . .'

Yan looked around as her father spoke on and on. For some reason she, again, couldn't comprehend, why the Americans seemed to believe every word he said, even though it sounded so obviously prewritten and rehearsed to her.

'I thank the people of America for all their help and support. It would be impossible for me to be here today without you. You have no idea how much this means to me. I can now reunite with my daughter and have my family back again.'

. . . *like an acceptance speech for the Oscar.*

Then, much to Yan's surprise, he began to cry. But it wasn't like what she saw at the hospital. This was for dramatic effect. For television. She could tell that it wasn't easy for him to let the tears flow freely, due to either lack of practice or a thespian's talent. Nevertheless, he managed to squeeze out a drop or two that drove the journalists crazy, and they began thrusting their cameras and smartphones even closer to their faces.

'Can your daughter say something too?' they began shouting the moment he ended his speech.

Terror seized Yan's throat.

Shit.

'No, no, I do the talking here—' Yan's father insisted.

'What's her name? How old is she?'

'Her name is Li Yan. She's almost twenty-one years old. She's the big sister of the family.'

Stop father. Yan prayed. *Someone, please stop him!*

'Do you look forward to meeting your sister?' A journalist directed the question at Yan.

'Of course, she looks forward to it! What kind of question is that?' Yan's father snapped at the journalist before Yan had a chance to speak.

'Are you planning to take Ying back to China?'

'It doesn't matter where we are as long as we're together,' he replied casually.

Smooth and nonchalant. Well done, father!

'Where's your wife, Mr Li? Why is she not part of this family reunion?'

'She . . . she's in a home. She isn't feeling too well, so she can't travel right now. We'll get her here as soon as possible—'

'Our investigation tells us that she once worked as a prostitute. Is that true?' a reporter began the first strike.

And, so it begins . . .

'What? Where did you get that information from? I'll not stand for such slanderous accusation—'

'If it isn't true, can you tell us more about her?' another demanded. 'And exactly where she is now?'

'As I said, she's in China. She'll be here when she gets better!'

Watch out, father! Your nose is starting to flare.

'You wrote on your Facebook page that you had tuberculosis. But you seem perfectly fine with no symptoms whatsoever of the illness . . .'

'I've received treatment, and it worked, damn it!' he said too quickly. Realizing that things weren't going the way he wanted, he tried to end the impromptu 'press conference' before the situation or his temper got out of control.

'Thanks to the kindness shown by the Americans, I managed to treat it in China. That's all I have to say. Thank you. Please let us through so that we can go meet Ying now.'

The press, however, didn't think it was over.

'How far are you in your treatment? It seems like you were able to recover rather quickly. People with TB usually need at least six months of treatment.'

Yan watched as her father wavered. She knew that he had underestimated the reach of the American media and its hunger for sensational stories. She felt as if both of them were being corralled by a pack of hunting wolves, waiting for the inevitable kill, to be torn apart so that everyone could have their share of a pound of flesh.

It was over. They were dead. But her father didn't know it yet.

'I'd rather not talk about it. It was a painful and difficult experience for me. Anyway, I don't care about my illness. It's my daughter that I think about all the time—'

'What's your plan after the reunion?' another reporter yelled.

'We're going to enjoy each other's company for a while before we decide what to do. We've seventeen years of catching up to do,' replied Yan's father, straining at the end of his tether.

'Surely, it's a dilemma, isn't it? You can't stay in the United States once your visa expires, and it's unlikely that your American daughter will live in China. What if she decides to stay with her adoptive mother?'

Strangely, Yan's father had never considered that possibility. Among all the questions, this one caught him by surprise.

'Stay with her adoptive mother? What do you mean? Why?'

'I don't know,' the journalist replied. 'But that's a possibility, isn't it? After all, she was brought up by her adoptive mother and had known nothing about you till recently. Are you saying you haven't thought of it before?'

The journalist's words silenced Yan's father, finally. As abruptly as it had begun, the press conference was over.

'No more questions, please. I wish to meet my daughter now.'

FAYE

Faye didn't know what was more nerve-wracking, meeting her biological father and sister for the first time or watching her adoptive mother crumble before her eyes.

While she didn't regret sending that letter to her father, and she wasn't sure what their first meeting would be like, it certainly wasn't what she had imagined it to be. First of all, the press. Why were they here? How did they know? Who told them? And why was her father speaking to them like he was going to be the next President of the United States?

It was impossible for Faye and her mom to get to her father and sister, engulfed as they were in a swarm of journalists who would sell their babies to the devil for a spot closer to them. And they couldn't get enough of him, feeding on his every word and asking ridiculous questions. It was baffling to see that such a man, such a small man, a nobody in his own or this country, could so quickly become a celebrity overnight here.

Since Faye couldn't get to them, she had to wait for them to come to her. It took them forever as he talked, laughed, cried, and scowled his way out. As she stood tensely and impatiently at the fringe of the crowd, she tried to imagine how the actual meeting would go and what this man who claimed to be her father would do. From where she stood, he looked small and lanky but carried a little potbelly. He looked very tan for a Chinese, but he certainly looked Asian. He sported salt and pepper hair, but it was wiry and unkempt. He wore a neat black blazer, but it looked old and ill-fitting. He carried an aura of confidence but was clearly ignorant. He seemed nervous talking to the reporters, and yet, she could tell that he was enjoying the attention. All in all, he looked, for the lack of a better word, unrefined.

Faye wasn't sure if her father was what she had expected. For the last few weeks, she had tried to imagine what her father would be like, but her usual imaginative self had lost its magical power. The reason was simple: she had never known a Chinese man before, and therefore, there wasn't a frame of reference for her. American Chinese, yes, there were plenty of them in San Francisco, but a Chinese man born and bred in China? Never. Sure, there were cooks and waiters from China in Chinatown, but her interaction with them was limited to ordering dim sum and fried rice. How could she picture a father from a place and a culture she had never known?

Faye couldn't say if she was disappointed with what she saw. Even if she were, she would never put it *that* way.

Her sister, on the other hand, seemed like the quiet and diffident one. Possibly, even dull. Faye looked at her and wondered if the Chinese girl was indeed her real elder sister.

I don't look like her at all, do I? Dear God, please tell me I don't look like that! Do I look like her and not know it? Faye panicked as thoughts— terrible, narcissistic, mortifying thoughts—surged through her mind.

Before she could fully subdue her panic, things began to happen.

'He's coming over right now, Faye. Get ready,' Sophia whispered as she straightened her brand-new jacket from Neiman Marcus. It was the most expensive piece of clothing Sophia had ever bought for herself.

Faye's father, with Yan scurrying behind him like a dangling appendage, fought his way out of the crowd and scanned the arrival hall desperately, trying to find a face he could recognize.

The media, however, was insatiable. Those few quotes from Li Fu wouldn't satisfy their editors, readers, or audience. No, they needed footage and photographs. They needed action and drama. They needed that moment when father and daughter locked eyes, tears rolled and arms embraced. They wanted nothing less than a Hollywood moment, preferably one with them walking out of the airport towards the setting sun as one happy family.

Faye's father had looked at his youngest daughter's photograph hundreds of times and memorized every feature, every shade, and every nuance of that face. He already knew her face before he saw it. As if his sixth sense told him where to look, he turned to where Faye and Sophia were standing, looked past Sophia, who was standing in front of Faye and set his eyes on his daughter.

He froze.

Yan followed his gaze and looked swiftly at her younger sister before averting her eyes furtively.

A self-esteem issue. We may have to fix that. Faye made a mental note. It's puzzling how random thoughts float into the mind at the most crucial moments of one's life.

At this point, everyone, *everyone*, at the airport arrival hall pivoted their cameras, lights, booms, recorders, and smartphones on Faye.

Breaths were held, and gasps were heard. Awaiting. Anticipating.

Faye and her father gravitated towards each other in silence, as if some kind of law of physics was at work to pull them together. Yan was a few paces behind her father. Walking beside Faye, Sophia clasped her daughter's hand firmly into hers—a little too firm for comfort—looking perplexed by the hullabaloo. Faye's father was in tears, genuine this time, pouring out seventeen years of pain and grief unabashedly and unreservedly. So was Sophia, weeping in shame and guilt. Yan twitched nervously behind the father as she darted glances around her.

Faye, however, was disappointing, failing to live up to everyone's expectations. As she looked at the stranger in front of her, she tried to muster up her emotions.

But she felt nothing.

She knew this small, frail Chinese man was her real father, her next-of-kin sharing her DNA, the person who gave her life, but what could she make of it? What did she know about him?

Nothing.

What am I supposed to feel? How am I supposed to behave? She thought as her heart pounded with a fresh wave of panic. *Why have I not burst into tears?*

She wasn't so sure about this meeting-my-family thing any more. She felt she wasn't ready, that she had rushed into this without giving it enough thought, that she should have been more prepared for this, especially if she had known that she was to do this in front of the entire fucking world. She turned to Sophia, hoping that she could magically erase this life-transforming-episode-turned-nightmare shit that was happening right now.

'It's okay, sweetie. Just say hello to your father,' Sophia offered instead.

Faye stopped and hesitated. The silence and awkwardness weighted palpably in the air, filling up the entire arrival hall and packing the lungs of the onlookers. Everyone was holding their breath for this moment, ready to be aroused by a collective explosion of feel-goodness, waiting to be coerced into believing in love once again.

But Faye remained rooted. She wanted to turn around and run, out of the airport, out of San Francisco, possibly all the way to Mexico. But Mexico had to wait.

Because her father made the first move to close up the distance between them.

'I've waited all my life for this moment. Ying, I've finally found you!' he said in his thick, country-accented Chinese.

And what was Faye thinking of? She was thinking how clichéd and unimaginative his first words were, albeit being well delivered with just the right amount of love and agony in his voice. She was thinking that her father might have practised it in his head for some time before this moment. She was thinking if she were in his shoes, she would probably say the same thing too.

Perhaps Faye was overthinking, or she wasn't thinking at all, because what came next became a mistake and a huge public embarrassment for her.

When her father came forward to embrace her, she flinched— flinched!—and pulled away.

If someone asked Faye afterwards why she had flinched, and if she was in a good mood, she would have deconstructed her emotion and given a detailed analysis of her reaction at the time. She would tell the person that she had flinched because it was an involuntary reaction of her body muscles. Her father was almost a stranger to her, and if an odd-looking stranger with a slight body odour came forward to hug her, she would viscerally pull away. But if she weren't in the mood to discuss the incident, she would simply say, 'I guess I freaked out.'

Either way, it wouldn't have mattered, because a huge mistake had been made.

The decibel level of the 'Oooooooo . . .' that registered at the arrival hall at that moment rivalled that of a fighter jet taking off.

When Faye realized what she had done, it was too late. She could tell that she had hurt and embarrassed her father, although he tried to put on a smile and said, 'My little girl is still a little shy. That's okay; it'll take us some time to get to know each other.'

'Yes, yes, she is indeed shy. And she doesn't like to be hugged. She does that to everyone, including me. Don't worry, she'll come around,' Sophia quickly interjected and offered her hand. 'Mr Li, it's nice to finally meet you. I'm Sophia.'

Sophia spoke slowly as if that would help him comprehend her language. Fortunately for her, the interpreter was still around.

'Sophia,' he repeated, taking her hand and shaking it vigorously. 'Thank you for taking care of Ying all these years. We're forever indebted to your kindness.'

Sophia turned to Faye with pleading eyes.

'Faye, please don't be rude. Go on, say hi to your father.'

A chance for redemption. Faye thought, almost relieved. *Take two. Here you go, the perfect reunion.*

Faye stepped forward and hugged her father. And he seemed truly grateful.

'Thanks for accepting me, my little Ying,' he said as he patted her back tenderly.

Once again, cameras and lights began flashing.

Chapter 10

YAN

She flinched. I saw it; in fact, everyone saw her pull away from papa when he tried to hug her the first time.

She. Actually. Flinched.

The scene replayed over and over again in Yan's head as Sophia's car pulled away from the airport's parking lot and into the highway. Although she didn't show it—why would she ever!—Yan was sorely disappointed by the whole reunion experience. Years of anticipation at her end had sharpened and detailed a specific image of what the reunion should be, and it was nothing like what she had just witnessed. Among the many scenarios Yan had conjured, none had Ying flinching when their father embraced her.

Also, Yan couldn't understand why Ying was so cold towards them. Was she not happy to see them? Had they done anything to offend her within such short a time? Yan had seen American TV shows before, and she thought White people—or people who lived with White people—liked to show their affection to others by hugging and kissing them, even to those whom they had just met.

So, why didn't Ying welcome their father's embrace?

She could also tell that her father was more disappointed than she was, although he tried his best to put up a brave front. Yan knew he had expected more, and Ying's aloofness must've bewildered him too.

On the way to the car, Ying had explained in halting Chinese that her adoptive mother would drive them to the hotel where their father had made a room reservation. Yan could tell that Ying was already straining her Chinese conversational ability. Coupled with the strange *laowai* accent, it was difficult for Yan and her father to understand her, although they were relieved that she could at least speak some Chinese. They had heard of many Chinese diasporas in America who couldn't understand a single Chinese word and wondered why these people didn't bother to learn the language of their ancestors.

Ying said very little since leaving the airport, and since Sophia couldn't converse with Yan and her father at all, the journey was filled with pockets of uncomfortable silence. Everyone seemed to be either absorbed in their thoughts or exhausted from the long flight or the intense experience at the airport.

Not that Yan cared much for conversations. Moreover, she was captivated by the passing scenery outside the window as the car approached the city centre. She was awed by its beauty. Indeed, unlike Ying, San Francisco did not fail to deliver. It was as ravishing a city as she had seen on travel brochures and television. She wondered what it would be like growing up in a lovely place like this where everyone looked so beautiful, so vibrant, and so happy.

She glanced at her father, and she knew that he was equally mesmerized by the city's charm. He seemed curious about everything. Occasionally, unable to hide his excitement, he'd ask Ying a question or two about this and that. He had transformed from a loving father into a child at Disneyland's threshold, brimming with exhilaration as he waited to be allowed into the happiest place on earth.

The car finally stopped at a place that seemed awfully familiar to Yan, even though she had never once set foot in it. With many of the shops, restaurants, and buildings displaying signage in the Chinese language, Yan figured this must be Chinatown. Ying pointed at a building across the street, it was their hotel. It looked a lot less posh than some of the buildings surrounding it, but it was more than Yan could ever ask for.

As they checked into their room, Yan decided in her mind that it was, without a doubt, the most luxurious accommodation she'd ever stay in. For one, it had 24/7 air-conditioning—air-conditioning!—with an en-suite bathroom. There were also two nicely made beds with fresh sheets and a big flat-screen TV.

It's smart of you, Papa, to book a nice hotel. Yan wanted to praise her father. *Now, Ying and her mother wouldn't look down on us!*

Yan looked longingly at the bathroom. She hadn't showered since they had left the apartment for the airport, which seemed like a lifetime ago on a different planet. She plucked her courage and asked Ying how much it would cost them to take a shower here. Ying gave her a weird look and told her that everything except the minibar—wait, there was no minibar in this hotel!—was already included in the price of the room.

'You mean I can use as much water, soap, shampoo, and all the other stuff as I wish?' Yan asked incredulously, promising herself that she'd take as many showers as possible during their stay here.

'Yes, just ask housekeeping for more if you run out of soap, shampoo, and towels,' Ying replied, just as incredulous.

'Towels too? Wow!'

'Don't get too used to this, okay?' Yan's father whispered to her once Ying was out of earshot. 'This is only temporary. We'll move in with Ying as soon as we get a chance to.'

But even that couldn't dampen Yan's elevated mood. She, Li Yan, a nobody from the Beijing slumps, was staying in a hotel in San Francisco. That meant her social stratum had just gone up a notch. A huge notch.

Maybe coming to America wasn't such a bad idea after all.

FAYE

It was probably the most agonizing ride of Faye's life.

The drive to the hotel wasn't exactly short, and the conversation flatlined after a few polite exchanges. Faye had so many questions that needed answers, but it was so fucking hard for her to converse in Chinese. With her father's thick accent, she could barely understand what he said. And neither her father nor her sister could make sense of Ying's pronunciation, which they amusingly deemed as incomprehensible *laowai* Chinese.

What's worse, Sophia couldn't contribute to any of the sporadic exchanges. Faye tried to translate, but that only resulted in killing the conversation as she had to stop to explain to her mother what was being said. Snippets of small talk soon fell away, leaving only the buzzing of the engine and hissing of the air-conditioning.

Faye wished Charlie was here. He would know how to keep the party—or, at least, the conversation—going, but he could only join them at the hotel later on. On second thought, she wondered how her boyfriend could ever converse with her family. She knew that Charlie would be too unmotivated to do something like learning another language; his French classes were already torture to his lazy American tongue. She wondered if her father and sister would be bothered enough to pick up English. Either way, her wandering thoughts were not helpful to the situation at hand because the atmosphere in the car had become deader than dead.

Faye looked at Sophia as her mom focused on the road and gave her a this-is-not-going-well look. Sophia smiled weakly, squeezed her daughter's hand, and whispered gently, 'Don't worry, it'll get better.'

When they arrived at the hotel in Chinatown, Faye was even more dismayed. Of all the hotels in San Francisco, or Chinatown for that matter, her father had booked the dingiest and the most horrifying. It was ugly and sleazy on the outside, and uglier and sleazier inside. She tried to tell herself to stop being a snob, that her father was likely on a budget since he was relying entirely on donations for this trip, but the smell of a concoction of rotten fish, sour beer, and vomit in the building made her feel sick to the stomach. The room wasn't an improvement either. It was poorly lit, decorated with crumbling fixtures and stained carpet, and looked as if the housekeeping crew hadn't cleaned it for the past decade. The bathroom was grimy and hard for Faye to even look at. And the stained bed linens? Burn them. Burn them all before whatever deadly bacteria that was on them infected all of them with an incurable disease!

Faye wasn't an expert in these things, but she was pretty sure the hotel rented out its rooms by the hour.

'Looks good, looks very good! This hotel's economical yet has a high standard,' said her father said as he inspected every corner of the room to his satisfaction.

Help me, God! Faye screamed in her head as she watched Sophia put on her best smile and nod politely.

YAN

'There's so much to say . . . I don't even know where to begin.' Yan's father smiled for the umpteenth time as he sat on the bed next to Yan facing Ying and Sophia who were sitting on the edge of the other bed, looking as if they were trying to position their butts in such a way that minimal contact with the bedsheet could be maintained.

'Why didn't mom come with you? Is she really a prostitute like what the reporter said?' Ying asked the most pressing questions in her mind as soon as he settled down.

Yan's father looked partly surprised and partly offended by her candidness, but he tried to let it slide. He lowered his eyes and said sombrely, 'Honestly, your mother's not well in the mind. She's resting in an institution. No . . . I'd say more like a hospice. I don't want people to know because I don't want her to be disturbed by reporters or fraudsters; we've come across quite a few since our story has gone public. Even Yan doesn't know about her situation and whereabouts. But your mother is getting better, especially since she now knows that you're alive and well. She'll join us soon, so don't you worry.'

Half-truths. Yan thought as she listened quietly to his little monologue. *Papa's go-to solution to all his problems. But it's still not a lie—a sign that he's playing his cards cautiously.*

'But was she really a—' Ying pressed on, but her father was determined to deflect the conversation.

'Let me tell you what you were like when you were a child—' he interrupted. He started recounting stories of Ying's childhood.

He was a good storyteller, and he made the two short months she had spent with her real family sound like a lifetime. A lot of what he said didn't really happen—at least not to Yan's recollection—but it captured Ying's attention. Ying listened intently, smiling, and asking questions occasionally. He sobbed a little now and then, but her eyes remained dry.

When he had finished with the two months of good times as father and daughter—there was only so much that could've happened within the short period—he moved on to their extended family. He had packed their only family album, which contained pictures of their maternal and paternal grandparents, granduncles, uncles and aunts, nieces, nephews, and a bunch of other relatives whom Yan and her father hadn't contacted since they had run out of favours and handouts from them. But his narrative skills moulded the relationship into a tight-knit family that had supported him every step of the way.

'You'll love the family. They can't wait to meet you, Ying. Nothing can replace the love of a real family . . .'

'Can you tell me about my abduction? Why was I taken away? And what exactly happened on that day?'

Her father seemed glad that she had asked, for he was losing steam in his stories. His smile faded, and he began the real story. He told it as it was—no lies, no half-truths, and no exaggeration. And there was something about his low, raspy voice that had a hypnotic effect when employed in telling the truth, and his audience was captivated, in fact, infatuated, by the candour of his suffering and the harshness of the life he had led and the hatred he felt for those who had brutally wronged the family.

This was a side Yan had seldom experienced—the honest, truthful Li Fu. And this was the side that she loved and missed most.

As he finished his recount, he let out a little sigh and said, 'That's why your mother can't join us now.'

'I . . . I don't know what to say. There's just so much to think about. Poor mother! She must've gone through hell!' Ying seemed overwhelmed by what she had heard.

'Don't worry. When she can, we'll get her over, and we can all live here and be a family again.'

'Well, I don't know about that . . . There're immigrant laws to consider—' Ying, surprised that her father had brought up such a delicate matter so soon and so abruptly, looked to Sophia to support her. But before she could say anything else, the door to the hotel room flew open, and a tall and blonde young man with a wide grin on his face entered. The brightness of his hair, his beautiful smile, his handsome face, and his cheerfulness lit up the room immediately as if the scene of a musical play had changed and the song had transformed from the sombre rendition to a happy, snappy tune.

Yan stared and stared. She had never been in the same room with a White man before. The only White men she had ever seen were on TV and occasionally, at Wangfujing Street and the airport. Charlie's chiselled good looks; tall and athletic body; and tanned, olive skin reminded her of the Greek god Apollo she had once read about in a storybook.

'Sorry for being soooo late. I was delayed at school,' Charlie said in a cheery, breezy voice, a little breathless but perfectly at ease with the curious stares directed at him. 'Hi everyone, who am I looking at?'

'Let me introduce you to my boyfriend, Charles Murray.' Ying stood up quickly and rushed to Charlie's side, relieved at once for the distraction.

'Charlie, this is Mr Li Fu, my fa . . . my biological father,' she hesitated.

Li Fu stood up and scrutinized the boy from head to toe, weighing and judging his worth in a split second. He decided he liked what he saw, and engulfing Charlie's hand in his callused palms, he pumped it fervently.

'Nice to meet you, Mr Li! Please call me Charlie, Sir. Everyone does.'

'And this is my elder sister, Li Yan,' Ying turned to Yan and put her hands on her sister's shoulders.

Charlie walked towards Yan, flashed a brilliant smile, and embraced her with a warm hug. Yan didn't know what to do—no one had ever hugged her before, so she stood still like a soldier at attention while he gave her his three-second, very-nice-to-meet-you hug. She could feel his breath on her neck and his muscular arms around her back and taste his light, musky cologne. Her mind raced in confusion as she felt her legs buckling, her heart pulsating, and her face turning crimson. To her, it seemed like a lifetime, and she wished he wouldn't let go.

In those three seconds, she was someone who mattered. In those three seconds, she forgot she was Yan.

'It's good to finally meet Faye's sister. I can't wait to get to know you better,' he said. Then, he went to Ying and kissed her on her lips.

Yan was shocked by the public display of the two lovers' affection. *On her lips!*, she thought with indignation. *Right in front of everyone! And why isn't Sophia stopping them? Abomination!*

'Charlie, what do you do for a living?' Her father, while equally disapproved of their casual act of physical intimacy in full view, decided to overlook the small things and pick his battles carefully.

Charlie couldn't understand Chinese, so Ying interpreted.

'I'm a high school student like Faye, but I'll be going to college soon.'

'College? That's good, that's very good. What about your father? What does he do?'

'He runs a business conglomerate. He has business dealings everywhere, even in China. By the way, he sends his apology for not being here today. He and my mom are currently in Canada. They wish to invite all of you to dinner once they're back.'

'Good, good. I'll be happy to meet them. What kind of business is he in?'

'Mainly financial, equity, bonds, etc. . . . oh and property too.'

'Excellent, excellent. That's big business. Very lucrative,' Li Fu said almost reverently. 'Any brothers and sisters?'

'Just an older brother. He's . . . well . . . sort of an artist and resides in Thailand at the moment.'

Li Fu nodded earnestly as he took in and evaluated the information, looking very pleased with what he had learnt about Charlie and his family so far and approving of his daughter's well-to-do boyfriend.

'I was just telling Ying—' Li Fu began.

'Ying?'

'That was my name when I was a baby, dumb dumb,' Ying pretended to be annoyed. 'Don't you ever pay any attention when I talk?'

'Oh yeah . . . sorry—'

'Ying, don't be so harsh on Charlie! Chinese names can be confusing to White people,' Li Fu had already decided whose side to be on. 'Anyway, I was just telling Ying that we could all stay here in San Francisco now that we're united as a family. Since your father is in the property business, perhaps he can let us a small apartment at some discounted rate or something—'

'Wait, I'm sorry, but I don't think it's a good idea to talk about this now,' Ying interrupted immediately, looking aghast at the audacity of the idea.

'Why not?' asked Li Fu.

'Well, first of all, Charlie's dad deals with very expensive houses and commercial properties that are way out of our price range. Also, I don't like to ask for favours from him just because Charlie and I are dating. And, about you and Yan staying in San Francisco—'

'I'm sorry, but what's going on here? What are you talking about?' Sophia, sensing the tension that had built up based on the tone of the conversation, decided to jump in. Ying quickly translated.

'It's a little too early to talk about these things,' Sophia added quickly, looking afraid that Ying might get a little too hot-headed and say things that she'd regret later. 'Let's focus on getting to know one another better first.'

'That's right,' Ying said as she translated her mom's words back to her father. 'By the way, how long are your visas good for?'

'Oh, those are just details. The important thing is that we're here. Anyway, I heard it's not difficult to get a couple of green cards if you have some money if you know what I mean,' Li Fu insinuated with a rattling laugh.

But no one was amused. The mere suggestion of an illegal activity killed the conversation right away. Yan looked around the room as the knots of tension tangled more tightly around everyone's throats, and suddenly, no one could think of anything else to say.

'Look, I'm just saying—' he said defensively.

'No, please don't suggest anything,' Ying whispered, surprising even herself at her insolence. 'As for the reunion, let's not be too hasty. We'll talk when we're ready.'

Li Fu didn't seem to comprehend her words. For him, there wasn't even a need for a discussion.

'What do you mean? Are you saying you don't want us to stay here?' he persisted. 'If you like, we can go back to China. I'd prefer to start a new life here, but if that's what you want, it's no problem. We can work it out.'

'No, it's not so simple,' Ying said, avoiding her father's gaze. 'Please try to understand, it's too soon to talk about living together as a family. For as long as I remember, my only parent was Sophia, and I love her so dearly. I can't even begin to think about leaving her. And I barely know you—'

'You don't want to live with us? You want to stay with Sophia? But you haven't met your real mother yet,' Li Fu looked as if he had been given the death sentence.

'Sophia's my real mother too. And no, that's not what I meant either. I'm saying we don't have to decide now. I need time; we need time. Time to get to know one another first, time to adjust, time to think things through. I'm sure Yan needs some time to cope with a new sister in her life too. It's unreasonable to expect me to go and live with a bunch of strangers just because you're my real father.'

As soon as Ying said those last few words, Yan could tell that she regretted and wished to take them back. She didn't mean to be harsh, but she was afraid. She was afraid of losing the life she was living and was even more afraid of losing Sophia.

All of a sudden, Li Fu looked as if he had aged ten years. He didn't see this coming. He had been so fixated on the perfect picture he had created in his mind that there wasn't any room for alternatives. He could handle the many obstacles and setbacks, but it looked like he had finally been beaten by his own daughter. He seemed like a wounded puppy, abandoned and left to die. It was hard for Yan to watch.

'I'm really tired from the long trip. I think Yan and I need to get some rest. Why don't you leave now,' he mumbled slowly as he crawled under the blankets, curled into a foetal position, and closed his eyes.

'What's going on, Faye? What did you say to your father?' Sophia asked worriedly.

'Let's go, Mom. I'll tell you on our way out. C'mon, Charlie,' Ying said. She started towards the door. When she got there, she turned around and looked at her father as if she wanted to say something. But her father's eyes remained shut. He was lost in his devastated world.

Left with no choice, she turned to Yan and said, 'Please try to make father understand that I'm not deciding on anything right now. I need time. I don't know what he's expecting, but we've just met. And we're so different in so many ways, like how we think and live. It takes time to adjust, you know?'

'I understand. Don't worry about Papa. He'll bounce back. Nothing can get to him,' Yan said without really believing her own words. But she wanted to sound adult-like, and adults often said things like that. She was, after all, the big sister.

'That's good. I'll call you tomorrow, okay? Maybe we can hang out or something,' Ying said, trying to sound cheerful.

Chapter 11

FAYE

Faye held up long enough till she got home. She was a proud girl, and she didn't want to lose her composure or display any emotional vulnerability, especially not in front of her new family. But the moment she set foot in her bedroom, tears gushed out like the Niagara Falls. A confluence of conflicting thoughts and feelings of disappointment, anger, and guilt swamped her mind, pushing her to the verge of an epic meltdown.

She was devastated. But exactly by what she wasn't quite sure. It could be that the whole thing didn't go as well as she had expected, or rather, it didn't go well at all. Or, it could be the family she had in her mind was light-years from the real family she had just met in that dirty, sleazy hotel in Chinatown. Or, perhaps she felt guilty and angry with herself because she couldn't reciprocate the love her father had for her.

No, that wasn't true.

The truth was she didn't feel anything for them.

She didn't feel anything for them—not her father, her sister, not even her mother, although she had only seen pictures of her. For a short while—a very short while—when she was listening to her father's recount of her abduction, she nurtured a strange admiration for this stranger in front of her. She liked him in a way that she couldn't quite grasp herself. She liked him like how she liked Tom Hanks or Jackie Chan—a safe, distant, surreal appreciation that she could easily disassociate from or tuck away and get on with her real life. But it wasn't close to her heart, and it certainly wasn't love. And that, too, vanished as soon as his real personality took over.

She wondered why she was such a cold-hearted bitch who couldn't share the joy her family, or, at least her father, had so openly expressed. Shouldn't she be dying to spend every waking hour with them, asking questions about her childhood over and over again until they got sick of her? Shouldn't she feel like she finally had a family? Shouldn't she feel whole?

She didn't.

She felt nothing. They were no different from strangers to her— strangers she could've crossed paths with and never taken a second look at. In fact, she was a little disgusted with her father's behaviour, at how he had hogged the limelight with the media and how he had asked for a favour from Charlie's parents even before meeting them. Unbelievable! As for Yan, there wasn't any connection there either. She had hardly said a word except for right before they had left the hotel room. And, she had acted so weirdly and uncomfortably with the others that, if Faye were to be honest with herself, she would go as far as saying that her big sister gave her the creeps. She wondered if it was just her family or if all Chinese families behaved like that.

Faye had no idea how to deal with the situation that she had got herself into. She shivered at the thought of having to face them the next day, the following day, and possibly the rest of her life. She was only seventeen; her life hadn't even begun, and it was already falling apart. It couldn't possibly be fair for her to have to handle this alone.

And now, she found herself wallowing in self-pity, something she despised. Faye always told others that only the weak and the narcissistic feel sorry for themselves. So which one was she?

As she reached for a new box of Kleenex, she heard a gentle knock on the door, followed by, 'Hey, it's me. Can I come in?'

Mom.

Mom with her beautiful smile and fat-padded shoulders to cry on. The only person Faye wanted to call family now. But she was ashamed to face even her.

'Please go away, Mom. I'm tired. I just want to sleep, okay?' She didn't want her mom to see her in such a distraught state. On the other hand, she was dying to talk to her. So Faye sent an I-wanna-see-you-but-I-can't-say-it message, and Sophia got it immediately.

'I know, honey. I'm sorry to disturb you, but I need to talk to someone. I feel so confused . . . and . . . and . . . I thought we could talk about, you know, stuff?' Thoughtful as ever, Sophia made herself look hapless so that her daughter could feel better.

'Okay, but just for a while,' Faye capitulated quickly, as intended. She loved her mom so much now that she could hug her forever.

She opened the door slowly, letting the light from the hallway into her dark, cheerless room. Standing against the light, Faye could only see her mom's silhouette, but she didn't fail to notice that she had put on quite a few pounds lately. The love handles were thicker than ever, and those broad hips of hers were straining the pant's zipper almost to a breaking point. Stress-eating had always been a problem for Sophia.

Ironically, Sophia couldn't find the right words to say once the door was open. All she knew was that her daughter was in pain, and she had to help her, never mind the fact that Sophia herself was miserable, and no one had asked if she was all right. She decided the best thing to do at such a time was to play mom.

'Are you hungry? Would you like me to whip something up quickly?' she asked as she sat down on Faye's unmade bed.

'Mom!' Faye cried in dismay.

'So that's a no? Okay, sorry.'

Silence.

'You know, there's never a right or wrong way to meet people, even though they're your family—' Sophia began. Then she decided those weren't the best lines to comfort her daughter.

'What I'm trying to say is . . . it's not your fault, okay? It's not your fault that any of these things happened. So stop beating yourself up over it.'

'You don't understand! You don't even . . . like . . . know how I'm feeling right now,' Faye said despondently.

'Tell me then. Tell me how you feel. I'm listening.'

'I'm . . . I'm . . . I don't know . . .'

'There's nothing wrong with feeling upset or confused right now. I think most people would probably feel the same.'

'Oh yeah? I bet they don't feel guilty. I bet they don't feel—'

'Feel what?'

'That they don't love their family.'

'Is that what this is about? Oh, honey! It's absolutely fine to feel that way! I mean, you didn't know them before, and you've just met them today. It'll take time to connect and bond with them. You can't expect to love somebody instantly, I mean, not unless he's Brad Pitt—'

Faye rolled her moist eyes. Even her mom's choice of Hollywood studs was outdated.

'It's not just that. They said they wanted to stay here and expected me to live with them. How could they assume that it was a good idea? Did anyone ask me what *I* wanted?'

'Do you want to live with them?' Sophia asked quietly. Faye noticed she held her breath while she waited for the answer.

'I don't know. I think it's too premature to even bring up stuff like that. I mean, it's a life-changing decision, don't you think?'

'Yes, it is,' Sophia said reassuringly, letting out her breath slowly. 'And you should take as much time as you need.'

Faye paused for a while, wondering if she should continue.

'And if I don't, is that okay?'

'Of course, it's okay! You can stay here with me for as long as you like. Stay forever!' she cooed, stroking her daughter's long, jet-black tress as she heaved a sigh of relief.

But these comforting words didn't offer much solace to Faye. Beneath her soul harboured her darkest, ugliest secret. A secret that said: *I'm repulsed by my family, and I don't want to have anything to do with them.*

A secret that would brand Faye as the worst she-devil in the history of mankind if it ever got out. She kept it from her mom because she knew she wouldn't even begin to understand it. She was sure Sophia would tell her that the feelings would go away and that any misgivings could be attributed to differences in culture and lifestyle. That she would eventually get used to them once she knew them better.

But Faye didn't want to get to know them better or get used to them. Because her deepest fear was that she would become—God forbid!—one of them. The very thought made Faye feel nauseated.

'Where's Charlie?' Faye decided to change the subject.

'I sent him home. It was getting late, and I didn't see the point of him hanging around. Look, why don't you get some rest? You'll feel better tomorrow, I promise you.'

While Faye knew Sophia said those words with the kindest intention, she didn't believe her. She knew that tomorrow would be just as bad if not worse than today. But she needed to sleep. She needed to fade into nothingness and forget about the nightmare that she was living in.

SOPHIA

Sophia's loving smile melted from her face the moment she shut Faye's bedroom door. Replacing that smile was a diabolical fear that almost crippled her. Faye was right about one thing—this was not going well. Never mind that Sophia couldn't communicate with the Li's at all—why didn't she drag her sorry butt to the Veronica Ip Chinese Learning Centre with Faye? And, all she could do was smile and nod like a dumbass all the time; let alone the fact that Faye was so ill-prepared for the meeting that Sophia wasn't sure what her greatest mistake was any more—not telling Faye that she was possibly abducted or telling her the truth. And amidst the frenzy of feeling guilty and trying to do the right thing, she had forgotten to consider the one thing, the one crucial thing that meant more to her than her own life. Like Li Fu, the possibility that she could lose Faye forever hadn't crossed her mind.

Until now.

Since the moment Li Fu had mentioned taking Faye with him, terror had rapidly seized Sophia's heart, constricting it from pumping blood into her brain, sending her into a state of terror. She remembered sitting on that possibly bed-bug-infested bed in the hotel room—smiling widely and reassuringly, of course—as the world she knew collapsed right in front of her into a hell hole, which was where she would remain if Faye were to be taken from her. A part of her told her that she deserved it, *for shame on you for not coming clean with your daughter when you had the chance to.*

On the other hand, Sophia couldn't possibly let that happen. She had worked too hard and loved Faye too much to let her go. Faye was all she had all these years, and she had given the best years of her life bringing her up in the most comfortable environment and giving her the best things in life. Surely she deserved some credit? Surely that could somehow absolve her of her sin? Comparing Faye to her elder sister—what's her name? Yan?—surely Sophia had proven herself to be a much better parent?

Surely she didn't deserve to lose Faye?

What can I do? Sophia wondered as she crossed the hallway into her bedroom, allowing her tears to now flow freely on her face, creating little rivulets that ran along her deep crow's feet. She could sabotage Faye's relationship with the Li's by whispering tiny devilish suggestions now and then into Faye's young, inexperienced ears. Surely she could convince Faye to stay with her rather than with the Li family. Or, perhaps she didn't even need to. Faye was already so uncomfortable with them. She could just let Li's unpleasantness unfold itself, causing their demise.

No, she wouldn't be able to live with herself if she had allowed herself to do any of these things. She was guilty. At the point of offering the bribe to the orphanage manager, she had crossed the Rubicon. She had blood on her hands in bringing down the Li family. How could she possibly do even more harm to them?

What should I do? What would Jesus do?

YAN

Yan's father remained in a foetal position on the bed long after Ying and the others left. Yan wasn't too concerned about his state of being, but just to be sure, she listened for his breathing in the quiet room. Relieved that it was still heavy and regular, she stepped into the bathroom and took a long, hot, satisfying shower.

She had seen him in this state before. She had even coined a name for it. She called it the High-Expectation-Followed-By-Great-Disappointment Syndrome. The cause was apparent: unexpected bad news leading him to a massive shock and rendering him temporarily immobile. Not very different from his state of drunkenness, except that she didn't need to clean up his vomit or nurse a hangover the next day. Her prognosis? He should be up on his feet after a night's rest.

She walked across his bed and lay down on the one parallel to his, enjoying the cool air-conditioning and the quietness of the room. It was already nighttime, but from the look of it, dinner seemed out of the question. She remembered the roasted ducks hanging by their necks inside the glass panes at the entrance of a Chinese restaurant across the street and imagined what they would taste like. It made her hungry, but she would have to deal with it. As she closed her eyes, she concentrated on the filtered noise from the downtown traffic and the Friday-evening revellers through the double-pane window, wishing that she could go downstairs and take a walk around the blocks to experience America. But with her father in his catatonic state, it was impossible to leave him alone in the hotel room.

Exhausted from the long trip and the excitement of the day, she started drifting into sleep. Then, she heard her father speak, 'You need to learn to dress better and act like you belong here.'

'What?'

'You have to start dressing and behaving like your sister. And start acting . . . what do they call it here? "Cool", that's right. The outfits you've brought with you won't do, they're too outdated,' he continued mumbling without moving a muscle. 'That's probably why Ying was so reluctant to stay with us. Girls here are very particular about such things—looks, makeup, clothes, and all that. If you don't learn to be like her, she'll never like us. You know what? We'll get some new clothes tomorrow and start dressing like the Americans.'

Yan stared at him, amazed and hurt that he was blaming it all on her.

'And stop behaving like a mute. For heaven's sake, say something intelligent once in a while. You need to have opinions here, you understand?' he rattled on. 'We've got to look more respectable, and less like hillbillies. We've got to get our act together.'

'I think she's just not used to us yet, that's all. Like she said, we have to give her some time and space,' Yan replied.

'What do you know? Time? What does she need time for? I think we're giving her too much time. That's why she's overthinking stuff. In fact, you just gave me an idea. We can't sit here and wait for things to happen. We've to take initiative. I know exactly what I need to do now,' he said, sitting up suddenly. He put on his shoes, straightened his clothes, and left the room.

Yan knew it was a bad idea even before she found out what he wanted to do. She knew it was such a bad idea that she didn't dare to ask what it was.

And he didn't even use the free shower, she thought.

FAYE

'Hey Faye, can I take a picture with you?'

A girl Faye didn't recognize came up to her the moment she stepped out of her car.

'For my Instagram,' the girl said with a ready smile as she thrust her face right next to Faye's and snapped a couple of pictures before Faye had a chance to say no. Among the many things Faye didn't want to do today, taking pictures was at the top of the list, not with her puffy eyes and dog-tired face.

'Thanks,' the girl said breezily. She walked away, uploading the pictures instantly without giving Faye a second look.

'What the hell was that all about?' Faye whispered to herself indignantly.

As she walked towards the school building, she gradually came to realize that many of the kids who were hanging around were staring at her, openly or furtively, and parting ways as she crossed the lawn as if she was Moses crossing the Red Sea. Some gave her the thumbs up, but most just gawked unashamedly.

Several girls walked past her and whispered to one another, 'She's the girl I was talking about. How I wish I were her. She's so lucky!'

'What? Are you crazy? She's an attention-seeking bitch!'

'Who does she think she is . . . like . . . with her fifteen minutes of fame or something?'

'She thinks she's Kim Kardashian – famous for being famous!'

'Well, her ass is starting to look like Kardashian, for sure!'

Faye felt as if she had walked into one of her parallel universes. She had been studying in this high school for years, but no one had ever noticed her the way they did today. She laughed bitterly in her head at the thought of it. She was popular now because of what happened yesterday—not because she did anything worthy like discover a cure for cancer, find a solution to poverty, or win an Olympic medal for her country. But there she was, almost a celebrity, simply because she was on television.

People always say be careful of what you wish for because you may just get it. Like any teenager, Faye had dreamed of being famous, but within five minutes, she already knew that fame wasn't as fabulous as she'd expected. The attention she was getting from her 'celebrity status' was turning into a nightmare almost as soon as she started enjoying it.

Faye walked quickly into her classroom, leaving the haunting giggles behind her. For the first time, she chose a back seat, pulled her sweater hood over her head and tried to be as inconspicuous as possible.

She texted Charlie.

Where the hell r u? I m dyin here.

It took him a full minute—a full minute!—to reply.

@ my locker. B there in a min. Luv ya.

Yeah, you better be here soon enough, she thought miserably as she noticed from the corner of her eye that someone else had slipped into the seat next to her. It was Michelle, one of Faye's best friends.

Michelle was half Singaporean-Chinese and half American. Born and raised in Singapore, Michelle had lived in several Asian cities growing up as her American investment banker dad moved his family from country to country every few years to assume new postings. Two years back, her family had finally settled in San Francisco and got her enrolled in Faye's high school.

Faye had felt a kind of kinship with this lonely and eccentric girl and was instantly attracted to her. Michelle was weird and quirky, optimistic and sad, resilient and vulnerable, witty, whimsical, and mischievous all at the same time (think Katy Perry meets Puck in *A Midsummer Night's Dream*). Faye had befriended her and helped her adapt to her new environment. Being practically a foreigner in her father's country, Michelle had found the transition particularly tough. Her strange accent, idiosyncratic ways, short stature of five feet two inches, small bosoms, and a peculiar and eclectic wardrobe had made her the target of bullies and an unpopular girl among the popular girls. Despite being laughed at, Michelle insisted on dressing differently because it was, in her own words, a way to forge her own identity.

Michelle had gratefully accepted Faye's friendship, but soon, her sense of self-deprecating humour and winning personality started attracting friends of her own, despite her unconventional fashion style. But Faye would always be Michelle's BFF because of the kindness Faye had shown her when she had needed it most.

'Hey you, my celebrity friend! What's it like to be famous?' Michelle thrust her head, freshly styled with a pixie cut, underneath Faye's downward-facing and gloomy face, her half Asian exotic countenance gleaming with mischief. When she saw Faye's red, sleepless eyes, she stuck out her tongue, made a face, and whispered 'whoops' underneath her breath.

'Miserable, huh? Let me guess, fame brings you not just admiration but jealousy and trolling as well?' Michelle said, as she abruptly withdrew her head and slouched ungracefully on the chair, sinking into her super oversized chequered shirt, which she'd decided was a good match with her ankle-length, multi-coloured flared skirt.

Faye didn't answer her.

Seeing how dejected Faye was, she stopped teasing. 'Listen, don't let those bitches in the hall get to you. You know they're just jealous of you—'

'It's not about that. I don't care about them,' Faye blurted sullenly.

'No? Okay, so things didn't go well yesterday then. Am I right, or am I right?' Michelle sprang upright from her chair again. 'I called you last night, but your mom said you were asleep. Best to leave you alone.'

'Yeah. Thanks.'

'So? What were they like?'

'I don't want to talk about it.'

'You sure? 'Cos you look like a train wreck.'

'I don't want to talk about it.'

'Okay, but you know I'm always here if you . . . like . . . need something, right?'

'Right.'

They were quiet for a minute. Michelle remained in the chair even though she knew Charles would come in any minute to kick her out of it. Faye was glad she didn't leave because she needed to talk to her, but at her own pace and not before she was ready. But it didn't take her long this time.

'You promise you won't tell anyone, okay? Swear on your . . . your grades,' Faye said.

'I swear that if I ever tell anyone, I'll get an A-minus for Math.'

'Wow . . . brutal! An A-minus? That's like failing to you!'

'See? So pray tell!'

'They were terrible! And I was awful.'

And so Faye told Michelle everything, from the meeting at the airport to the conversations in the hotel, sparing no details. Michelle listened without interrupting, but all this time looking not at her friend but at Instagram posts on her phone, liking and commenting on some of them occasionally. Faye took no offence at all, for she would've done the same if Michelle had to recount a long story.

'That's typical,' Michelle whispered nonchalantly when Faye had finished. The teacher had already entered the classroom and so had Charlie, although he was oblivious to their conversation.

'What's typical?' Faye whispered back.

'Their behaviour. They behave like that because they have a very different set of expectations and needs from you guys.'

'It can't be!'

'Look, I've seen enough of them to know how they think and behave. They are, after all, Asians, and guess who else is half Asian? I should know, right? But you know what? It's not really their fault. Blame . . . like . . . Communism if you want,' Michelle waved her hands casually.

'What the hell has Communism got to do with my problem?'

'Everything! Your family comes from a place where there are too few resources for too many people. It's terribly competitive, and everyone has to fight really hard for their survival. And because your dad has nothing, money and face are everything to him.'

'Face?'

'C'mon Faye, don't you have . . . like . . . weekly Chinese lessons? How can you not know about face?'

'Well, I don't, okay? Just tell me!' Faye whispered a little too loudly. A few heads turned, and the teacher looked up from her desk.

'Anything interesting you wish to share with us, Faye?' the teacher glared. 'Perhaps your encounter with the media yesterday?'

'Sorry, Mrs Irving,' Faye replied.

That ended the conversation.

After class, Faye told Charlie to wait for her in their next class while she caught up with Michelle in the hallway.

'You were saying something about face?'

'Face? What face?'

'Hello? You said something like money and face are everything to my family?'

'Oh yeah. I did. Okay, let's start with the obvious. The Chinese are very particular about how they look in front of others, right?'

Faye looked lost.

'Oh God, please say you know—' Michelle gasped and looked mortified.

'Duh! I'm not a total idiot!' Faye rolled her eyes with mock exasperation, although she had no idea what Michelle was saying.

'They need to appear respected, well-to-do, and all that shit. That's face. And they expect people to give them face, especially those younger than them. They also expect their kids, that's you, to be filial to them. No matter what happens, you need to be on your parents' side. It doesn't matter whether you think they're wrong or stupid; that's beside the point. The point is, they're right, and you're wrong. The filial thing also includes taking care of them when they're old. So, I think your father was already planning for his retirement when he met you and Charlie.'

'You're kidding, right?'

'Nope, never been more serious in my life. The media thing? That's a face thing too. Your father finally had the respect and attention of everyone, and that made him feel like a million bucks—above everyone else. Capeesh?'

'But I'm so young, and we've . . . like . . . just met! How can he expect *me* to take care of him?' Faye exclaimed.

'E-vent-ual-ly. He's thinking long-term. My guess is, he likes Charlie, doesn't he?'

'I think so.'

'Of course, he does.'

'Why?'

'Why? Let's see, how can I put it without sounding too offensive? Hmm . . . well . . . Charlie's family is bloody rich. Figure that out. I've got to go. Late for another class!'

Before Michelle disappeared into the crowd, she turned and offered an ominous warning.

'I'll be careful if I were you. Choose your words carefully and don't commit to anything unless you're absolutely sure.'

* * *

There was luggage at the front door when Faye got home. She knew whom they belonged to, although she hoped that she was wrong. However, the conversation with Michelle that was still echoing in Faye's ears told her she wasn't.

She closed her eyes and counted to ten. Then, she counted another ten, just to be on the safe side. She opened and closed the door as quietly as possible to not arouse anyone. Her dumbass plan of avoiding everyone, escaping to her room, and staying there till they left was proven a failure immediately.

'Faye, is that you?' She heard Sophia calling her as she was creeping halfway up the stairs.

Fuck.

Defeated, she turned around and stomped back down, and tried to look mortified.

'Mom! What's going on here? No, no, don't tell me—'

Sophia looked hapless. She didn't need to utter a word because the loud conversations, or rather, the *one* loud voice delivering a monologue in the kitchen said it all. To top it off, Faye could smell Chinese cooking permeating the house.

'They're here—' Sophia mouthed in dismay.

With perfect timing, Faye's father joined them in the hallway. He smiled like he had learnt to smile from a manual.

'Oh good, you're back! We've great news for you. Sophia has kindly opened her home to us, and we've gratefully accepted her generosity. Do you know how much money it'll save us? The hotels here are so expensive, and I think it's crazy to spend so much just for a place to sleep. This way, we can spend more time together to get to know each other better, like you said we should,' he said, his smile still hanging desperately on his face. 'Come on in, you must be hungry. Yan and I are making dinner. We'll show you what a real Chinese meal is like!'

'Why don't you guys go ahead? I'll just run up to my room to freshen up. Won't take long.' Faye forced a smile and sounded cheerful.

'We'll wait for you. Our first dinner as a family should be taken together. This is so great!' He clapped his hands and popped back into the kitchen.

Faye looked daggers at Sophia, stabbing her thousand times over.

'How could you invite them to stay with us? Do you know what you've got us into?' Faye went ballistic.

'Shhh . . . keep it down, will you? They can hear us.'

'They don't understand English, remember?'

'I'm not too sure about that. Your sister understands a little. Anyway, it wasn't me. I didn't invite them to stay with us.'

'*He* just said you did!'

'Well, I didn't! They just showed up at the door in a taxi with their luggage and stuff. What was I supposed to do?' Sophia whispered defensively.

'You could say no!'

'Really, I could? Why don't you go into the kitchen and tell them to leave then?'

Faye opened her mouth, but she could think of nothing clever to say to her mother.

* * *

There was only a spare room with a single bed, which was the home office slash guest room, so they had to put Yan up in Faye's room. Faye surprised herself when she realized she wasn't resistant to the idea of sharing her room with her sister. Having given some thought to Michelle's insight about the Chinese people, she wanted to give her family a chance, perhaps even to form some kind of relationship with them, and she thought she could start with her sister. Yan was younger and probably more open-minded. Faye might have the opportunity to have a decent, one-on-one conversation with her without their father jumping in all the time and answering questions on Yan's behalf. Over dinner, Faye had been annoyed by his constant interruptions whenever she had tried to talk to Yan.

'Yan has enough rice, don't worry.'

'Yan does most of the cooking at home, although I'm the chef of our family when it comes to real Chinese gourmet!'

'Yan doesn't have a boyfriend yet. Do you have someone in mind?'

It had been hard for Faye to remain polite when what she really wanted to do was to ask her father to shut up. But the phrase 'giving face' had repeatedly popped up in her head. And since they had had such a bad start, she didn't want to make the situation any worse than it already was.

Faye, however, was worried about her mom. Sophia had been very quiet throughout dinner. Although she had attributed it to her not understanding the conversation at the table, Faye knew there had to be more to it. Sophia was just not telling.

Faye's bed wasn't big enough for two people, so she offered it to Yan while she snuggled into her sleeping bag. Once they were in bed, Faye began casually.

'Are you comfortable there, Yan? Do you need more pillows?'

'I'm comfortable. Thanks,' Yan said.

'It must be exciting for you to be in a country that's so different from China. Isn't it great to see so much new stuff?'

'It's okay.'

'Do you go to school in China?'

'No,' Yan started giving monosyllabic answers.

'I guess you're done with school, huh?'

Silence ensued.

'Do you have a job?'

Another pause. A longer one this time.

'No. I take care of papa.'

And so on and so forth.

The one-way conversation soon became tedious for Faye, and she wondered if it was due to her barely comprehensible Chinese or if her sister had a low IQ, for both seemed highly possible to her. Soon, she gave up and stopped talking altogether. She needed sleep, but she found herself staring at the ceiling, battling insomnia. After a long time, she heard a low, barely audible whisper.

'What's it like to be you?' Yan asked. At first, Faye wasn't sure if it was a voice in her head or her sister had actually asked her a question.

'I'm sorry, did you say something?'

'I asked what it was like to be you. What kind of life do you have?' Yan replied, slightly more confident this time.

Faye was surprised by the profundity of the question.

'Well, it's like, stressful most of the time, I guess. I mean, between the school work, the household chores that Sophia . . . like . . . makes me do, and the editorial work for the school magazine, it's a lot to handle. Plus, I'm going to university next year, so I've to make sure my grades are good enough for the school I'm applying to, which is UCLA, by the way. Sometimes, I wish I had more than twenty-four hours a day.'

She could tell that Yan was listening intently, but she wasn't sure if it was the answer she was looking for.

'What about you? What kind of life do you have?' Faye asked her in return, glad that they were finally talking.

'I don't. After you went missing, you got to live. I didn't.'

Chapter 12

YAN

It had been more than a month since Yan and her father had moved into Sophia's home. Yan's father liked it here; he had told Yan that this was the best way to experience America and learn about its people and culture. He had maintained that it was vital for them to know the real America if they were to be accepted by the people here. He had also said that if they had stayed in Chinatown, they would be mingling only with the Chinese immigrants, and that would serve them no purpose.

But so far, the friends they had made here were all Chinese immigrants—legal or otherwise. Almost all of them lived in Chinatown and attended English lessons at the Veronica Ip's Learning Centre, where Yan and her father also dutifully went three times a week.

So, Yan knew that everything her father said was bullshit. He was thinking only of Ying when he had said 'the people here' and was doing everything he could to gain her acceptance. He was also trying to figure out a way to get green cards for both of them. Yan wasn't sure about that; she'd heard that it wasn't easy to get a green card in this country unless one had a unique skill or lots of money to invest. They had neither the skills nor the money to offer America. Besides, time was running out;

with less than two months left before their visas expired, she seriously had doubts about their chance of obtaining any legal status in this country.

As a part of his 'strategy' to integrate into the American culture, he had insisted on speaking only English when they were at Sophia's home and trying to make conversations with Sophia and Ying as much as possible. Yan confined her conversations to pleasantries such as 'good morning', 'how are you?' and so forth, but she enjoyed watching her father trying to prolong excruciating conversations with either Sophia or Ying because it was just so funny and painful. Sophia did her best to try to understand him, but Ying wasn't always patient. She was seldom patient. She'd become edgier since their arrival, and her discomfort with them being under the same roof as her had been obvious. Yan had eavesdropped on her sister's conversation with Sophia the other day, and she had heard her going on and on about 'not getting any privacy in this damned house'. Yan couldn't understand why, of all things, Ying complained about space because the house was many times bigger than their apartment in Beijing. Yan thought that if anyone in this house had the right to complain, it was Sophia. Poor woman! Caught between a rock and a hard place. Not only did she have to face the possibility of losing her daughter, but she also had to put up with them, the very people who might take her daughter away. But unlike Ying, she'd shown them nothing but kindness—not a mean word, a sullen face or a reluctant hand had ever been offered.

It turned out that Ying wasn't as nice as Yan had thought she would be. But in all fairness, over the years, she'd built up such a perfect idea of a sister in her mind that anything less than perfection was a disaster. In Yan's eyes, Ying was often moody and ill-tempered. She cursed and swore a lot for a young, educated lady, and often complained about the incompetence of her teachers and friends. She was so obsessed with her phone that she wouldn't even look up when their father entered the room. How insolent! Yan wondered why a person like Ying who had so much could be so unhappy.

Because Yan and her father were almost always at home—without money, where else could they go in San Francisco?—Ying had been spending less time at home and more time at Charlie's place.

Perhaps her father was right. They didn't understand the Americans.

FAYE

It was a Saturday.

Faye and Sophia didn't have to go to school or work, and as always on weekends, Faye slept in. Yan had been up at dawn, and she had prepared breakfast for everyone—her usual pot of chicken porridge—way before Faye, still in her pyjamas, sauntered into the kitchen at almost ten o'clock with dishevelled hair and a sleepy face, yawning lethargically and reaching for the pot of coffee. She looked at the porridge in disgust. They had been eating porridge almost every day since Yan had taken over the duty of preparing breakfast, and Faye was sick of it. She opened the upper kitchen cabinet and went for a box of cereal hidden behind a big bag of rice—a recent addition to the grocery list—and poured herself a generous serving.

While she ate, her eyes glued to the phone, she noticed from the corner of her eye that Yan was doing the laundry and cleaning the house. Yan always did the chores despite Sophia's repeated protests. Her father had insisted that Yan help out in the house, but Sophia insisted back that she rather Yan didn't. Faye knew it wasn't out of politeness that Sophia didn't want Yan to do the chores. Sophia hated people touching her stuff, but she was too embarrassed to explain to the two strangers in her house about her idiosyncrasy. So, the daily struggle continued—two people trying to get to the chores first or stop each other from completing the housework. It had been playing out so frequently that Faye had stopped finding it amusing.

It seemed that Sophia had lost the battle today, for she was out in the backyard re-potting plants. For her, the backyard was the last paradise in the house that hadn't been invaded by her Chinese guests. Curiously, neither Yan nor her father was interested in gardening or spending any time in nature. And thus, Sophia was seen more and more often in her garden, expanding her collection of lilies, lavenders, black sages, and blue elderberries.

From the lung-rumbling smoker's coughs, hawks, and spits, Faye could hear her father on the front veranda, enjoying his morning cigarette. Smoking in the house, according to Sophia's house rules, was strictly prohibited. So, Faye's father would be out on the veranda often enough to be a familiar sight to their neighbours. Faye could tell he liked getting to know the neighbours, although his limited English vocabulary confined him to mere common greetings.

His hearty 'good morning!' and 'how are you?' could be heard now and then, and Faye's brow furrowed viscerally every time he greeted someone.

The house was peaceful, almost normal.

Almost.

Until Faye sprang from her chair and yelled 'WHAT?' She looked up from her phone and glowered at her father reproachfully through the front windows. Yan stopped her dusting and stared at her while Sophia walked briskly back into the house.

'What's the matter?' Sophia asked as she pulled her garden gloves from her fingers. Faye ignored her mother and took a deep breath. Shaking with fury, she marched straight to the front door and opened it forcefully.

'Father, may I speak with you, please?' she said with restrained politeness, but her eyes were filled with abhorrence.

'Talk here. I'm not done with my cigarette,' he said as he billowed smoke out of his mouth and nostrils.

'Not here, father. Trust me; you don't want the neighbours to hear what I'm about to say. I need you *inside* the house *now*,' she articulated her words slowly between her clenching teeth.

'Okay, okay. I know you people here throw away half-smoked cigarettes but not me. I smoke till the last bit. I don't waste anything,' he grumbled as he stepped into the house. 'What is it? Look, if this is about the cigarette butts, I don't throw them out on the street any more, okay? I put them out in the ashtray and dump them in the trash like you told me to.'

'This is not about the cigarettes,' Faye said, nostrils flaring.

'Then what is it, sweetie?' Sophia asked.

'You should ask him. Go on, ask him what he has done!' Faye raised her voice.

'I don't understand—', her father looked confused.

'You're scamming innocent people on the internet! You're collecting donations from people for reasons that are totally untrue. You'll go to jail for something like that!'

'Scamming? What do you mean?' Sophia looked from concerned to frightened.

'He's still appealing to people on his blogs, Facebook, whatever, for money. This time, he says he needs to pay for my college education!'

'No, Mr Li, you don't have to do that. I've already put aside a college fund for Faye. We talked about it the other night, remember?'

'Oh . . . he has no problem remembering that, Mom! He's asking for money for his own use. That's wrong, WRONG!' Faye spat out, pacing back and forth in the living room like a caged animal.

'How did you find out?' he asked quietly.

'I received a message from a stranger asking me where she should wire her donations. I found that weird, so I checked out your latest updates. Lo and behold, there you were, begging, no, cheating, kind people's hard-earned dollars. You must be super rich now, huh? How long do you plan to milk this cash cow of yours?'

He sat down on the sofa and buried his face in his hands.

'Tell me, how did you manage without a computer? Smartphone?' Faye asked.

'I've a friend in China. He helps me with these things,' he answered softly.

'Ah! A collaborator! I thought so too!'

'Mr Li, you can talk to me if you need money. This is not the way to earn a living!' Sophia added, distraught.

'So? Do you have anything to say about this?' Faye asked again.

. 'I'm only doing this for you and your sister!'

'Don't! Don't you dare use us as your reason! That's just pathetic!'

He looked up, his countenance transformed from one of shame to defiance.

'It's easy for you to say, you with your Westernized holier than thou ideals and your virtue signalling. But take a good look at me. What good am I? I couldn't get a decent job in China, and I bet I wouldn't get a decent job here even if I had a green card. Do you have any clue how expensive this city is?' said Faye's father, speaking rapidly in Chinese so complex Faye could barely understand.

'That's still no excuse for your lying and cheating—' Faye interrupted.

'I only had a few thousand dollars in my pocket when I came here. I thought it could keep me going for a while, but it took me no time to realize that it wasn't enough, not in this city. You think I don't know that I'm imposing on Sophia? You think I don't know that you despise us for being here? I may be uneducated, but I'm not a fool. But what else is there? I don't want to cheat people either. *I* want to get a job, any job, so that Yan and I can move out of here. But without a work permit, what can I do? And trust me, I've looked everywhere in Chinatown. I'm willing to do anything—wash dishes, wash cars, cook, clean—*anything*, but nobody would hire me.'

'Still, it's not right—' Faye said defensively.

'You think I don't know what's right and wrong? It may not be the right thing to do, but maybe, just for once, you should stop thinking about yourself. Look at Yan. What does she have? I've spent so much time looking for you that I've completely neglected her. She has no education, no looks, no prospects. Don't you think she deserves better? If you don't want the money, let her have it. Let her go back to school and learn a skill or two.'

Finally, Faye had nothing to say.

'What's the big deal in taking a few bucks from these rich people anyway? It's not like we're stealing from the poor. Americans have so much to spare.' Faye's silence gave him the courage to push on.

'That's not the point,' Faye fought back. 'It's criminal, no matter your intentions. If they find out, they'll put you in jail. You have to stop, right this minute.'

He hesitated but decided not to argue. 'Okay, if you feel so strongly about it, I'll stop. I'll call Liu later to remove everything from the internet.'

'No, call him now.'

'But it's the middle of the night in China!'

'I don't care. Call him.'

He looked annoyed, but he took out his phone and dialled Liu Gang's number.

YAN

That night, for the first time since arriving in San Francisco, Yan's father came home drunk.

Fortunately, Ying had gone out on a date with Charlie, and Sophia was already fast asleep in her room. How he had managed to hitch a ride back home from Chinatown—Yan guessed that that must have been where he'd gone for his fix of alcohol—she had no idea. He stumbled upstairs to Ying and Yan's room. Yan was already in bed, and from the smell of it, she could tell he had consumed enough alcohol to make up for months of abstinence. She prayed that he wouldn't do something stupid that would get them kicked out of the house. She liked this house; it was the nicest house she'd ever lived in, and she didn't want to be out on the streets in a foreign land. She could handle the streets in China—she had practically grown up there—but here, she wasn't sure if they could survive.

He made lots of noise as he fumbled and knocked around in the dark. When he realized that Ying wasn't in the room, he looked disappointed.

'Where's your sister?' he slurred.

'Out with Charlie,' she replied, reluctantly throwing off her warm blankets to help him back to his room.

'Don't get up. I'm fine. I'll go back to my room in a while. Let me stay here for a couple of minutes,' he said, eyes and face red with intoxication. He sat down clumsily on Ying's sleeping bag that was rolled up in a corner.

'If you need to throw up, you'll have to go to the bathroom. Ying will be mad at you if she finds out . . .' Yan warned, already anticipating what might happen next.

'I said I'm fine, fine—' he mumbled as he drifted off into unconsciousness. Yan wondered what to do. She regretted not getting him back to his room while he was still conscious. There was no way she could wake him up now, and he was too heavy for her to drag him across the hallway. So she did what she had always done, staying awake until he came around, which he sometimes would after a quick nap, and hoping he would do so before Ying returned home.

Thankfully, Ying was out late tonight—way too late for a young girl like her in Yan's opinion. She wouldn't have approved if she were her mother. But things were different in America. Teenagers here did whatever they pleased, and had little regard for what others thought of them.

Anyway, Yan couldn't go back to sleep with her father in the room. It was strange because she had slept in the same room with her father for as long as she remembered. Now, it seemed weird. Maybe it was because of the mortified look Ying had given her when she had asked her about their living conditions in China. Yan had told her sister that they shared a tiny bedroom and Ying had laughed. And, when she had realized Yan wasn't joking, she had given her a puzzled look, as if she had more unanswered questions in her mind but didn't dare to venture further. Yan had also realized later that Ying believed they had crossed some taboo threshold. In America, the need for privacy was almost constitutional. Yan and her father's living conditions were unacceptable. Sacrilegious even. It didn't matter that millions of other Chinese had lived or were still living in similar circumstances.

So, what had been normal in the past suddenly became discomforting for Yan. She worried that someone might bust in and arrest them for transgressing some US privacy laws. So she stayed awake, listening to the sounds of the night.

Soon, she heard Charlie's car pulling into the driveway. She waited for the sounds of Ying opening the front door and coming up the staircase. For a whole ten minutes, nothing happened. What's taking her sister so long? She decided to check it out. Silently, she crept out of bed, passed her snoring father, tiptoed downstairs and out through the front door.

The night air was cold, very cold, and she only had her thin pyjamas on, but the chill cleared her sleepiness and heightened her senses.

Charlie's car was parked in front of the garage. Although the full moon was particularly bright that night, the car was shrouded in darkness.

Then, she heard them.

They weren't loud. In fact, she could tell they were trying to keep it down. But Yan had the ears of a cat—a nocturnal skill she had honed over the years of sleeping on the streets.

What she heard were sounds of animalistic nature, of primal yearnings. She had been introduced to such noise before, for her father was no saint. Prostitutes hung around bars and street corners, and her father had patronized them once in a while. There had been times when Yan would sit in the waiting room together with the other customers who were waiting for their turns, listening while her father 'consumed' his purchase.

Yan snuck closer, peeped through the windshield, and saw in the car Charlie and Ying, intertwined in pleasure, amid their carnal act. Charlie was on top of Ying with his tan, brawny back facing Yan, his trapezius muscles bulged prominently like the wings of an angel as he pushed Ying's bra aside and caressed her breasts lustily while he nibbled her neck. Ying moaned softly with her eyes closed, like the cheap whores on the streets of Beijing.

In the heat of their passion, they didn't hear or see Yan standing next to the car, watching their lascivious act almost with disinterest. She neither stopped them nor made a scene. As quietly as she came, she sneaked back into the house, up the stairs, and next to her father, who was still asleep. That would change in a minute, but in the meantime, Yan needed to put on an innocent face.

'Papa, wake up, please, wake up,' she shook him forcefully.

He woke with a start and, for a while, seemed to wonder where he was.

'I heard something outside,' she whispered in a concerned but innocuous voice.

'It's probably nothing. Maybe a neighbour's out walking the dog or something,' he murmured. Yan knew that by now, the alcohol would've hurt his head badly, and all he wanted to do was to sleep it off.

'You're right. It's just that Ying isn't back yet, so I thought it might be a good idea to check it out. But like you said, it's probably nothing—' she said nonchalantly.

That did it. He shot up like a deflating balloon.

'Where did you hear the noise? Show!'

Quietly, Yan led her father out of the house into the crisp night.

'There, I heard something there—' She pointed at Charlie's car.

Then, she heard them again. Her father heard them too, the soft groans, the heavy breathing, and the wet kisses. He ran towards the car, and the sight of the two half-naked young bodies made him yawp like a caveman. Yan followed closely behind, savouring every moment of her delectable victory.

'What the fuck—' Yan heard Charlie's yelling before he was yanked out of the car and on to the pavement with his pants down to his ankles and half his balls hanging out of his underwear. Yan's father was a strong man, albeit his age and the bulging belly. He began to punch Charlie with his bare fists.

Ying, naked from waist up, tried to cover her bared breasts as she stumbled out of the car and screamed, 'Father, stop! Stop it now!'

'Mr Li, you have to stop right this moment, or I swear I'll fight back,' Charlie shouted repeatedly between the punches.

But Yan's father wouldn't stop, and Charlie had had enough of it. He stood up, grabbed the older man's palm firmly, twisted it into an unnatural position and locked it behind his back, making him squeal in pain.

'You fuck my daughter,' Yan's father yelled in broken English. 'She good gal. She now broken.'

'Charlie, let go of him,' Ying cried in desperation as she struggled to put on her clothes. By now, Sophia and the entire neighbourhood were awakened by the commotion. A gathering crowd had formed, some with phones on hand to record the scene.

'Don't worry, baby. I know what I'm doing. I won't break his bones. I had to stop the punching, man. It hurt like hell!' Charlie said as he tried to use his other hand to pull his pants up. 'Mr Li, don't move or you'll be in greater pain. Now, I'll let you go if you promise to calm down and stop acting like a crazy person, do you understand?'

'You fuck my little girl,' Yan's father screamed again.

'Stop saying that, for Christ's sake! Where did you learn to say something like that?' Ying cried.

'From the language centre. From Veronica Ip!' Despite his compromised position, her father was proud to share his recent academic advancement.

'And she taught you the word "fuck"?'

'Look, now's not the time to discuss this, okay?' Charlie interrupted.

'Father, Charlie wasn't "fucking" me. We were just making out. Do you understand the difference?' Ying said.

'All right! Everyone, please stop using the word "fuck"? What's wrong with you?' Charlie said again.

'The two of you get married as soon as possible,' Yan's father said. Upon hearing the words 'get married', Charlie reflexively twisted harder, making the old man wail in greater agony.

'No way, Mr Li! We're not getting married now. It's not like I knocked her up or something—'

'Papa, calm down, all right? That's not how it works here. People here do stuff like that all the time—' Ying said in exasperation.

'Tell him to let go of me first,' Yan's father ordered furiously.

Charlie finally let go but remained in a combat position in case he had to fight the crazy Chinese man again.

'Now, apologize to Charlie and me for what you just did! You've no right to humiliate us like that!' Ying growled.

Yan's father looked at them, incredulous. 'You want *me* to apologize? I'm protecting your reputation, your chastity. And you want *me* to apologize?'

'Listen, father,' Ying piped down a little. 'We didn't do anything wrong, okay? We're in love, and that's what people do when they love each other. And we didn't have . . . like . . . intercourse. So please don't make a big deal out of it. You don't have to apologize to me if you don't want to, but please, just say sorry to Charlie and let him go home.'

Yan, who had been thoroughly enjoying the scene she had single-handedly created, couldn't believe what she had heard either. She thought their father had done the right thing—'intercourse' or 'no intercourse'.

'You know what I think?' her father replied, his eyes burning with rage and humiliation. 'I think you're a whore.'

With a thousand other unspoken words, he turned and walked away with as much dignity as he could muster, leaving his stunned daughter outside the house.

* * *

When Ying and Yan returned to their room, they found a card and a bunch of roses on Ying's sleeping bag. The card read:

My dearest Ying,

I don't know how to express my love for you. We don't openly do so in our culture, but I know it's important to you. So I use flowers instead. I just want to tell you that I love you, and I'm very happy that I've found you.

Your father

Their father had gone up to their room to give Ying the roses and the card, and when he had realized she wasn't there, he had decided to wait for her.

Ying buried herself under the blanket and wept.

Chapter 13

SOPHIA

If Sophia could turn back time, she would go back to the unpleasant night and stop the awful incident before it turned into such an abomination. She didn't know how she would do it, but she just would, for she couldn't bear the thought of it any more. Right in front of her house with the neighbours as witnesses! It wasn't just the embarrassment but also the hostility in the house in the aftermath that she had to contend with. The silence, the tension, and the strained politeness. The pretence that nothing had happened and that all was well. It was intolerable.

She had seen less and less of Faye since the night, and although they were supposedly staying in the same house, it would be days before she had a chance to catch a glimpse of her daughter. She knew Faye had been trying all ways to avoid her father. Sometimes, Sophia could hear her waking up at the crack of dawn and leaving for school before anyone saw her. And she would either stay in school after class, conjuring up some excuses like extra classes or practices, or head over to Michelle or Charlie's place, where she would remain till late at night. During weekends, she would stay over.

Her daughter was alienating everyone in her family, including Sophia, and this was worse than anything Sophia had had to deal with. She felt that she had already lost her daughter.

Sophia had never felt lonelier.

And as if things weren't already bad enough, the Li's visas had expired a week before, and Li Fu hadn't planned to leave the house or the country. No amount of gentle reasoning with him that he was breaking the law and would go to jail for it could convince him to change his mind.

'If we return to China, the Chinese authorities will never allow us to leave again. We can't go back. We're staying here until we get our green cards,' he would say with finality, although he hadn't had any idea how he could obtain citizenship for him and Yan.

The situation had left Sophia feeling extremely anxious because she was officially harbouring illegal immigrants in her home. She had never broken a law in her life, not even a speeding ticket. Not until now. She wanted them to leave, but she didn't know how to do so without literally throwing them out on the streets. And she couldn't bring herself to do that, not after she had taken their baby and broken their family.

She wondered how much more atonement she would have to make for her sin before she could be forgiven. Sophia was not coping well. In fact, she felt she was one conflict away from reaching a breaking point. Perhaps, it was her turn to have a meltdown. Why not? No one thought she was entitled to a meltdown. This would show them that they couldn't possibly put all their burdens on her shoulder and expect her not to break. The cross was too much to bear.

What's worse, no one had asked her how she had been feeling lately. Certainly not the Li's. But more depressingly, not even Faye. Faye had been busy feeling so sorry for herself, she couldn't find the time to ask how Sophia was coping.

Perhaps that was the price of her atonement.

Sophia wiped away her silent tears, tears she shed only in the privacy of her bedroom. If there was a price, Sophia was determined to pay it in currency rather than with her daughter. She picked up the phone and dialled a familiar number.

'Hey, Julie, it's me. I think I need that favour after all. Could you please call that Chinese restaurant about the job? Yes, I'll pay the "introduction fee".'

FAYE

After the incident, Faye had refused to talk about it with anyone, not even with Charlie, although she had been spending a lot of time with him. Not that Charlie had noticed her reticence; to him, the whole thing was over and he had already moved on. He would talk about how *funny* it was, how he had his balls hanging out half the time, and how he had almost broken her father's arm—but he wouldn't talk about his or his girlfriend's feelings and emotions. He called these things 'Nancy boy' stuff and he hated every minute of it. He also had no idea about the emotional trauma his girlfriend had experienced that night, although he had noticed one thing—the physical alienation. He didn't understand why Faye had found making out with him so revolting all of a sudden. It was exciting at first, her playing hard to get, but it got old after a while, after a very short while. It didn't help that Faye had been sleeping over at his place most weekends after that night. He was, after all, a young man, a very young man high on libido and hormones. How long did he need to observe this abstinence thing?

Faye, on the other hand, had found it incredulous that Charlie couldn't understand why she wasn't interested in making out with him after what had happened. Didn't he hear her father calling her a whore? Wasn't he there when her father yanked them out of the car, half-naked, right in front of the entire neighbourhood? Didn't Charlie feel any shame?

Apparently not, because Charlie didn't seem to be affected at all.

The only person with whom Faye could find solace was Michelle. Michelle seemed to be able to empathize with Faye's feelings and completely understood what Faye meant when she bitched about her Chinese family.

Above all, Michelle wasn't interested in making out with Faye.

So Faye hung around her best friend like a puppy, following her around at school, following her to the mall after school, and following her home when they had spent all their money at the mall.

And this went on for several weeks.

'Don't get me wrong, I love you and everything, but when do you think you'll be ready to face the music?' Michelle asked Faye at lunch after weeks of being inseparable. 'I mean, you can't avoid your family forever.'

'I don't know. I'm not sure if I ever will,' Faye replied, picking at her food.

'Okay, walk me through. What's the one thing you're most afraid of?' Michelle pressed on with her mouth full. 'Also, are you going to finish your chips?'

'Take the chips. You know what I'm afraid of.'

'No, I don't.'

'What're you talking about? He called me a whore.'

'That's what traumatized you most. Well, that and being naked. What are you really avoiding?'

'I don't know. Them. Everyone. Everything.'

'No, Faye. Think harder. Be specific.'

Faye paused for a long time as she stared at the mob of teenagers at the cafeteria.

'You know I've been reading about this being filial to your parents' thingy, and I found out that this philosophy came from Confucius. Unlike what most people think, he was a grumpy old man who had an unsuccessful political career. And then he went on to teach others how to live their lives.'

'So?'

'You see, his father died when Confucius was a kid, and because his mother was a concubine, he and his mother only had each other. When his mother died, and listen to this, he was already in his twenties when it happened, he became so depressed that he mourned for his mother for three years. Three *freaking* years, can you believe it? He quit his civil service job, wore nothing but rags, sat at home, and mourned.

A little too obsessed, don't you think? Freud would have a lot to say about that . . .

'Anyway, he began to expound on the idea that the relationship between a parent and a child was the very foundation of society, and filial piety became . . . like . . . his main teaching. Shit like one must be loyal, obedient towards one's parents, blah, blah, blah. So basically, we have to be our parents' slaves, just because they're our parents, no matter who they are or what they've done.'

'Are we getting somewhere with this story?' Michelle finished her lunch and started devouring Faye's.

'You asked me what I was most afraid of, right? Well, I'm terrified of being stuck with my family forever,' Faye replied, her eyes reflecting the fear in her heart.

'I know how you feel, but don't you want to give them another chance? Sometimes, in relationships, you just have to try and try until—'

Faye's cell phone rang, interrupting Michelle. It was Sophia.

'Answer it,' Michelle urged. 'Start facing your worst fear.'

Faye knew Michelle was right. She had avoided the whole thing long enough. She couldn't be on the run forever.

'Hey Mom,' she picked up the call, her tone pitched in determined cheeriness.

'Hi, sweetie. Why don't you come home for dinner tonight? We've some good news.'

* * *

That night, Faye went home for dinner with Charlie. Charlie had agreed—with great reluctance and only when Faye had threatened to break up with him if he didn't—to apologize to her father for almost breaking his arm. Faye had also hinted that if he could give her father 'face' just this once, things might improve on the intimate side of their relationship. She had also promised Charlie he wouldn't be the only one who had to give her father 'face'. She, too, would apologize for screaming at him.

Sophia was thankful to be able to see her daughter and was cooking up a storm when Faye and Charlie stepped into the kitchen.

'Hey sweetie, come over here and give me a kiss,' she exclaimed with joy in her eyes, but her voice was strained and her eyes tired. And when she hugged Faye, she held her so tightly and for so long that she almost burnt her roast dinner.

Seeing Sophia's unhappiness, which she tried by all means to conceal, made Faye feel even guiltier than before. After all, she did the irresponsible thing of dumping her family on her mother and walking out. She knew it was unfair, and she promised herself not to do that to her mom again. Somehow, she had to find a way to mend her relationship with her father before it got any worse.

'Hello Sophia,' Charlie greeted her warmly with a peck on her cheek. Charlie had always liked Sophia and vice versa. 'Man, that roast beef looks awesome! Always love your cooking. I can't wait to dig in!'

'Thanks, Charlie,' Sophia turned to Faye and said. 'Your father and sister are in the living room right now, pretending to watch television. Do I dare to ask you and Charlie to join them?' she asked with pleading eyes.

'Do I have to?' Faye moaned.

'Yes, you have to, to make amends. That's what you're here for, remember?'

'Yeah, yeah... you're right... you're always right,' Faye surrendered. She got up reluctantly from her seat and walked to the living room slowly, with Charlie a few steps behind her.

Yan looked up as they entered the room. She neither smiled nor said anything, merely acknowledging them with a look of recognition. Her father pretended not to see or hear them and went on watching television. *The Big Bang Theory* was on. Faye wondered how in the world they could understand the comedy.

'Hi, Papa,' Faye said, sounding like nothing had happened between them.

The wrong way to start a conversation with her father. Dead wrong.

'"Hi, Papa"? Is that what schools in America have taught you? Just "Hi, Papa"?'

Every atom of Faye's self-control was engaged in stopping herself from starting another argument with him. She sat down, closed her eyes, and counted to ten.

'Sorry. How are you, Father?' she tried again, mindfully directing her facial muscles to stretch and form a resemblance of a smile on her face while nudging Charlie to say something.

'Hello, Mister Li. Good evening. It's an honour to see you again.' Charlie stood up and bowed, his words laden with sarcasm. Faye glared. She wanted to stab her bare fingers through his torso, pull out his heart and devour it at that point. Fortunately, her father couldn't comprehend the sarcasm.

'That's more like it!' he nodded, pleased with the 'respect' he got from the two.

Faye's mood changed from trepidation to amusement. She couldn't help but stifled a chuckle as Charlie nodded comically like an Eton-educated aristocrat.

Yan stared at them stoically.

'Mister Li, I'm very sorry for what happened the other night. But you were beating me up so badly I had to react without thinking—a reflex, you know? But surely I couldn't possibly have hurt you, could I? You seemed so strong, and I'm still bruised from your punches—' Charlie said with a straight face as he improvised his 'apology'. Faye could barely stop herself from laughing as she interpreted for him.

'No way you could have hurt me! Not at all! It'd take an ox to take me down. I hardly felt anything when you locked my arm. I let you do it on purpose so that I could calm myself down in that situation—' said Li Fu, as he rotated his still-stiffed arm to demonstrate that he wasn't affected by the fight.

'That's good, Mister Li. I feel so much better knowing that you're fine.'

Charlie's words instantly boosted Li Fu's ego and lifted the dense atmosphere in the room. Light conversations began to flow. Li Fu even managed a smile and talked about how he enjoyed his time here and his plan to enrol Yan in a night school.

When Sophia stepped into the living room to announce that dinner was ready, she thought she had walked into a business meeting: smiles hanging tiredly on the faces—except Yan's—mixed with occasional bad jokes and forced laughter. Yan, like usual, didn't join in the conversation but held her gaze at Charlie and Faye like a stalking psychopath eyeing her target.

The determined politeness continued at dinner. As Sophia served the pasta, Li Fu lamented how he missed Chinese fares back at home.

'Chinese food is far superior to any cuisines in the world. Don't get me wrong, Sophia, I enjoy your cooking very much, but nothing beats an authentic bowl of noodles. That's the real soul food,' he boasted.

'I think the Chinese restaurants in Chinatown are pretty authentic. You can get a bowl of wonton noodles for less than ten bucks,' Faye murmured under her breath.

'That's different. Home-cooked Chinese food is still the best. By the way, have you learnt to cook?' he asked, thinking it was safe to assume his authoritative figure again.

'Well, I can make a ham and cheese sandwich—' she chuckled, trying to steer the conservation to a lighter trajectory.

'Barely!' Charlie jumped in quickly.

'That's not good. A woman needs to know how to cook,' Li Fu bemoaned. 'You should start learning from your sister. Yan is so much better than you when it comes to domestic matters.'

'Learning to cook is not exactly my priority now,' Faye sounded a little vexed, the defiance in her rising. But as soon as she began, someone kicked her in the shins under the table. She bit her lips and looked around for the culprit, and saw Sophia mouthing a silent 'shut up' to her.

It looked like the night was to be *The Tonight Show* starring Li Fu.

For her mom's sake and her own mental well-being, Faye decided to shut up, no matter what her father said.

'Anyway, I've some excellent news to announce,' Faye's father continued cheerily. 'I've found a job! I'm helping out at a Chinese restaurant in Chinatown. And, it's a rather posh one, with tablecloths and cloth napkins and everything.'

'That's . . . great! How did you manage that without . . . proper documentation?' Faye was truly surprised.

'Like I've always told you, all you need is to make friends with the right people. Who needs a visa when you've got the right connection?' Faye's father bragged brazenly. 'And that's not all. I've more good news.'

The room was filled with anticipation as Faye's father paused for dramatic effect.

'Yan and I are moving out. My new boss has recommended a little apartment not far from the restaurant. The rent is incredibly cheap, so I should be able to afford the place easily.'

It was the best news Faye had heard in months. Not as good as them leaving the country, but considering the circumstances, it was more than what she could hope for. She was so happy she almost wanted to kiss her father. As she congratulated him heartily, she stole a look at her mom, who appeared almost serene, like a Madonna, smiling peacefully as she murmured what Faye believed to be praises to God under her breath.

The worst is over, Faye thought with tremendous relief as she vaguely registered in her mind her father's more boasting about how much the boss must've liked him.

Maybe this is a chance for Papa and me to start over. Perhaps this time, I won't screw up as much as before.

Maybe.

Chapter 14

YAN

Her father's announcement at the dinner table about his new job had taken even Yan by surprise. She had seen him looking very hard, going to the restaurants regularly to scout for job openings after their English class, but nothing had ever come through. While these restaurants did hire illegal immigrants, buddying with the right people and greasing their palms with the right amount of money were the real qualifications needed to get employed. But her father had neither the money nor the palm to grease. How he had managed to secure a job remained a mystery.

Regardless, Yan was glad that the job came through with an apartment of their own. From the way things were progressing, Yan thought that it would only be a matter of time before they got kicked out of the house. And it wouldn't necessarily be Ying who would do the kicking although her father would've lost face in every possible way if that had happened. Yan could tell that Sophia, while patient and long-suffering, was on the brink of a breakdown hosting a couple of freeloaders cum illegal immigrants who were a constant embarrassment to her family. Not just that, she had to also put up with their strange antics and questionable personal hygiene. They had overstayed their welcome. Like a long time ago.

So Yan's father had, in some way, restored some credibility—and a whole lot of dignity—by securing that job. Although, even when everyone thought there was no way he could've made it work here, Yan hadn't lost faith in him. She never did. She had always believed that he'd bounce back. He always did. After all, he was Chinese, and by definition, a survivor who would thrive in the most adverse circumstances.

A week later, Yan and her father moved out of Sophia's beautiful Victorian house in the Sunset District into a tiny, dingy, second-floor apartment in Chinatown. It wasn't that far in terms of distance, but it was a world apart. The so-called apartment was more like an enlarged single bedroom that came with a noxious stench of greasy fried chicken soaked in overused oil, urine, and week-old socks and a lovely view of the narrow back alley lined with trash bins and drunken hobos. If you were lucky, which was often, you could see the hobos peeing or hurling vomit out of their mouths. Welcome to Chinatown! The whole place was dark and dirty, for no one had bothered to clean out the filth that had accumulated over the decades and the only natural light that came from a small window was filtered through by a thick layer of dirt on the panes. Not that it mattered, because the window couldn't be opened. The only working ventilation was from the Vietnamese restaurant downstairs, which steadily blew greasy smoke out of their kitchen into the apartment. The few pieces of furniture, consisting of a stained couch with torn fabrics mended with duct tapes, a three-legged coffee table, and an old Cathode ray tube TV, looked like rejects from The Salvation Army. The 'bedroom', was so small that only a queen-size bed and a narrow wardrobe with a missing door could fit in, and it was separated from the living room by a thin, see-through curtain. No door. The communal toilet and kitchen, shared with the other tenants in the building, were, of course, always filthy and the plumbing was in dubious working condition. It was bad even by Yan and her father's standards. But they took it because her father said this was all they could afford.

They didn't take long to settle in because there weren't many things to unpack. Ironically, Yan's father was happier here despite the apartment's appalling condition. He was once again among his kind, for the other tenants were mainly retired, first-generation Asian immigrants and new migrants who came here to work as dishwashers and busboys. They came from his land, spoke his language, and ate his kind of food. He could talk to people once again. He finally felt he belonged, although he would rather stab himself than admit it.

'This neighbourhood is good, Yan,' he declared shortly after they had moved in, directly contradicting what he had said a few months before. 'You know our neighbour, Old Wang? His village is only about eighty miles from ours. What a coincidence! And he works in the same restaurant. We should've moved here a long time ago. I think things are finally looking up!'

Yan was relieved that her father was cheering up. With all the clashes that he had had with Ying, he hadn't been quite himself lately. Now, things did seem to be getting better, at least for now. The job at the restaurant had kept him busy; sometimes, he worked up to twelve hours a day. Although it paid below the minimum wage and had no job security, for once, Yan's father didn't complain.

'It's better than nothing. And it's just temporary anyway until I find something better. I heard that construction here pays so much more. I just need to find the right connection,' he justified.

Ying visited them regularly after they had moved out of Sophia's place. They had been seeing Ying more than when they were staying with her. She took Yan and her father to several places of interest in San Francisco like the Fisherman's Wharf and even got Charlie to drive them all the way to a forest to look at some really old, tall trees. It seemed strange to Yan that Ying had taken the initiative to build a relationship with them *after* they had moved out. Why the sudden and newfound interest? Guilt, perhaps? Anyway, these visits and tourist activities kept her father really happy, and so, Yan had no reason to complain.

At times, Charlie would come with Ying during the visits. It was obvious that Ying hated the apartment and she tried to over-compensate her repulsion for the place by talking non-stop about this and that, walking around with her nose in the air, and behaving like a snob. She wouldn't even drink from the cup that was offered to her because it was chipped, and would breathe through her mouth so that she would not gag from the room's pungent smell.

Charlie, on the other hand, was pleasant and easy-going. He seemed intrigued and genuinely charmed by the place and repeatedly professed that he didn't know such an 'exotic and charming' place existed in San Francisco. Yan couldn't understand what Charlie saw in Ying and thought that they were completely different people and that Charlie deserved someone better. Perhaps one day, she thought, she could help him realize his mistake.

On this particular visit, he brought along his camera—not a camera phone, but a real camera with removable lenses and other professional photography gadgets. Yan's father was still at work, so Ying decided to go for a walk while Charlie stayed behind. He took numerous pictures of the place—odd things and people, in Yan's opinion. The stairways, the wrinkled face of a centenarian living next door, their laundry, for instance. These things and people seemed more interesting to him to shoot than, say, a family portrait, which, in Yan's opinion, would be a lot more useful. He told Yan—through a combination of simple English, lots of gestures, and the use of Google Translate—that when he captured something in a picture, it was like freezing and immortalizing that moment. It all sounded so profound and intelligent to Yan. He also said he was putting together a 'portfolio' on his website so that people could see his body of work. Yan didn't realize that shooting useless people and everyday objects could be accounted for as 'work'. Nevertheless, she was fascinated by the way he worked, the way he held his expensive-looking camera to his inquisitive, intense face; the way he climbed the rusty, rickety fire escape ladder just to capture a photo of more rickety fire escape ladders, and the way his blonde bangs would fall over his eyelashes, but he would take no notice of them.

Yan must've been staring at him while he worked—she often did that to people without realizing—and that must've made him uncomfortable. She had that effect on people: making them uncomfortable with her stares. He stopped working, smiled sweetly at her, and started taking pictures of her. For a moment, Yan thought he had mistaken her for Ying.

'You're so shy,' he said as he put down his camera gently after he was done. 'So different from your sister.'

'Different?' Yan ventured. 'Good different?'

'Just . . . different,' he replied, surprised by Yan's question, and changed the subject quickly. 'Want me to show you how the camera works? It's fun.'

'Yes,' Yan replied softly. All she could hear was her pounding heart.

'Come over here and sit next to me. See this dial here? That's for—'

Yan didn't hear the rest. She was lost in his sonorous voice, his fragrance at the back of his neck, and the soft touch of his fingers as he guided her hands.

He smelt of a beautiful and fortunate life.

Under his tutelage, Yan managed to take some photographs of Charlie and one with both of them together. He promised to print a copy of these photographs for her.

For the first time in her life, Yan felt like a true human being.

With perfect, movie-like timing, Ying returned from her walk and saw Charlie and Yan sitting intimately, looking at the camera screen.

Too close for Ying's comfort, it seemed to Yan, for her sister's face turned dark.

'Hi,' she said tartly. 'Having fun, are we?'

Yan could taste the acidity in her sister's voice.

'Hey! I was just teaching Yan how to work the camera—' Charlie explained casually.

'That's great, but we've to go now. I've a lot of homework to do tonight,' she interrupted Charlie, feigning a smile.

FAYE

'Faye, are you even listening to me?' Michelle tapped on Faye's shoulder repeatedly.

'Yes, of course—' Faye lied, eyes dazed and mind fogged. She wasn't listening. She was replaying in her mind the scene she had witnessed of Charlie and Yan laughing together at her father's apartment, again and again.

'No, you're not!' Michelle slammed her locker door hard as she watched Faye struggle with the lock on hers. 'What's up with you? I thought things were good in the family department. You're finally free from your father and sister, and you're even trying to have . . . what was the word you used? . . . that's right, a relationship with them. Why the moody face?'

'Can you keep a secret?'

'Please! That's all I do lately. Keeping secrets! What do you think I've been doing? Telling everyone about your sad, tortured life?'

'I can do without the sarcasm, okay?'

'Tell me already!'

'All right,' Faye held her breath and blurted. 'I think Yan has a crush on Charlie.'

'Wait . . . Charlie cheated on you?'

'No, it's nothing like that. I think it's a one-way thing—'

'That's a lot less scandalous,' Michelle said, sounding disappointed. They paused while someone opened the locker next to theirs.

'How do you know Yan likes Charlie?' Michelle asked immediately after the person left.

'It's just a hunch. Charlie and I were visiting my father's apartment yesterday, and he brought his camera to take photographs for his portfolio. You know how he is when he thinks he sees some "artistic angles in exotic places".'

Michelle giggled and nodded rapidly in agreement, her head bobbing like the needle of a sewing machine.

'Anyway, he was teaching Yan how to use his camera. I swear Yan was so-oo smitten by him. So . . . love-struck.'

'How long has this been going on?'

'I don't know, but come to think of it, she has always been sitting in corners and staring at Charlie whenever he's around. I thought she's just shy—'

'Do you think she stands a chance with Charlie?' asked Michelle.

'Why?' Faye stared at her, mortified by the thought.

'The answer determines whether you need to act on your hunch or not, so you've to be completely objective about this. Does. She. Stand. A. Chance?' Michelle said, matter-of-factly.

Faye thought for a long time, digging through every memory of the time they had spent together, trying to remember Charlie's face in each of these moments.

'No,' she concluded. 'Charlie's not remotely interested in her. I think he was just being nice, taking care of her because she's my sister.'

'Okay, then. You don't have a problem. It's just a crush. This too shall pass,' Michelle said. 'You know, you ought to have more confidence in yourself. You're a beautiful girl, and everyone knows Charlie's crazy about you. I've not met Yan, but from your description of her, it seems unlikely that he'll fall for her.'

'Thanks, Michelle,' Faye smiled, reassured.

Another silence ensued.

'What if there was more to it? What if Yan decided to make a move on Charlie? She hasn't done anything so far, but what if she did? What would you do if you were in my shoes?' Faye asked.

'Me? I'd be ruthless. I'd do whatever it took to protect what was mine.'

Chapter 15

FAYE

Faye's little talk with Michelle had left her feeling more unsettled than before. She thought about talking to Charlie about Yan but quickly decided against it. She knew he would probably laugh in her face and call her ridiculous and paranoid, and the conversation would deteriorate into a nasty fight.

She thought of bringing it up with Sophia at dinner that night. But, ever since Faye's father and Yan had moved out, Sophia had been happy to have her old life—and home—back to where it used to be. She would avoid any mention of the troubled times she had endured, skirting conversations that hinted at Li Fu and Yan, and at times, even went as far as pretending that her daughter's other family didn't exist. This made it difficult for Faye to steer the conversations to the topic without bringing up the miserable times.

With little else she could do, Faye thought her last resort was to visit Yan while she was home alone and see if she could fish anything out. Yan would probably draw a blank face like she always did. But it was worth a try. She also wondered how much of the deadpan look was just a pretence and whether behind that naivety harboured a sly and boyfriend-stealing slut.

And, so, she did.

It was a Thursday afternoon and a sunny day. Faye felt almost silly as she climbed the stairs to the apartment.

They were probably just having a laugh, she thought as she reached the door to the apartment. *Why do I feel so insecure about the whole thing?*

But a persistent, nagging feeling drove her on.

Her father had given her a set of keys to the building's gate and the apartment's door. For privacy reasons, Faye had never used it; she had always called beforehand or buzzed at the gate. Her father had found her respect for their privacy puzzling, in fact, a little annoying.

'Use the damn keys. No one here cares, and it saves us the trouble of answering the door every time you come here,' he had said.

'But I don't live here . . . it isn't right,' she had protested.

But her firm stand on personal privacy couldn't stand up to her desire to spring a surprise on Yan. Faye was curious about what her sister did when she was alone, not alone in Sophia's home kind of alone, but alone, alone. And a small part of her had expected to see Yan and Charlie together, enjoying another photography session. Or, a different kind of activity. Some terrible activity.

The building stood quiet. Apart from some rustlings now and then, the place was like a graveyard. A few residents, retired Chinese men who already knew her, stared stoically as she walked by their open front door. She smiled and mouthed 'hello', and was rewarded with a nod or a wave of acknowledgement. She stopped at the front door of her father's apartment, inserted the key quietly into the recently-oiled keyhole and pushed the door slightly ajar.

What she saw in the next five seconds would stick with her for the rest of her life, perhaps a few lifetimes thereafter. It was so horrific she wanted to gouge her eyes out.

She heard the moans first. The wall was thin and rotting and barely offered any sound insulation. They were moans of a man and a woman, the woman of a louder and more dramatic sort. She knew the moans, but they didn't stop her from looking at the dark, shocking skeleton in the closet. Unfortunately, the skeleton turned out to be scarier than expected.

The scene was as grotesque as it sounded: through the translucent curtain, Faye witnessed her father fornicating with a woman, presumably a prostitute, in the bedroom. They were in a doggy position, stark naked, and he was thrusting vigorously into her again and again, panting noisily as his hands groped her large, sagging breasts. The prostitute, an Asian woman in her fifties who was clearly not enjoying the act, moaned and faked her ecstasy as he moved his hands from her breasts to her butts.

However, that wasn't the hardest part for Faye to take in. Beyond the bedroom, a thin curtain away, was Yan on the old, stained couch in the living room with her skirts pulled up and panties down. She, too, was moaning softly while she masturbated with her eyes closed, holding pictures of Charlie in one hand and her groin in the other.

Faye wanted to flee before anyone noticed her presence. But it was too late. Before she could close the door, Yan opened her eyes and saw her sister's stunned figure. She pulled down her skirt in shame and sprang up. But, when she realized what Faye had seen, her shame gradually turned into a triumph, as if she had finally succeeded in squeezing her sister out of her father's life. She looked down at the pictures of Charlie in her hand and up at her sister again, smiled lopsidedly, walked towards her, and tossed the photos one at a time at her sister's pale, sickened face.

'Do you see? Do you finally see? This is how we live, princess. Aren't you glad that you were abducted?' she giggled maniacally.

Hearing Yan, their father looked up, but he was climaxing right at that point, and he couldn't, or wouldn't, stop. He continued humping the old whore as he looked at Faye, horrified and ecstatic.

Faye fled the apartment. She was too shaken, too revolted, and too appalled to think. What she had seen was a new level of repulsion, so repelling that it made her want to peel the skin off her body.

* * *

Faye drove straight home after her hasty retreat, manoeuvring the traffic carelessly as her mind wandered from her driving to that horrible scene again and again. She couldn't concentrate—the brain seemed to have decided on a coup d'état, seizing the operation of her thoughts and going on different paths that led her to dark and abominable places.

Along the way, her phone rang non-stop. It was her father. There was no way in hell she would answer his calls.

She didn't want to ever see them again. If she had ever considered for the fleetest moment the possibility of living with them, what she'd just seen in that filthy apartment sealed that fate forever.

On the other hand, sick as the situation might be, she was relieved that she no longer had to agonize over the remorse she had been feeling about abandoning her family. She wasn't the guilty one; no sir, not any more. The verdict had been made. She had won. Vindicated. All charges against her were dropped. Finally free to leave the courtroom.

How Faye managed to get home safely she did not know. But no one was there. She called Charlie, but his phone was off. It then dawned upon her that Charlie was on his way back from New York with his parents—most likely on the plane right now. So she called Sophia and Michelle using the home telephone—her cell phone hadn't stopped ringing—insisting that they dropped whatever they were doing and came over immediately.

'What's so secretive that you had to call me on a LAN line? My God, you guys still have them? That's so cool! I forgot those things existed—' Michelle chirped as she sashayed into the house, imitating the Southern belle accent and the dramatic manner. She was in the mood for one of her many shenanigans.

'Oh good, you're here too. Now Faye can tell us what's the matter with her,' Sophia emerged from the kitchen with a glass of water for her daughter.

So began Faye's recounting of the horrifying scene she had witnessed to Sophia and Michelle, amidst the many gasps and the oh-my-gods from her appalled audience.

'The image of Yan . . . God, I can't say that word in front of Mom . . . lusting for Charlie . . . yuck!' she grimaced. 'I don't think I'll ever recover from that!'

'I'm sure it's just an infatuation. Nothing has or will happen between Yan and Charlie. I know Charlie. He was nice to her because she's your sister,' Sophia said.

'Yeah, but she was actually holding his pictures as she touched herself—'

'Stop thinking about it, okay. Thinking about it won't help,' Michelle said.

Faye's cell phone rang again.

'He won't stop calling. It's so annoying!' Faye said, vexed. 'I'm not speaking to him, ever!'

Michelle took the phone from her and switched it off.

'There!' she grinned.

'I wish Charlie was here,' Faye said. 'He'll know what to do to make all these terrible things go away!'

'Well, he's no wizard,' Michelle said. 'Besides, you can't just tuck these things away. You need to deal with them before they fester and spread and become something bigger than you.'

'What should I do?' asked Faye.

'Maybe you want to talk to them,' Sophia offered carelessly.

'Are you crazy? After what I've just said?'

'You're right. I'm sorry, sweetie, I don't know what I'm thinking—'

'You may want to think about severing all ties with them,' Michelle said.

'Uh . . . I don't know about that, Michelle. That's a big step. Maybe we need to take a deep breath and talk things through. I think I'm going to call Julie over too. Four brains are better than three,' Sophia said as she picked up her cell phone. She called Julie's number, but her phone was switched off.

'If you do so, it needs to be quick, like pulling a Band-Aid. Painful but effective,' Michelle ignored Sophia and continued.

'I don't know if that's the right thing to do,' Faye said, wavering a little.

'It's your decision,' Michelle slumped her tiny body into the couch resignedly. 'All I'm saying is if you want to cut them out of your life, it has to be absolutely clean. There must be no turning back, no chance of them coming here looking for you or trying to explain what really happened, and then you'll be, like soppy and forgiving, and like "Uh . . . I'm not sure if I should do this" . . . you know, the emotional mumbo jumbo? You have to be firm. Pull the plug, move on and forget about them,' said Michelle with drill sergeant-like instructions.

'Michelle! I don't think we need to make that decision now,' Sophia said while texting Julie, clearly against anything hard-line or radical.

'It's okay. Let her talk. I need advice,' Faye said.

'Think about it,' Michelle sprang from the couch with a fresh burst of energy and paced the room. 'How can you make them disappear forever from your life?'

'I don't know . . . maybe Sophia could talk to them to leave me alone?'

Sophia stopped texting and looked at Faye, mortified. Talking to them after hearing what they'd done was beyond her capability. And her imagination.

'That's one way, but there's no guarantee that they'll oblige,' Michelle said. 'Plus, I don't think Sophia is up for the task.'

'I can call Julie—' Sophia offered again, clearly not thinking straight.

'I'll write to them and tell them I don't want to see them again,' Faye tried again.

'Writing a letter? You think that's effective?'

'Why don't you just tell us your idea? I don't think we are in the mood to play your guessing game—' Faye said brusquely.

'Okay, okay. Didn't you say their visas expired?'

'Yes.'

'So . . . they're like illegal immigrants now?'

'I think so.'

'So?' prompted Michelle.

'So what?' Faye was perplexed.

'If the authorities know about their illegal status, they'll do something about it, won't they? Like deporting them back to where they belong . . .'

'Are you suggesting that I snitch on them?' Faye's mind churned in tumult.

'Well . . . "snitch" may be too strong a word. Just a call to the Immigration Department informing them of a couple of suspicious aliens staying in a particular apartment.'

'I think that's a bad idea, girls,' Sophia said firmly. 'That's wrong, no matter what they've done.'

'We're just brainstorming. I'm merely suggesting that there're tools that you can use. Whatever,' Michelle shrugged.

'I wouldn't do that, Faye. This is your family we're talking about here,' Sophia insisted.

'Do you have any other suggestions?' Faye asked quietly.

'What?' Sophia was surprised.

'If you think that's not a good idea, what do you suggest we do?'

'Well, I think we should all sit down and discuss this matter carefully instead of making any hasty decision—'

'That's what we're doing now, Mom—sitting down and discussing this.'

Sophia paused. The house became quiet and still.

Suddenly, the doorbell rang.

'Don't answer the door. It's probably him,' Faye said, starting to panic.

'It could be Julie,' Sophia said, walking briskly to the front door. The bell rang and rang. She looked through the peephole.

'It's him,' Sophia turned around and whispered urgently. 'What should we do?'

'Ignore it.'

'We can't do that. He knows we're here.'

'Tell him to go away. I don't want to talk to him,' Faye said, cold sweat began forming on her brow. She dashed to the phone and picked up the receiver. 'It's time to cut the cord. I'm doing it.'

With shaking hands, Faye dialled the deadly numbers and waited for someone to answer at the other end of the line.

Chapter 16

FAYE

It was happening too fast, and sooner than Faye had expected.

The police arrived just when she saw Yan staring at her through the apartment's window. Faye was crying her eyes out while hiding in the building's fire-exit stairway landing. Charlie, her pillar of strength, stood behind her as she leant against his warm body for support.

'It's okay. It'll be over soon,' his soft, familiar breath offered little comfort to her troubled soul.

The high-pitch sirens, crackling feedback from the walkie-talkies, and shouting drifted in before the homeland security officers showed up. Faye remembered thinking to herself that if the sound always comes first, won't it give the people they are arresting a chance to take off?

Soon, the apartment door was broken down, and her father and Yan were led out of the filthy hellhole amidst shouts of pleading, warning, and reading of rights. Her father's pants looked wet, and the officers pinched their noses and walked quickly away from him.

Yan continued to fix her gaze on Faye as she was being led away. Her eyes burnt with such hatred Faye could barely meet them. She looked away, into the darkness.

But her father didn't let up easily. He was shouting something about being famous and having an American daughter named Faye Williams. Faye was horrified that her name was brought up and prayed that the officer would shut him up. But God does not help the sinners. One of the homeland officers seemed to recognize her father and suggested that he call her to bail him out.

The irony of it all.

Fortunately, her father didn't understand what the officer said, who soon gave up and walked away.

'Hey boss, how did we find them?' the voice of the officer reached Faye's ice-cold ears.

'Tip-off.'

'Who called?'

'Dunno. Some girl. Left the address and hung up.'

'Yeah? Maybe it was his American daughter who got tired of her old man,' he chuckled.

* * *

The police station called again. They repeated the same message they had been conveying throughout the past week—Li Fu had asked to see his daughter, Miss Li Ying. And like the calls before, Faye adamantly declined. She didn't see the point of meeting him. He had to understand that it was over, that she didn't want to have anything to do with him or Yan any more. She just wanted them to leave her alone and go back to China.

But deep, deep down inside her, Faye knew the real reason for rejecting his request, although she would rather die than admit it. She refused to see him because she couldn't face him. She was too ashamed of herself. She had been stubborn. She had been selfish. She had been judgemental and unforgiving. She had made up her mind about them before they had even begun. They didn't stand a chance right from the start.

So once again, Faye fell into a maelstrom of guilt, self-blame and abhorrence of her family's existence. For a week, she refused to get out of bed, go to school, or even talk to anyone. She cried whenever she thought of the phone call she had made. Then, she cried some more as she remembered the fear in her father's eyes as he got into the police car. Things didn't get any better, whether they were in her home, away from her home or away in jail. Things couldn't get better unless she fixed herself.

About a week after the arrest, two officers from the Homeland Security arrived at their door. Sophia, who had answered the door and invited them in, had rather forcefully pulled Faye out of her bed before whispering crossly, 'Stop acting like a baby and take responsibility for your action. I'm here for you, but I can only do so much. Now, go talk to the officers!'

So, Faye decided she would stop acting like a baby and start acting like an asshole. Still in her week-old, stinking pyjamas, complete with dishevelled hair and a tear-stained face, she lumbered downstairs to meet the officers.

'Good afternoon, Ma'am. I'm Officer Anderson, and this is my colleague, Officer Harris. We're from the Homeland Security Department—'

'I'm not bailing them out if this is what you're here for,' Faye said curtly, trying to look proud and disinterested with her jutted chin and firm jaw. 'I don't have that kind of money anyway.'

The officers looked at each other, like how good partners in the movies did. Silently, they were warning each other of the speed bump ahead.

'Well, Miss Li—' Anderson began.

'Williams,' Faye interrupted at once.

'I'm sorry?'

'The name is Williams,' she said emphatically.

'Oh . . . I'm sorry, there must be some mistake. It says here that your father's family name is Li.'

'Yes, it is. But mine's Williams. Can we move on, please?' she urged impatiently as she slumped into a couch and melted into it. She was so tired; she had no energy or will to stay standing. Even speaking was arduous for her.

'I apologize for her rude behaviour, officers. Please, sit down. Can I offer you gentlemen some coffee?' Sophia said as she continued to glare at her daughter.

'No, Ma'am. This won't take long. Okay . . . Miss Williams,' Anderson heaved a deep sigh and made a steeple of his fingers as he spoke. 'I'm not sure if you're aware of the situation. Your father and sister have been taken into custody by the Homeland Security and charged with overstaying illegally in the United States of America without valid visas. They're currently incarcerated in one of the Federal Bureau of Prisons and will be deported back to China in the time to come. And just for your information, there's no "bailing?" for them.'

He paused for a response but was rewarded with none. Faye looked down at her pyjamas and played with a loose thread.

'Your father's last request before he leaves the country is to see you again. He has been asking, or rather, demanding for you incessantly. He refuses to eat or answer any questions unless he sees you. He says he would rather die if can't speak with you one last time, and we've every reason to believe that he means his words. So far, he only accepts water; he hasn't consumed food for a week. I'm afraid he's already in a critical medical condition and may soon lose his life if he carries on this way.'

'I don't wish to see him,' Faye replied defiantly after a long pause, but tears began rolling down her sunken cheeks. 'Just send him back. He's better off where he came from.'

'But Ma'am—'

'He's just playing games with you, with all of us. He'll come to his senses eventually and eat. If he doesn't, just force-feed him.' Faye wiped her tears away and stood up to show the officers to the door. 'Thanks for coming.'

'Don't be rude, Faye. Let the gentlemen finish what they have to say first,' Sophia cajoled.

Faye was too weak to argue with Sophia. Like her father, she had hardly eaten anything in the past week, and her depressed state had sapped all her strength. She sat down again, closed her eyes, and listened to Officer Anderson's plead.

'Ma'am, I don't know what's going on in your family, and frankly, it's not our job to intervene. But your father's condition is deteriorating rapidly, and nobody, not even your sister, can convince or force him to eat. We have a doctor in the prison where he is incarcerated who can verify that he'll be . . . beyond saving soon if this continues.'

'We know it's hard for outsiders like us to understand your family circumstances. We appreciate that, Ma'am, but this is a serious case that can't be ignored,' Officer Harris added.

'If he dies, it's on me. I'm to be blamed for everything. No one cares about another dead Chinese illegal immigrant anyway,' Faye said, as she felt the tightness at her temples. Insomnia and too much sleep at the same time had drained away her ability to think or feel.

'I'm afraid it is our concern, Ma'am,' Harris said. 'He's relatively known to the media, and if they get wind of him dying in prison, there'll be trouble. I don't know if you can appreciate the political and social consequences we're dealing with here, not to mention further souring of an already rocky relationship we have with China if anything bad were to happen to him. This is beyond your just "family affair".'

'Are you serious?' Faye opened her eyes incredulously.

'Let me put it this way, Ma'am. If you refuse to go, the press will eventually hear about this, and they'll put your "family affair" in the limelight again. And this time, it may not be so pleasant for you or your family—'

'Are you threatening me?'

'No, Ma'am. Absolutely not! I'm just laying out the consequences for you to weigh against your decision.'

'Go, Faye. Go and hear what your father has to say. You can't move on with your life until you have closure. I know that, and I know you know that. I didn't raise you to be this rotten kid you're pretending to be right now. I raised you to be a responsible person who faces your problems, not run away from them,' Sophia added, this time rather sternly.

'I'm not pretending, Mom. I'm a rotten person,' Faye said, the corners of her mouth turned down, ready for another round of weeping. 'I'm the most rotten person in the world.'

'Sweetie, don't think so highly of yourself. Yes, you did a pretty awful thing to your family, but you're still not the worst person in the world! And you know what I've learnt? When you do a terrible thing, you make amends. You do the right thing and fix the damage. Not hide in your room in your pink pyjamas, feeling sorry for yourself and telling the whole world to leave you alone!'

'Who are you to lecture me? You did wrong things too. You brought me here and lied and—' Faye fought back.

'Bringing you here wasn't a mistake, and you know that. And I brought you up with all the love I could give. Yes, I lied, but I've paid a heavy price for it. I've to bear the consequence of my stupidity for as long as I live. That's why I don't want you to go down that same path. I don't want you to have the same guilt and shame, which I promise you'll feel if you don't look into your father's eyes again.'

Sophia paused and then said, 'That's all I have to say. It's up to you now.'

Turning to the visibly uncomfortable Officer Anderson and Harris, Faye said quietly. 'Officers, could you please give me a minute while I change out of my pyjamas?'

* * *

The visiting centre at the prison was a capacious, function-over-form hall painted almost exclusively in white with more white ceiling light flooding the area, giving the place a fake sense of cheeriness. Cafeteria-style stools and round tables in groups of four and five seats were neatly placed in rows with ample space in between to allow prisoners and their visitors some level of privacy. The place reminded Faye a little of her high-school cafeteria, except for the several uniformed officers walking around, keeping a close eye on every person in the room.

The hall was almost empty, and Faye waited impatiently alone. Out of respect for Li Fu's request to have only Faye in the visitor's area, Sophia had offered to wait in the car.

Then, Faye's father appeared from one of the doors, handcuffed and in prison clothes.

He was a bag of bones and needed assistance in walking—he had refused a wheelchair—as he shuffled to the table where Faye was sitting. He was also without Yan, who was presumably locked up in a women's detention centre. And he seemed genuinely happy to see Faye.

'I knew you would come! I knew they would succumb to my protest. My goodness, how could they do such a thing, stopping you from seeing me! And to think that America is a free country! Did they lock you up too? No? Well, you've lost a lot of weight. Did they question you endlessly and not give you enough to eat? You can tell me. When I get back to China, I'll get Liu to write about it and post it on the internet for the world to see—' he said in a low, crackly voice.

Faye looked at her father, gaunt, emaciated but proud that he'd won again. She said nothing.

'Yes, I know. It's not convenient to talk here. They're likely listening, so just hear me out and don't say anything,' he lowered his voice further.

Still, she said nothing.

'Listen, I'm terribly sorry about what you saw the other day. I didn't know you were coming. I wouldn't have hired her . . . you know who . . . if I'd known that you were there. Anyway, that hideous whore! I think she was the one who called the police. It's just terrible luck.'

He doesn't know. Faye thought, surprised. *He hasn't realized it was me.*

'Bad luck follows me when I'm doing well. The job at the restaurant was fine, and I was able to make my rent this month, actually—' he continued, unfazed by Faye's silence.

'You asked to see me. What do you want?' Faye said coolly, trying not to look him in the eyes. She knew that would trigger a meltdown. Not now. Not in front of him.

'You're right; we don't have much time. Listen very carefully to what I've to say. It's very important,' he pressed on despite looking slightly affected by Faye's coldness.

He waited for her to acknowledge, but Faye had already turned on her coping mechanism, crossing her arms and looking at him as if she was watching a bad movie. She had a name for her coping mechanism. It was called Put-On-A-Bitchy-Front Syndrome.

'There is a tin box—'

'Li, you've five more minutes. Say what you want to say now. You need to get to the hospital for your drip, as you've promised,' the Chinese American officer in charge of the visiting centre said in bad Mandarin. Faye felt nothing but immense gratitude for the officer.

Only five more minutes to bear, she told herself.

'Okay, okay,' her father grinned and bowed subserviently.

He turned to Faye and whispered, his grin vanished. 'Ying, do you still have the key to my apartment?'

Faye nodded slightly, her countenance not giving anything away.

'Now, I want you to go there with Charlie in the night. Don't do it during the day because everyone will know you're there. You need to be very vigilant about this, okay? Make sure you enter the apartment without anyone seeing you. And you need to do this very quietly because the walls are very thin and the neighbours can hear everything you do.'

Faye listened with raised interest. She had no idea where this was leading to.

'There're a few cookie tins under my bed. Pick the blue one; the rest are just decoys. When you open it, you'll see some cookies; remove them. Then you'll see something wrapped in red paper. Those are American bills, about twenty-five thousand dollars in all. I want you to take the money and leave the apartment as quietly as you entered it.'

Faye thought he had gone demented on her.

'Where did you get so much money from?' she said a little too loudly.

'Shh . . . don't speak!' He looked around to make sure no one was listening. 'They are mostly from online donations before you shut my operation down. The rest is tips and salary from the restaurant. I haven't spent much since I arrived here, except on an occasional meal or two for Yan and myself. I've been lying all along about spending all my money away because I wanted to save as much as possible for your dowry. You see, Charlie comes from a good family. They'll look down on you if you don't have a decent dowry when the two of you get married.'

He paused as if talking was too much work for him.

'I know what you're thinking. What about the prostitute, right? That was a gift from a co-worker at the restaurant. I didn't have to pay, so I agreed to it. You know, sometimes, men have needs—'

'Stop,' she urged at once, disgusted even by the idea. 'I don't want to hear or know anything about it!'

'Okay, okay . . . I understand,' he said, regretting that he had brought it up.

'Nobody knows about the money, not even Yan. If you must, you tell Charlie and Sophia that I left you with only a few hundred dollars. Don't let them know how much money there is in the tin,' he continued.

'Use the money as you see fit, maybe on a nice wedding dress or jewellery or something. You know, you need to look wealthy, even though we don't have as much money as Charlie's family. You must never let people think that you've nothing,' he said, almost to himself.

Faye came here without meaning to say a word. Now, she was too stunned to. She wanted to say something, anything, but she could think of nothing. What was she supposed to say? Thanks, Papa, for the twenty-five thousand dollars? By the way, I was the one—not that hideous whore—who betrayed you? So long, and thanks for all the fish?

She didn't have to struggle for long because before she had a chance to respond, the officer-in-charge came up to them again. 'Time's up, Li. Say your goodbyes now.'

'Wait a minute, I've two minutes left!' her father protested.

'I'm sorry, my brother. Doctor's order.' The officer's shrug and tone were nonchalant.

'Oh, just so you know Miss Li, your father's leaving as soon as he's well enough to get on a plane. So, this may be your last chance to say goodbye.'

The officer's words caused a sudden panic in her father. He looked as if he was drowning, and Faye was standing at the side of the pond, watching him go down. He seemed like he had more to say, but he couldn't do so with the officer right next to them. So, he uttered meaningless phrases like 'Take good care of yourself' and 'Don't worry about me. I'll find my way back to America.'

As he was being led away, he began sobbing like a child.

'I'm sorry, Ying,' he wept. 'I should've been more careful. I'm sorry I've to leave you again. It's all my fault.'

Faye could still hear his cries even though she couldn't see him any more.

She could still hear him long after she had left the detention centre.

Chapter 17

YAN

Two US Immigration and Customs Enforcement agents were walking them, the illegal aliens, to the departure gate at the San Francisco International airport for their commercial flight.

Today was the day. Yan and her father were being deported back to China.

It was another media fiesta, much like the first time they had arrived, although the number of reporters at the airport had dwindled to about a third of the former.

Yan supposed her father had lost his media appeal. His story was no longer sensational. After all, how many more exciting stories could a reporter file on a middle-aged Chinese man who had found his long-lost daughter in America? Did the readers really care if he was returning to China? Sure, he had to be deported—that part was somewhat scandalous—but hadn't he already found his daughter and had his reunion? And let's not forget the possible backlashes that the newspapers and TV stations would receive from the xenophobic, illegal-immigrant haters who believed that the foreigners were taking over America. Yan and her father were, undeniably, illegal immigrants who had overstayed in their country. There was no escaping on that one.

For Yan, she was glad that they were finally going home.

Free at last! Free at last! Amitabha, we are free at last!

She couldn't wait to get on that plane, away from Ying, Sophia, and the rest of the red-hair barbarians. All she wanted was to return to where she belonged, the ugly, cold, miserable apartment, which wasn't unlike the last apartment they had stayed in, in Chinatown. She didn't mind going back to eating rice with soya sauce or food scraps and leftovers or wearing almost everything she owned to keep warm because they couldn't afford the heating facility in the apartment. She almost missed washing laundry with her bare hands in winter, the freezing water that set her fingers ablaze with blinding pain, letting it scorch her skin red and purple and waking her every sense. It wasn't a comfortable life, but it was hers.

She didn't tell her father that she had seen Ying standing on the stairway with crocodile tears rolling down her pretty cheeks when they were arrested that night because she knew that his deluded mind would vehemently deny it, even though it couldn't be more obvious that it was Ying who had reported them to the immigration department. Her father had come up with a list of possibilities, none of which included Ying: it was the prostitute who wasn't happy with the tip; a restaurant patron who had overheard his conversation with someone about getting a green card; or a co-worker who was jealous of him. Anyone but Ying.

Yan wished he could look at the evidence. The officers had arrived the same night after the 'incident', and they had known exactly where to look for them, even though there were at least a dozen other illegal immigrants in the same building. But once again, she had underestimated her father's love and obsession for Ying, and the power she still had over him.

At least Yan had her father all to herself now. She was sure that by now, he must've given up all hope of having Ying in their lives. In Yan's small, small world, she believed she'd won.

But no one else knew. And no one would applaud her.

Her father, on the other hand, only cared if Ying could make it to the airport to see him one last time. He didn't even notice the journalists' presence. Much as the media had had enough of him, he, too, had had enough of the media. They were a liability now that there was no denying his crime of overstaying in this country.

'Mr Li, would you care to make a statement before you get on the plane?' asked a reporter.

Yan's father wasn't interested in making a statement or answering any questions. Ignoring everyone, he craned his neck anxiously in search of his daughter's face in the crowd as he was led to the departure gate with the journalists in the wake.

'Mr Li, will Ying be joining you in China?' another reporter tried.

It was in vain. In his eyes, they no longer existed.

'Are you looking out for your daughter? Is she coming?'

'It's unlikely that she's coming, Mr Li. My colleague who's stationed outside her house just told me she was still in there. She hasn't left the house since last night,' another reporter volunteered the information.

Li Fu looked surprised and hurt, and lashed out at the reporter.

'You leave my daughter alone—you hear me? This has got nothing to do with her. If you harass her even just a bit, I'll break your neck!' he glared.

'Oh yeah? That's a threat, Mr Li. Do you know that I can sue you for threatening me in this country?' the reporter decided to provoke him, hoping to squeeze a little action out of the otherwise dull story.

'Shut up!' one of the Immigration and Customs Enforcement agents intervened. 'Mr Li, I want you to ignore the reporters. Just keep walking, you get that?'

'Why isn't she here? Does she not want to see you any more? What have you done?' The reporter didn't let up.

'You piece of shit!' Yan's father yelled. 'I told her not to come to avoid motherfuckers like you! So, shut the fuck up! If I ever see you in Beijing, you're a dead man—'

'That's another threat, Mr Li. By the way, I heard from a source that it was a young lady who tipped the law enforcement off about you and your daughter. Do you think it was Ying who made the call?'

That did it. He took the bait. Blinded by rage, Yan's father suddenly struck a blow on the reporter's face, knocking him down. The other reporters rushed to film the victim, while the agents pulled Yan's father away as quickly as possible.

Scurrying behind her father, Yan heard the assaulted reporter asking his cameraman, 'Did you get that on camera? You did? That's awesome, man!'

FAYE

Faye, too, was blinded, although not by rage but remorse. It was overwhelming, devastating, and it was eating her alive. There was no getting away from it; it became her entire being, and she could think of nothing else but a crushing sense of utter shame and regret.

Once again, she was downright miserable, despondent even, and a complete human wreck.

She had gone to the apartment like her father had asked her to. She had found the blue cookie tin and retrieved the package wrapped in red paper. There were indeed stacks of hidden bills, twenty-five thousand American dollars in all, not a dollar less.

He hadn't lied.

What did that make her? Perhaps the biggest asshole in the world? A humongous, colossal, epic rat who squealed on her own father, a man who saved up every dime he had so that he could provide her with a decent dowry.

A decent dowry. That was laughable. She wasn't sure if her relationship with Charlie would survive college. Marriage was so far away on the horizon that it wasn't even a speck from where she stood.

Needless to say, Charlie and Sophia were sick and tired of her 'episodes' by now. Her refusal to function normally and the guilt and emotions she constantly wore on her sleeve had made her very unpopular, to say the least. Their patience for her was fast running out.

So they left her alone to 'get a grip on herself' and got on with their lives.

But Faye was still unable to 'get a grip on herself' on the day of her father's departure, and so, going to the airport was out of the question. For one, she couldn't face the media that camped around the clock outside their home. They had been ringing the doorbell, knocking on their doors, peeping through drawn curtains, and asking endless questions. Faye and Sophia were so strung up by these invasions of privacy that they jumped at any sound inside and outside their house. The Police were summoned several times—they couldn't do anything if no one had violated the law—and neighbours were sought to politely or impolitely ask the journalists to please go away or fuck off. But mostly, Faye didn't see the point of going to the airport because she hadn't decided what to do. What would she say to her father? That she had betrayed him but had been regretting it every day, and oh, have a great life by the way? Or, should she just lie and tell him she'd miss him dearly and hoped to reunite with them soon?

Neither seemed appealing to her. She wasn't ready for any kind of conversation.

She did, however, watch the telecast of his departure on the news, which was repeated several times throughout the day, newsworthy once again because of the brief brawl. It had been reported as 'the use of violence against our correspondent'. Faye was appalled not by her father's use of violence but by the reporter's hint that she might be the one who made the report—how dare he say such a thing!—conveniently forgetting that she had indeed made the call.

She cried and cried while Sophia shook and shook her head as they watched Faye's father punch the reporter, and then some.

After their departure, Faye moped around the house and once again grew squalid in her habits. She was a pile of melancholic mess, crying to the lyrics of sad songs and pouring over the pictures of her father and the only note he had written to her. Besides going to school, she would find herself slumped on the couch and binge-watching entire seasons of Netflix series. When she had finished a series, she would move on to the next, choosing one with the highest number of seasons. She hardly went out with Charlie or hung out with Michelle, and when she did, all she wanted to talk about was her father.

Her father had become her obsession, her only preoccupation.

This went on for weeks until Sophia decided that Faye wasn't about to 'get a grip on herself'. She needed to do something about it.

So one Friday afternoon, Faye found Charlie chasing her down the hall after class. His TV had broken down, he said, and he so wanted to finish the final season of *Narcos* this weekend. Wasn't she watching the same season? Why couldn't they watch it together? He was sure Sophia wouldn't mind him being there at all.

Faye was a little perplexed. *Like, how many TV sets does his family own? Why would he want to come to her place just because one of them is broken?*

Nevertheless, she agreed. It was only when she stepped into her home that she realized it was a trap.

On the couch sat Sophia and Michelle. Even Julie was there.

Oh my God, I used to laugh at this stuff on TV. And now, it's happening to me!

'Hi Faye, please take a seat and join us.' Julie stood up and ushered them to the seats in a dramatic manner.

'What's this? This isn't an intervention, is it?' Faye asked, bemused.

'Yes, it is. Please, take a seat and listen to what your loved ones have to say,' answered Julie, trying to sound professional.

'Don't be ridiculous! I don't need a freaking intervention—'

'Just. Sit. Down,' Julie insisted, teeth clenched.

Faye threw up her hands and slumped into the only seat left.

Michelle began reading from a letter she had prepared. 'Dear Faye, I'm sorry I pushed you to make that call. I know that it was the wrong thing to do now. It was my mistake, not yours. I understand you need time to grieve, but you mustn't dwell. It's time to forgive yourself. I love you, and I'm here for you, standing next to you, waiting to help,' Michelle looked up meekly at Faye.

'Faye, please let the others finish first before you say anything,' Julie offered. 'Charlie, you go next.'

'What happened to the strong, self-assured Faye whom I knew and loved? Did you kill her?'

'Uh, Charlie, you're not supposed to say things like that—' Julie interrupted.

'It's okay. Let him say whatever he wants. I know what he's trying to do,' Faye said, her eyes softening a little. Charlie might not be good with words, but at least he used the honest ones.

'I see that you're hurt, but you've built this wall around you and you're not letting anyone in,' Charlie continued. 'It breaks my heart to see you go through this shit. So, I think you need to face your monsters . . .'

'Demons, Charlie! Face your demons,' Michelle jumped in, rolling her eyes.

'Okay, okay, demons. Thank you, Michelle, but I'm trying to talk to my girlfriend here if you don't mind—'

'Sorry, Charlie. Just trying to help.'

Charlie turned to Faye, annoyed to be made to look like an idiot. 'You need to face your demons so that you, no . . . we, can carry on with our lives. Together, you know. As a couple. So do it.'

A mist began to form in Faye's eyes. While it was hard listening to Charlie read his badly structured letter, she believed it had been harder for Charlie to write it.

'Dearest Faye,' Sophia began, already tearing up. 'You're the love of my life, and you know that I'll do anything for you. I raised you, so I know you more than anyone here, including yourself. I know that you can't get over yourself unless you do what you think is the right thing, even if that involves taking the difficult but right path. I'm so proud of who you are . . .'

Sophia paused, buried her face in her hands, and sobbed, her shoulder shaking violently. Julie, who sat next to her, embraced her tightly.

Sophia composed herself and continued, ' . . . and I believe you have the courage to walk that path. I'm telling you now that you need to do something to get out of your current state, but know this: whatever your decision is, I'm here to support you entirely. No matter what.' She put down her letter and started wiping away the tears that had formed again.

Julie, who saw herself in the interventionist role, spoke next. 'So Faye, what do you think?'

'Well, first of all, I think this is the worst intervention ever,' Faye said with a grin. Everyone laughed, some a little too loudly to hide their relief.

'But I love you all for doing this. And I think you're right. I need to do something, and I've just decided on what that is.'

Silence ensued. All eyes were focused on Faye.

'I'll do the unthinkable. I'll look for my father and return him the twenty-five thousand dollars. And I'll tell him I was the one who made the call.'

More silence, this time not with anticipation, but with hesitation and uncertainty.

'In China?' Charlie asked incredulously.

'Yes, that's where he is now, isn't it?' Faye replied.

'You'll break your father, I mean, utterly break him if he knows you betrayed him. But if that's what you're going for—' Michelle began.

'It may break his heart, but he has the right to know. I can't live with myself unless I do this. I can't explain it, but I *have* to do this,' Faye said.

'Are you sure this is a good idea?' Charlie ventured.

'I'll go with you,' Sophia said suddenly.

'Really?' Surprised, Faye spun around and looked at her mom.

'Yup, I'll go. I've learnt my lesson about not telling the truth, and I don't want my daughter to repeat the same mistake,' Sophia said.

Chapter 18

FAYE

Beijing was not what Faye had expected. It couldn't be further from her imagination.

From the airport to the hotel, all she saw were new superhighways, shining skyscrapers, and ultra-modern shopping malls that housed international high-street fashion brands such as Louis Vuitton, Chanel, Rolex and Armani. It looked like any big city in America. What happened to the stuff that Americans like her look for? Where were the ancient sites and historic buildings so beautifully depicted on tourist websites? Where would she find the unique cultural experience that was supposedly so well preserved in the capital city?

'That belonged in the past, Miss. If you want to see the old stuff, you can visit the Forbidden City, the Great Wall, etc. For tourists like you, they're better than Disneyland because this is the real stuff! But Beijing is a modern city now, and we've made many changes and progress in the last twenty years,' boasted the taxi driver who was driving them to their hotel.

'I remember visiting the Great Wall when I was here the last time. It was magnificent!' Sophia chimed in.

'In fact, we've had double-digit economic growth for a very long time.' The driver ignored Sophia and rambled on like an economic commentator. 'Here, we've some of the biggest companies in the world. You must've heard of Alibaba and Jack Ma, haven't you? Have you heard of the One Belt, One Road initiative? Very soon, we may even surpass the US as the biggest superpower in the world.'

Faye had lost count of the number of times he used the words 'modernized' and 'growth'.

Even taxi drivers are talking in economic terms, Faye thought. *But who's to say that the Chinese can't be as rich and powerful as the rest of the world? After all, they had suffered enough in the past century. The country had endured civil war, foreign invasion, Maoism, famine, and poverty. Maybe this is their time to shine.*

But Faye wasn't sure if it was a good or a bad thing. She was disappointed that her idea of China, the China she had seen and read in movies and books—she loved the works of Lu Xun, the film *The Last Emperor*, and admittedly, even the new *The Karate Kid*—no longer existed. This was post-Communist China, with much of the old 'Chineseness' stripped from the country and its people. It was a city that was so determined to move on—to modernize and prosper—that it was willing to do so at all costs, including burying its past.

As she entered the city, Faye realized that for the first time in her life she looked like any other person on the street—the same black hair, the same yellow skin, and the same flat nose. Yet, she shared neither their language nor culture. She had never felt so much like a foreigner before.

Sophia, on the other hand, seemed exhilarated to be back here. Although she tried to contain her excitement—she didn't want to look like she was enjoying her time here because of her daughter's circumstances—it was not hard to tell that she couldn't wait to show her daughter the China she had once loved. Or, what was left of it.

But Faye wasn't interested in sightseeing; it was the last thing on her mind. She was anxious about meeting her father and sister again. She was still hesitant about what she would say to them. But despite Faye's reluctance, Sophia dragged her to the usual tourist traps—the Great Wall, the Forbidden City, the old, narrow streets of Hutong, and the rest, reminiscing upon the few good times she had overseas. She wanted to show Faye her heritage. She wanted her to see the place where she was born and how her life would've been had she not been taken to America.

To please her mom, Faye tried to show some enthusiasm, but she hated every minute of it. Like what the taxi driver had said, the Great Wall, the Forbidden City, the old, narrow streets of Hutong had become the 'Disneylands of China'. She disliked the crowd. She detested the indifferent attitude of the service staff. And, she was constantly wary of swindlers who preyed on tourists, and unfortunately, Sophia's naivety was as apparent as having the words 'gullible tourist here, please scam me' printed on her T-shirt.

She wasn't sure if Sophia was innocent or innocuously manipulative, but if she had planned this to make Faye appreciate her decision of adopting her and taking her to America years ago, it worked marvellously. Faye had never felt more grateful. She didn't belong here. Neither did she have any desire to live here. All she wanted was to do what she came here to do and go home.

A few days after they had arrived in China, they finally got in touch with Liu Gang, the young man who had helped Faye's father with all his endeavours, the mastermind behind the whole operation. All thanks to the great detective work of Michelle, who had proven once again to be extremely resourceful. She was amazingly good at looking up people on the internet. Creepy, actually. Liu Gang's profile, which barely existed, was listed only in Chinese on Chinese social media sites. Considering the many obstacles, including the fact that it was a common Chinese name, Michelle had pulled an almost impossible feat.

Initially, Liu Gang wasn't interested in meeting them. In China, it would be considered 'wise' to cut off all ties with convicted criminals like Li Fu. He didn't want to have anything to do with Li Fu or his family any more. He admitted he hadn't yet found full-time employment, but he had moved on to other 'projects', although he had left out the details of what those projects were. Fortunately for Faye, they managed to convince him. Not with her charm or emotional appeal, but with a high-end Alienware laptop and a special edition iPhone that wasn't available in China, courtesy of Sophia who had dug deep into her savings account.

They agreed to meet in a café at Wangfujing Street, a place chosen by Liu Gang. According to his theory, it would be safer if they were seen in a place commonly visited by tourists. No one would suspect when he talked to a couple of foreigners there. Faye and Sophia had arrived early and picked a quiet table at the back of the café. They were nervous about the meeting because they had no idea what Liu Gang was like. They had talked about him a lot in their hotel room the past few nights and imagined him to be this burly man akin to a bully and prayed hard that he wasn't a member of a Chinese triad.

How surprised they were—they didn't even bother to hide it—when a small, scrawny man who seemed barely out of his teens showed up and sat at their table. He looked like he had just woken from his sleep, his hair tousled and uncombed, his shirt creased, and his face tired-looking. There was even eye-booger stuck to the corner of his eye. It was apparent that this man-boy did not have a woman who looked after him—no mother, wife, or girlfriend by his side.

Faye almost laughed aloud as she recalled the anxiety and trepidation she and Sophia had undergone. This guy? She could take him down with one hand!

So rather than a triad member, they found themselves looking at a stereotypical nerd, a tech guy, albeit a brilliant one. He was soft-spoken, non-threatening, tensed, and behaved as if *he* was afraid of them. He sat down and nodded at them, but avoided eye contact as much as possible.

'So, you're the daughter Li Fu had been looking for all these years,' he said in heavily accented English.

'Yup, I'm afraid that's me,' Faye said, almost ashamed to admit it. 'And this is my mom, Sophia.'

'Hello, Miss Sophia,' he nodded and gave a nervous smile. 'By the way, how did you manage to find me? Was it Li? What did he tell you about me?'

'He mentioned you a few times,' Faye said vaguely, not wanting to reveal too much too soon.

'Did he accuse me of anything? Let's just lay it out, okay? I didn't do anything illegal. I was employed by him to help out only with the technical stuff, that's all. I was broke at that time and—' he started to sound frenzied.

'Relax, Liu. This is not what we're here to talk about.'

'No?' he said, looking instantly relieved. 'What's this about then?'

'We'll get to that later. First, here are the gadgets we've promised you,' Sophia, sensing the tension, chimed in. She signalled to Faye to hand the bagful of boxes to Liu. That cheered him up and took the edge off him a little.

'And let's order you some beverage. What would you like to drink?'

'Coffee, please. And thanks for the gifts,' he said, looking like a boy on Christmas morning. 'You know . . . this meeting has kept me up for quite a few nights. I'm just glad this isn't about . . . well . . . what I thought it was.'

'Us too!' said Faye. 'We thought you were some kind of thug.'

'Thug?'

'A violent person. A criminal.'

Liu laughed softly, followed by Faye and Sophia, relieving some of the awkwardness between them.

'Poor Li . . . things didn't work out the way he wanted, huh?' Liu Gang offered.

'Yes, we're very sorry that he had to be deported. But if you break the law in the US, you need to face the consequence,' Sophia jumped in, sensing Faye's hesitance.

'It's none of my business, really,' Liu shrugged. 'But I kind of expected something like this to happen. I mean, so many Chinese tried to get a green card every year, and most of them are smarter and more educated than Li Fu. What made him think he could succeed when so many others have failed?'

'Was that what he was after? A green card?' Faye asked. Even at this point, she was still suspicious of her father's true intention.

Liu Gang regarded her again, this time with slight disdain. 'No, he went to America to look for you. I know Li has many faults, but his intention was pure. Even I could tell.'

The remark stung, but Faye knew she deserved it.

'You asked to see me. What can I do for you?' Liu was eager to get down to business.

'We want to see my father, sister, and mother. If possible, I wish to see their living quarters here. We're hoping you can help us arrange that,' Faye said. 'Of course, we'll pay you for your service.'

Liu Gang looked surprised at first. Then, he shook his head slightly, bit his lower lips, and murmured something in Chinese. Faye couldn't catch his words, but she knew he must be thinking, *what a nutcase!* First, she rejected her family. Now, she wants to get to know them.

'You want to be with your family again?' Liu questioned.

'No, I don't.'

'Why do you want to meet them then?'

'I want to return something to my father. And I want to know who my mother is.'

'What are you returning?'

'That's for him to know.'

'Fine. But you know that'll hurt him again, right?'

'Probably. Yes, it's very likely.'

'Then why do you still come? Why can't you just leave him be? Do you hate him that much?'

'I don't hate him. I'm here to set things right so that we can move on with our lives.'

'For him or you?'

Faye paused, careful not to reef off into anger as she held Liu Gang's blazing gaze. She could tell that he wasn't fond of her father, but he seemed highly protective of him.

'He needs to know the truth.'

'Can't you write to him?'

'No, it's too important.'

'What truth?'

'That I was the one who turned him in. I was the one who called the immigration department and got him deported. Happy now?'

People like to say it is almost impossible to read a Chinese face. But for a brief moment, Liu Gang's face was like an open book: first, the judgement and the contempt for her audacity, then came the abhorrence of her betrayal, and finally, his respect for her courage.

He contemplated for a full minute. He didn't move, speak, or look at either Faye or Sophia. He simply stared out of the window, looking at the cars zipping by. The café was getting noisier and more crowded, which made his silence even louder.

'I'll help you,' he finally decided. 'I want you to know that I don't agree with what you're doing, but I respect your honesty and your courage to face your mistakes. I don't know a lot of people like you these days.'

'Mistake,' she corrected him.

'We'll see about that. I can take you to his apartment now if you want. It's vacant at the moment, but you'll see how they used to live. Things are kept exactly as they were before your father and sister left for the US. And I'll arrange for you to visit your father and Yan at the prison. You can ask them where your mother is when you see them, and I'll take you there.'

'Thank you. I appreciate it,' Faye said, relieved.

'As for your compensation—' Sophia began.

'That's not necessary, Ma'am. It's the least I can do for Li Fu. Although we had our differences, I realize now he has something I don't. I've no idea what that is, but it must be something great because it brought his daughter here.'

'I'll tell you what he has,' Faye said. 'He has love. He doesn't show it, but it's right there.'

* * *

'Upstairs, second floor; that's where they lived.' Liu Gang pointed at a decrepit four-storey building in front of them.

As soon as they stepped out of the taxi, Faye and Sophia knew they were on the wrong side of town. It even smelt like it, for the stench of humanity hit them hard at once. Every street, every corner reeked of decay; even death. The foul odour of unwashed humans, filthy waste, and rotting food strewed on the sidewalks stung their every sense. Faye held her breath for as long as she could, and when she could no longer do so, she silently prayed for an end to this olfactory assault while inhaling through the very mouth she whispered those prayers.

As she caught a glimpse of the building Liu was pointing at, she could see new and disused antennae, wires, and other questionable objects zip-zapping the skyline, almost like an ugly yet permanent avant-garde art installation project that people pretended didn't exist. Together with the laundry that was hanging to dry outside every other household, the place looked busy even though they hadn't seen a soul since their arrival.

'Come on up. I can let you into the apartment. Li gave me a set of spare keys before he left.'

'He didn't give up the apartment?' Sophia asked breathlessly as she precariously made her way up the narrow and uneven rotting wooden stairs, testing every step with her weight and expecting to fall right through the planks.

'No, he didn't. I don't know why. I guess he wanted to keep his options open. It's not easy to find an apartment in Beijing, let alone a cheap one. If you find a gem like this one, you better keep it,' Liu said matter-of-factly.

A gem? Faye thought incredulously. *He calls this place a gem?*

Somehow, they managed the perilous stairs and reached the front door of the apartment. Liu wasted no time; he jammed the key into the keyhole, and the door opened right up.

Faye braced herself for the worst, and she was glad that she did.

It *was* a shithole, albeit a tiny one. The one-room apartment consisted literally of only four damp and grimy walls. A few posters of Hong Kong celebrities from the 80s and an outdated lunar calendar were duct-taped onto the wall—a miserable attempt to hide the holes and the mould that thrived in the apartment. The room was sparsely furnished, consisting only of a wooden table that had seen better days, a few mismatched stools, a bunker bed, and a tiny wardrobe. The air was musty and smelt like shit, and Faye was sure that she would find excrement left behind by some rats or other unknown creatures somewhere in a corner. She didn't go look. She didn't want to.

She thought the place they had rented in San Francisco was bad. This was a whole new level of worse! How could they live like this? How could anyone live like this?

From their disgusted faces, Liu knew they were appalled by the living conditions. Rather than feeling ashamed, he was offended by their repugnance, their turned-up noses, and their prosaic view of poverty.

'This may seem unacceptable to you, but it's already not too bad for our standard. A lot of people live like that. My apartment is at least an hour and a half away from downtown Beijing, half the size, and I've to share it with three other guys to afford the rent.'

'I . . . I don't know what to say—' Faye stammered.

Perhaps, that's why papa tried so hard to get out of here. This apartment, this poverty. Can I blame him for wanting more? I suppose not. Who then can I blame?

Piled neatly on the floor were a huge number of old books and magazines, occupying almost every square inch available. Faye picked up a few of them to scan through. They were literature of all kinds— history, science, medical, religious books, novels, and magazines, in Chinese and English languages, carelessly discarded by others but carefully saved by someone living here. She opened the pages of some of them and saw that Yan had written her name on the first page of every book. The books belonged to her now.

As Faye flipped through the pages, she noticed that they were marked, underlined, or highlighted with notes on the margins in Yan's handwriting. Yan had read, or attempted to read, these books. Her quest for knowledge was almost palpable throughout the pages.

Suddenly, Faye felt nauseated from the filth and the foul air in the apartment. She rushed out of the door, down the fleet of stairs, and on to the street. There, she vomited, hurling out the sickness of poverty, the despondency, and the hopelessness that still hung in the apartment.

She had had enough. When Liu and Sophia came down shortly after her, she gathered her strength and said, 'I don't think we need to go back there. I've seen what I came to see. Let's go.'

YAN

Yan was shocked beyond words when she saw Ying hurling at the street side below her apartment, looking pale and sick. She thought she was hallucinating. But when Liu Gang and Sophia emerged from the building after Ying, she had it figured out. For reasons Yan couldn't fathom, Ying must've decided to come to China and get in touch with Liu.

What Liu and Ying didn't know—at least not at that point—was that Yan had already been released from prison. Deemed as an accomplice rather than the mastermind, she was given a lighter sentence than her father. She did go to prison but like many state-run institutions in China, the prison was overcrowded and underfunded. They didn't care about small-time criminals like her, and thus, they gave her early parole to ease the overpopulation. Having nowhere else to go, she went back to their old apartment. There were still no electricity and running water because she couldn't afford to turn them back on, but she could sustain her basic needs there, at least for now. She didn't want to think about the imminent winter; she wasn't sure if she could endure another Beijing winter without any heating.

The last people she wanted to deal with right now were Ying and Sophia. She had other things to worry about, like food and money. She thought she had gotten rid of Ying for good, but there she was, right below her apartment, looking all nice and pretty, probably trying to patch things up with her father. Liu must've used the set of spare keys her father had given him to let them into the apartment.

Traitor!

While she felt upset and betrayed by Liu, an idea struck Yan. It could work. It could solve her problems, but she had to play her cards right. So right after Ying and Sophia had hailed a taxi and left the place, she emerged from the corner of the street where she was hiding and confronted Liu.

'What the hell! You scared the shit out of me,' Liu almost yelled.

'What is that woman doing in my apartment?' she asked, her face set hard.

'She wanted to see how you and your father lived, so I brought her here. When did you get out of prison? Are you living in the apartment now? Are you alone?'

'I got out about a month ago, and yes, that's my abode for now. What else does she want?'

'She wants to meet your mother, and visit you and your father. Well, since you're no longer in prison, maybe you can see her tomorrow—'

'What for?'

'I don't know,' Liu lied. He wasn't interested in getting involved in their weird and antagonistic family affair. 'She didn't say much, except about wanting to talk to your father and returning something to him. I suppose she wants to make good with all of you.'

'Oh? What is it that she is returning?'

'Hey, ask her yourself! I can take you to their hotel right now if you want. They just left—' Liu realized he had said too much.

'No, I don't want to do that; not right now.'

'My goodness Yan, you seem so different from the last time I saw you. You're so . . . level-headed and . . . well . . . a little scary. To tell you the truth, I'm a little afraid of you . . .'

'Sorry to scare you like this, but things have been tough without papa, and I need to take care of a few things,' she said matter-of-factly. 'When do you plan to take them to papa and mom?'

'I don't know yet. I need time to make the necessary arrangements. I don't even know where they are right now,' Liu confessed.

'I'll do it with you. Papa wrote me while I was in prison so I know which prison he was sent to. As for mom . . . I'll show you,' she said.

* * *

Yan made Liu arrange for her and Ying to meet first. After that, they would visit their mother together at the mental institute she was staying.

Yan knew that for her plan to work, she had to gain Ying's trust again, and that meant patching things up with her sister. It wouldn't be easy for her, and she knew it wouldn't be easy for Ying either. Yan went to jail because of her sister, and she attributed the years of having to endure a dysfunctional family solely to her abduction. The last thing Yan wanted to do was to have anything to do with her sister again. On the other hand, Ying saw her masturbating to the photos of her boyfriend. That incident spooked her so much that she went running to the immigration enforcement right away. So yes, this would be a tough one, but Yan had to somehow make it work for the sake of her family.

The meeting was set in the same café where Liu had met with Ying and Sophia. Liu rented a car to drive them around, at Sophia's expense, of course, and arranged to pick Yan up at her apartment in the morning. The night before, in preparation for the meeting, Yan had sacrificed some of the precious clean water she had salvaged to wash her body and picked the best set of clothes she owned—a decent but wrinkled white blouse and a pair of blue trousers. She had left all her other clothes in America when she was arrested. Not that she could wear any of the American-style clothes here anyway; it would only attract unnecessary attention from the local gangsters and the envy of the poor girls around her home. Yan wasn't sure who would be more dangerous—the gangsters or the girls.

Liu arrived on time at nine in the morning, and they drove in silence to the café. It was a weekday, and so, other than a few tourists, expatriates, and local rich housewives, the place was rather empty. Yan had never dined in a café this posh. Looking at the luxurious decorations and the well-to-do customers, she was very aware that the best clothes she had donned were possibly only good enough to be used as table rags here. Extremely self-conscious, she smoothened her blouse repeatedly as she stayed rooted at the entrance.

The waitresses at the service counter scowled as they noticed Liu and Yan. One of the staff left the counter to approach them. Before she could reach them, she noticed Ying waving to them and calling them over. Ying's American accent gave the staff pause. Looking rather confused, she turned back to the counter and left Yan and Liu alone.

'C'mon, let's go and meet your sister and get it over and done with. We've got lots to do today,' Liu said as he pulled Yan by her arm and headed towards Ying and Sophia.

There they were, the two sisters.

Face-to-face once again.

Images of their arrest and the humiliation Yan and her father had endured emerged in Yan's mind. Instead of the soft music in the café, she heard banging on the door and the screaming of the officers. In place of the aroma of coffee beans, her brain activated a whiff of pungent urine odour. Rather than Ying and Sophia, she saw her father peeing in his pants right in front of her.

But she knew she mustn't show the disdain she had for her sister. Not now. She had a plan, and she needed it to work. So against all her instincts, she managed a smile. A coy, furtive, uncertain smile. She didn't want the smile to be confident, for Ying would notice the change in her. A little furtiveness and uncertainty would suffice.

Ying looked uncomfortable and unsure of what to do. Yan was sure that the last image of her on the couch was still vivid in Ying's mind, and she wouldn't be surprised if Ying reached across the coffee table and throttled her. But Ying did no such thing. It seemed Ying had grown up a little too.

Like always, Sophia came forward to save her daughter's day.

'Ni hao . . .' In her attempt to ease the tense atmosphere, Sophia had finally said her first Chinese words, 'how are you?' She said she had just learnt it from Liu. After all those months of living together with Yan and her father, Sophia hadn't bothered to learn a word of Chinese to communicate with them. It seemed strange that she did so now. Why only now, Yan had no idea, nor could she be bothered to find out. She had bigger fish to fry.

Sophia then gestured for all of them to sit down and asked Liu to help her with the ordering of beverages, an excuse to leave Ying and Yan to talk alone.

And so, the sisters were alone, hating each other. Yan learnt somewhere that Americans needed this funny thing called closure, which she believed was what Ying was here for. Yan didn't understand it. Her idea of closure was to have Ying out of her life.

'I'm sorry about what happened. But I did what I had to do,' Ying generously began.

'What did you do?' Yan asked innocently. Obviously, Yan knew what Ying had done, but she wanted her to say it, to admit that she had wronged her flesh and blood.

'I . . . I . . . uh . . . I was the one who called the immigration department,' Ying said. She closed her eyes, bracing herself for an onslaught of outbursts from Yan.

It didn't come. Yan remained stony-faced.

'Again, I'm sorry. I shouldn't have done it, but after I saw . . . uh . . . you and dad and . . . uh . . . his temporary partner, I just lost my mind. I thought it was the best thing for all of us at that time,' Ying continued uneasily.

Americans. Yan fixed her gaze at Ying. *They can't stand silence, and they can't keep their mouth shut. They have to fill every moment, every space with words, actions, and things. Like their paintings, there isn't any white space in their lives.*

Yan decided it was time to make this easy for Ying. She needed her sister to let her guards down so that she could execute her plan smoothly.

This one's for you, Mom.

The images in her mind of their arrest were replaced with those of her mother standing outside the karaoke bar with her sequin dress and a cigarette in her hand, and of her in the wheelchair in the mental institute, barely holding on to her soul, with her husband kneeling next to her, weeping uncontrollably. Instead of letting her emotions get the better of her, Yan merely said, 'It's all in the past. Let's just forget about it and start over.'

Ying's face had relief written all over it. The reassurance, however, soon gave away to another old wound. Another closure was needed.

'About Charlie—' Ying began.

'Stop,' Yan said. 'I know what you want to say. I wasn't in love with Charlie. I was merely lonely.'

There, I said it, and I meant it. Yan simply had to satisfy her need at that time, and Charlie's pictures were, well, her tools. It was unfortunate that her sister appeared at the wrong time and the wrong place.

'Thank you for telling me that,' Ying said gratefully. 'Phew! That was much easier than I thought. Thank you . . . I mean, thank you for being so forgiving and for straightening things out for me. You're right; this is a new beginning.'

It was done. Yan believed she had said enough to earn that trust she needed. She smiled at her sister and relished in the thought of a new beginning.

Her beginning.

Chapter 19

FAYE

Things were going well.

The meeting with Yan had turned out to be much easier than Faye had anticipated—a tremendous relief for both Faye and Sophia. They had even arranged to visit their mother at the hospice the next day. Yan had mentioned the name of the hospice, and Liu had agreed to drive all of them there.

Faye took time in the afternoon to Google the name of the institute and read up on it. It turned out that the place was more of a mental institute than a 'hospice', but Faye continued to refer to it as so because it was hard for her to imagine her biological mother as a crazy person. Yan had said her mother's condition began soon after Ying's abduction, but when Faye poured over the details, there seemed to be a big gap between the day her mother left the family and the date of her admission to the institute. So far, no one could tell her what had happened during those missing years, but the vicious insinuation that her mother had been a prostitute clung to her mind. Perhaps her dad could sort this out for her, but she doubted he would speak the truth. As for Yan, the emotions between them were too raw. Faye didn't want to risk the connection they had just established with a misstep.

According to Yan, however, their mom was not exactly 'crazy crazy'; in other words, not the grass-chewing, naked-dancing, public-shitting type, but rather, her screwed mind simply made her sit, stare, and talk to herself occasionally. She wouldn't get up to eat, pee, or shit; she would go where she sat, and so required constant caregiving.

The night before, Sophia had decided to not go along with Faye. She had told Faye that she was unwell but her daughter knew that at some level, Sophia felt responsible for the fate of this poor woman and wasn't ready to face her. She doubted that Sophia would ever be ready. But she also felt that she had done enough for her on this trip and deserved space if she needed it.

For some strange reason unknown to Faye, Sophia's absence seemed to have a huge effect on Yan.

'Maybe we should go another day when Sophia's better,' Yan said after Faye got into the rented car at the hotel driveway and casually announced that Sophia wasn't coming.

Yan looked very disappointed, even upset.

'I didn't realize you've developed such an affection for my mom,' Faye exclaimed.

'Well. I just thought that she should meet my mom, that's all. For closure,' Yan mumbled.

'No, silly, I'm the one seeking closure, not her!' Faye laughed, trying to create a sisterly bond with Yan.

Yan managed an unhappy smile and said nothing for the rest of the trip.

The sisters got out at the entrance of the institute, and Liu drove to a nearby parking lot to park the car.

They walked into the building and arrived at a large reception counter, but nobody was there. In fact, the whole reception area was devoid of any activity. Faye looked for a bell to ring, but there was none. She cleared her throat and said loudly, 'Excuse me, is there someone who can help us?'

No one came. She turned to Yan, looking for an answer to such indifference in service attitude, but Yan just hung back and shrugged, as if she didn't want to be a part of the affair. It seemed as if she innately possessed some mutant power that allowed her to disappear into the background whenever she decided to.

'Excuse me, we need help here.' Faye had no choice but to yell again, this time, louder and more demanding.

Eventually, a nurse, or at least her uniform suggested so, emerged from one of the rooms behind the reception counter and walked slowly to the counter, scowling all the way. She looked annoyed to be interrupted by a couple of young girls.

'Who're you looking for?' the nurse hit a high-pitch, malevolent note. 'If you know the ward number, just go directly to the room, do you understand? We don't have time to serve you here.'

With that, she started to walk away, but something made her stop halfway, turned around, and gave Yan a second look. A glimpse of recognition. Her memory began churning. It struck her.

'Wait a minute! You were here two weeks ago, weren't you? Aren't you the daughter of Chen Mei Mei?'

'Yes, we're both her daughters. We would like to see her, please. If you could just tell us the ward she's in, we'll be on our way—' Faye began.

'Not before you pay her medical bills, no! Didn't I tell you when I caught you sneaking into the hospital?'

'What's she talking about?' Faye turned to her sister.

Yan shrugged innocently, 'I've no idea what she's talking about. I wasn't here two weeks ago.'

Faye looked askance at Yan with renewed doubt. *How can Yan not know about the hospital bills? Is this whole thing a setup to make her or Sophia pay the outstanding amount? Was that why she was so upset when she learnt that Sophia wasn't coming with them? Is Yan really smart enough to pull this off? If she needed help with the bills, why didn't she say so in the first place?*

There were many questions in Faye's mind, but this wasn't the right time to address them.

'Look, I've no time for this, all right? Settle the bill or you'll have to take the patient with you. We can't take care of her for free any more. You should be thanking us for not throwing her out of here already,' the nurse said curtly, arms akimbo.

'Isn't this still a Communist country? Isn't medical treatment free here?' Faye retorted brazenly, disliking the nurse immensely.

The nurse glowered at them.

'Shut up, Faye,' Yan whispered sternly. Like many foreigners, Faye had no idea that the gravest sin an outsider could commit in this Communist state was to talk about Communism.

'What's the outstanding amount?' Faye asked, less demanding this time.

Reluctantly, the nurse walked to one of the many metal cabinets behind the reception counter, unlocked it with a key hanging on her lanyard, opened one of the drawers, and started searching. It didn't take her long to find the answer.

'According to our records here, her statements have been outstanding for the past year . . .' The nurse read out the figure, tapping her fingers annoyingly on the table.

There was nothing Faye could do at that point except to pay up. Fortunately, she had some of the money from her father with her. Since she intended to return the whole sum to him, she was sure he wouldn't mind if she used some of it to pay for his wife's medical bills.

'Okay, I'll settle the bill now,' Faye finally said.

The nurse looked surprised, and so did Yan.

'We don't accept credit cards here,' said the nurse with high suspicion about her ability to make payment.

'I'll pay cash. American dollars.'

Yan couldn't stop herself from asking her sister, 'Where did you get that kind of money?'

'Not now,' Faye whispered guardedly, eyes on the nurse as she counted her bills inside her bag—she knew better than flaunting a huge pile of money in front of everyone—and drew out only what she needed. 'You'll find out later.'

It took another long squabble with the nurse, her superior, and her superior's superior to convince them to accept the American dollars. They were finally satisfied after Faye had agreed to give them more than what the exchange rate had indicated was the right amount. And it took even longer to get the paperwork done, but eventually, they were shown to their mother's ward.

The ward was deep into the building, and it took them quite a walk just to reach it. As they got further into the sprawling grounds, the rooms got dirtier, more crowded, and more despondent. The only other time Faye had felt this way was when she had visited an animal shelter, where unwanted, abused, or neglected dogs and cats were temporarily caged until they were adopted or put to sleep. At least the animals had a chance to find new homes and a better life.

Then, they saw their mother. She was left all alone in a wheelchair next to her unmade bed at the far end of her ward, one of the dirtier and more crowded ones. She sat like a piece of furniture; no one seemed to be paying her any attention as nurses and patients bustled around.

Faye knew instinctively that it was her—a mysterious yet magical experience she had never had. Instantly, she was drawn to her, and she felt a sense of closeness to this stranger in front of her, as if she had known this person her entire life. For the first time, Faye understood kindred.

Faye's father had shown a picture of her mother to her before, and she had remembered her as a strong, proud, almost-happy woman with a newborn in her arm. But this old gutted person in a wheelchair looked nothing like that. Faye was looking at an empty shell of a humanoid that was left here to rot away. The soul, tortured and destroyed, had left the frail, withered body long ago.

As they approached her, she slowly lifted her head, which was teetering precariously to a loose-skinned, brittle-boned neck so thin that Faye was afraid the weight of the head would snap it in half. Her dull eyes lit up for a second, and her mouth formed a shape that resembled a smile when she saw them.

She recognizes Yan. Thank God she isn't completely gone.

'You're back. Are you hungry? Would you like something to eat?' she uttered softly, her eyes vacant as she smiled.

'Mommy, I'm here.' As Faye held her mother's gaze, her eyes began to well up. She wasn't sure if they were tears of joy, pity, or compassion for this human being who had suffered immeasurably.

'Do you recognize me?'

Her mother ignored Faye completely as if she couldn't hear or see her. 'Are you hungry? I can whip up a bowl of noodles for you—' she said again.

'Mom, it's me, I'm Ying,' Faye tried again. She took her mother's wrinkled hands into hers and clasped them tightly as tears rolled down her Sephora-ed face. 'I'm sorry it took me so long to come here—'

It was no use. Faye soon realized her mother wasn't even looking at her. Her gaze was focused on Yan as if she was hypnotized by her presence. Yan, as usual, was quiescent.

'C'mon, eat something even if you aren't hungry. Better to have a full stomach than an empty one. I'll make you your favourite *yang chun* noodles,' her mother mumbled.

'Mommy, can you hear me?' Faye pleaded again.

As sudden as her apparent lucidity, Faye's mother stopped talking completely, closed her eyes, and went into a catatonic state.

'What's happening here? What's she doing? Why doesn't she answer me?' Faye turned to Yan and exclaimed, feeling a little hurt that their mother had ignored her completely.

'She's crazy, remember?' Yan said quietly. 'Crazy people do things that defy logic.'

'But papa said that all she remembered and thought about was me. Now that I'm here, why doesn't she even acknowledge me?'

Yan didn't answer her. Instead, she got behind their mother's wheelchair and began pushing her out of the ward.

'Let's take a walk, shall we?' she said.

They went to the so-called garden. It wasn't exactly the most pleasant landscape, not with its few withering shrubs, untended grass, and broken benches, but at least the air wasn't stagnant and miserable like in the ward.

They settled on a stone bench. Faye squatted in front of her mother and tried again.

'Mommy, I'm Ying. I'm your youngest daughter. Do you see me? I'm all grown up now, and I've come back to see you. Please tell me you recognize me—' Faye cried.

Their mother opened her eyes, looked past Faye, and said as if she was picking up from where she had left off. 'Ying, when you come home from school tomorrow, I'll sew you a new dress. It's almost time for New Year celebrations, and you haven't got a new dress.'

'Yes, Mommy, that's me. You do know me,' Faye said, tearing up again. She looked at Yan with relief. A strange sense of wholeness filled her. She felt that she was now part of something, a feeling she'd never had before. She felt she was part of this woman, insane as she might be.

'Not exactly. She knows Ying for sure—' Yan said elusively.

'What do you mean? I'm Ying.'

'Your name is Ying too? My daughter's name is also Ying, named after the eagle. We want her to soar as high as she can when she grows up,' her mother said.

Faye was confused and looked to Yan for answers.

'Mom doesn't remember she has two daughters. She only remembers Ying, and she thinks of her as her only child. She's been like that since I started visiting her almost daily after I got out of prison. And because I'm the only one who visits her, she thinks I'm you. In her world, I don't exist.' Yan sighed.

The revelation shocked Faye beyond words. For the first time, she felt genuinely sorry for her sister. Her pitiful existence, already choked with a lifetime of pain, chaos, and neglect was forgotten even by her very own mother. Yan couldn't imagine the kind of life her sister had lived, a life without an identity of her own. It was bad enough to have to tolerate their father's neglect, but having to pretend she was someone else in the presence of her own mother? How did she do it without turning into some psychopathic serial killer?

And yet, she didn't leave. She was still here, quietly caring for their mother.

Right there, standing in the garden of a mental institute, whatever angst Faye had felt against her sister instantaneously evaporated. Whatever wrong her sister had done to her was immediately forgiven.

'No, no, Mother. I'm Ying. You've TWO daughters, Yan and Ying—' Faye said in exasperation, wanting so much to make things right.

'Don't bother, Ying. She won't listen. Trust me, I've tried many times,' Yan said, trying not to show her pain. She got up from the stone bench and began pushing their mother back to the ward. As Faye watched her sister's slightly bent back, she could almost hear a part of her soul dying.

Chapter 20

YAN

Okay, the hospital bill is settled. That's one big, annoying problem off the list.
Yan thought with relief. It wasn't an easy stint for her to pull off, and
taking more of Ying or Sophia's money was the last thing Yan had
wanted to do. But she couldn't keep her mother in the institute any longer
without paying up, and with her father still in prison, there was no other
way to come up with that kind of money within such a short time.

Although, Yan was surprised that Ying had so much cash on
hand—and it wasn't even Sophia's money—that she could just give it
away without giving it a second thought. Where did she get that? Yan
was very curious, but she had to be patient because the next trip was
more crucial than the last one. She needed to concentrate.

Visiting their father in his prison was next. Liu Gang had arranged
for the visit a few days later. Yan didn't like the fact that Ying would
be seeing their father again, but she knew it was part of the deal she
had to honour. Personally, she was also interested to find out why Ying
had been so insistent on seeing their father after all that had happened.
(Did that have anything to do with the load of cash she was carrying
around?) Plus, although Yan had been corresponding with her father
through letters, she hadn't visited him since she had left prison.

Once again, the ladies piled into the rented car, this time with Sophia. It was a long drive, made longer by the silence in the car. Ying was unusually quiet. She seemed to be still upset by their mother's mental condition and, at the same time, nervous about the imminent visit. Her furtive eyes and frequent flipping of her hair told Yan that she was very anxious to see their father again. Occasionally, she reached out to clutch Sophia's hands and squeezed them tightly. She didn't seem to realize that she was doing it. To Yan, it seemed like an unconscious habit formed over the years. Whenever she needed reassurance, Sophia's hands would be there, ready for her to clasp.

As the old rental hummed loudly along, Liu Gang turned on the radio to break the silence. A Chinese pop idol was belting out a rendition of Chinese rap music. American pop, K-pop, J-pop, rap, R&B—these were the only music the young generation here listened to these days.

Ying had brought with her a large tote bag that she clung to tightly under her armpit throughout the journey. It was obvious to Yan that whatever Ying was carrying had to be something important, even valuable, and had a lot to do with their father. She wanted very much to ask Ying about the bag's content, but she didn't want to jeopardize the trust that she had earned from Ying. Besides, she didn't want to look too eager.

'Any plans now that you're out of prison, Yan?' Ying attempted to start a conversation either to fill the silence or take things off her mind.

'Look after father,' Yan replied.

'Sure, but other than that. Would you like to, say, go back to school or look for a job?'

'I don't know . . . maybe . . .'

'Night school, perhaps? That's good for you, isn't it?' Ying pressed on. She seemed to be unusually interested in Yan's future all of a sudden.

Yan didn't bother to reply. She couldn't imagine why someone who was supposedly so smart could be so stupid.

A long pause ensued. But Ying persisted.

'How did you do in school back then? Were you an A-student? Were there any particular subjects or areas that you were interested in?'

'I missed too many days in school to be able to qualify for an A-student.'

'But would you like to go back to school if you have a chance to? I noticed the many books you have at your apartment. You seem to enjoy reading a lot and these books aren't trashy novels—'

'Who wouldn't want to? But clearly, I can't afford it, can I? I don't have a rich parent or a rich boyfriend like Charlie to sponsor me, do I?' Yan answered curtly.

It worked. The mention of Charlie seemed to be able to shut Ying up immediately. Yan had hit a sore spot. Ying turned away and looked out of the window. It seemed that her relationship with Charlie had been on the rocks since she'd arrived here. Yan had overheard her squabbles with him on her fancy smartphone, and they didn't sound good to Yan. Like many foreigners, Ying and Sophia had grossly underestimated the time it would take them to get things done in China, and they had stayed on much longer than they had intended. And Charlie was getting impatient. He had wanted her to return home as soon as possible because he was going on a long trip to Europe with his parents. Following that, he would leave for Boston for college. He didn't want to leave without properly saying goodbye to her. Besides, his parents were going to throw a huge going-away party for him, and he 'couldn't be at his own big party without a date.' Ying had found his reasons for wanting her to return home 'ridiculous and shallow', and she couldn't believe that he 'would do this to her at such a crucial time in her life'. Each phone conversation would start cordially as they tried to be nice to each other and whispered sweet nothings about how much they missed each other, and as the conversation progressed, tempers would rise, and shouting and name-calling would follow. Before they could finish what they had started to say, they would hang up on each other, leaving Ying feeling more troubled than before.

The rest of the drive to the prison was once again filled with Chinese rap music.

FAYE

If the Grim Reaper were to drag Faye now through the gates of hell to face Hades instead of her father, she would gladly follow him. The Grim Reaper wouldn't need to do any dragging; she would walk ahead of him.

Just the thought of seeing her father again was nerve-wracking enough, not to mention telling him about the call she had made. At the looming sight of the Qincheng Prison, Faye's initial hope that the meeting would bring closure to this episode of her life was beginning to seem preposterous, even laughable.

Liu and Sophia had decided that they would wait in the car. Liu wanted to avoid the bad luck that he believed the prison would inevitably bring him, and Sophia wasn't quite sure about meeting Faye's father again.

The two sisters waited in the visitation room, sitting side-by-side, looking through a scratched pane of glass that would separate them from their father. Wardens were walking around, scrutinizing everyone, with eyes like predators.

It took a long time for the prison wardens to bring their father to them, which made Faye feel even more nervous. Every minute was like a ticking time bomb, ready to blast off her last ounce of will to stay.

Finally, he appeared. And Faye's heart sank.

The moment he saw her, he looked so happy like he could break into a song and dance, beaming and shaking his head incoherently as he walked briskly towards the two girls.

He wasn't making it easy for Faye.

'I knew you would come. I knew it! Nothing can tear our family apart, no, no, not even the American authorities!' he smiled widely at his youngest daughter without so much as a 'hello' to Yan. Faye noticed his head and hands were still shaking uncontrollably from his newfound happiness.

Fuck.

'Hello, Papa. How're you doing?' Faye eased into the conversation.

'I'm great. I'm doing well here. Believe me, I'll be out of here in no time,' he replied, still glowing.

'Well, the good news is, Yan has gotten out of prison early,' Faye turned to Yan, hoping to channel some of his positivity to her.

'Yes, yes . . . I know. Yan has been writing to me,' he said perfunctorily. 'Where are you staying again? I forget.'

'I'm back in our old apartment. No running water and electricity yet, but it'll do for now. Once I get a job, I'll be able to turn the utilities back on. I think the apartment will be a lot more comfortable by the time you get out,' she continued. Yan seemed eager to please.

Unfortunately, their father didn't seem impressed or interested. He nodded slightly and turned to Faye again.

'Remember I told you in my letters how I knew about mom's whereabouts and that I've been visiting her frequently since I was released?' Yan added quickly. She was grasping at anything to keep his attention on her.

'Yeah?'

'Well, I brought Ying to visit her a couple of days ago.'

'You did?' he exclaimed. 'That's great! How's she? Is she getting any better?'

It was too hard a question to answer. Yan deflected.

'And guess what? Faye took care of the hospital bills. We don't have to worry about mommy getting kicked out, at least not for a while,' she said instead.

'Really? That's just wonderful! How I wish I was there. It would've been even better if I were there—' He looked genuinely happy and unaware of the perfect storm that was coming his way.

'Yes, that would've been perfect,' Yan fanned his fantasy.

'It's okay. The important thing is that Ying has reconnected with her. She might seem a little off at times, but trust me, she'll get better as you spend more time with her.'

'I think she's more than "a little off", Papa! She couldn't recognize or even see me. And she thought Yan was me all the while! The whole visit was, well, not a success, if you ask me.' Faye decided to be honest. She was vexed by the false optimism and the trajectory of the conversation. It was making it harder for her to do what she came to do.

Although slightly taken aback by Faye's frankness, her father nevertheless tried to mollify her, 'That's what your mother needs to believe at the moment, Ying. Otherwise, she might do something foolish like harming herself, which she'd attempted before she was institutionalized. She couldn't live with the thought that you were taken right out of her arms. But don't worry, things will change. Perhaps you could visit her more instead of Yan. She'll come around eventually and start to see you as who you are.'

'No, that's not what I meant,' Faye said, exasperated. 'Never mind . . . whatever . . . forget about what I just said.'

The conversation died.

'Papa, I'm here because I've something to tell you—' she began.

'How long will you be here? Did Sophia come with you? Is she here? I've an idea. Maybe she can return to America first while you stay with Yan at the apartment—' he interrupted Faye as soon as she started to speak.

'I won't stay any longer than I can help, Papa. I'm here because I want to break this to you personally—'

'I understand. I forgot that you still need to attend school. You should go back first, and when I get out, we can make arrangements again.'

'Well, we'll see. I'll probably be busy applying to universities and stuff. I've already missed the admission for this year because of . . . all the things that happened.'

'Right, right, university. I can't believe my daughter's going to university soon! I've a better idea. Why don't you apply to the universities here? Beijing University and Tsinghua University are some of the best in the world, surpassing even . . .'

'Papa, please stop!' Faye said a little too loudly. A warden walked towards them; his interest in them increased in tandem with the decibel of Faye's voice. He stood behind her father for a long time before moving on, taking in and evaluating their faces, and warning them silently that he was monitoring their every move closely.

'Can you please listen to what I have to say?' Faye spoke quietly this time, eyes on the warden.

'Can you see that I'm trying not to?' he answered just as quietly. Suddenly, he looked like an inmate awaiting his death row, despondent but desperately trying to cling on to his last hope. His pardon.

Faye looked at him, and a revelation dawned on her.

He knew.

'You know why I'm here. And you know what I did,' she gasped, feeling every bit as foolish as she looked.

He heaved, let out a long sigh, gazed into Faye's eyes, and nodded ever so slightly. He leant back in his wooden chair and looked down at the floor, crestfallen, waiting for the inevitable.

'Why did you pretend that it didn't happen?'

'Some things are better left unsaid,' he said, his voice switched from upbeat to croaky.

A long silence. The buzzing conversations of the other inmates with their loved ones played up the uneasiness inside each of them.

'I didn't mean to hurt you. I just couldn't handle you any longer. I thought it would be best for all of us if you and Yan returned here,' Faye uttered the meaningless words.

He didn't move or say anything but continued to look down.

'We were thrown into a situation we weren't prepared for. And when I saw Yan and you and that whore—' Faye stopped herself. She had gone too far. She could see he flinched at that last word.

'Look, I'm not judging you or anything. And I'm not giving up on us. What I'm trying to say is that we're very different people who live very different lives. So rather than forcing ourselves to be together, maybe it is better if all of us go back to being who we are and start from there again.'

He stared at the floor with the eyes of a hurt puppy.

'You're here. It shows that you still care about us. You just don't wish to admit it because you're ashamed of us.'

'Maybe I still do. I don't know what'll happen in the future, but right, now, I need closure. I need to tell you that I'm sorry for what I've done. Can you forgive me, Papa?'

'Closure, huh?' he repeated, nodding slowly.

There wasn't any hope left. It was final; he was pronounced a dead man walking.

'And about the gift you've asked me to retrieve from the apartment,' she whispered, not wanting to draw any further attention from the warden.

Faye opened her tote bag slightly and showed him through the pane the stacks of dollar bills bundled in elastic bands.

'I came here intending to return it to you, but I've thought of a better way to use the money.'

Yan looked confusingly at the bricks of bills. 'Wait. What's going on? Where did you get so much money? How much is in there?' Yan demanded.

'Not so loud, Yan,' Faye said. She was very aware of the warden's renewed interest in them the moment he detected the word "money". 'I was going to tell you about this. There's twenty-five thousand in here, less the sum I paid for mommy's hospital bill. They are all from papa.'

Yan looked at her father as if the world had turned upside down, as if the right had become wrong, and wrong, right.

'You have so much money, and you give it all to Ying? I know all you care about is her, but you left nothing at all for me? Even when you know I've been struggling to survive? Even when you know she has everything and I have nothing?'

Again, Li Fu said nothing.

'I'm not returning the money to you, Papa. Sophia and I have already discussed this, and we've agreed that it's the right thing to do. We're going to set up a college fund for Yan so that she can continue her education. She's a smart girl, Papa, and she has the potential to do great things. Didn't you notice the books in your apartment? She'd read them, and from the notes on the margins of the pages, I can see that she understood a great deal of them. We'll use the money on her, and her only. If this isn't enough, Sophia is prepared to top it up with her own money,' Faye added.

Yan looked at her, too surprised for words.

Li Fu nodded without looking up. Slowly, he picked himself up from the wooden chair and turned to the exit door.

He left without another word.

* * *

The wind was howling outside the prison, blowing in the first winter chill from the ocean. As Faye and Yan walked towards the car where Liu Gang and Sophia awaited, Yan reached out and held Faye's hand. Faye was surprised, but she accepted the gesture gladly and grasped her sister's hand firmly.

Without turning, Yan said softly, 'Thank you, Sister.'

Faye smiled.

Chapter 21

YAN

Li Fu lit his first cigarette since leaving the prison and inhaled deeply, filling his lungs with toxic pleasure and taking the edge off his nerves. It felt relaxing and liberating. As he took another drag, he heard a familiar voice calling behind.

'Papa, smoking isn't allowed here.'

Familiar yet different.

He threw the cigarette on the ground, crushed it with the heel of his shoe, and smiled as he turned around.

'There, it's gone. Happy?' he said.

'No. You're supposed to throw the cigarette butt into a bin, not on the ground,' said the voice. She picked up the butt and dropped it into the empty paper coffee cup she was holding.

'My goodness! You look . . . you look so beautiful . . . so poised,' he gasped. 'What have you done to yourself?'

'Nothing! Well, nothing except getting myself an education, I guess.' She smiled as she walked over to her father and held his hand firmly. 'How are you, Papa?'

'I'm fine. I'm finally out! That's all that matters.'

'Wow, is that you, Yan? My goodness, I wouldn't have recognized you on the streets,' Liu Gang, who had just walked up to them, exclaimed. 'You're a completely different person from the last time I saw you, like, what? Two years ago?'

'Three. Good different or bad different?'

'Do you even need to ask? Good different, of course! Confident, beautiful, and so full of life!'

'Expect only the best from an Edinburgh University scholar,' said another female voice from behind. 'Hi, Liu Gang! Do you remember me? Yan's sister?'

'Ying! How can I forget?' said Liu, shaking Ying's hand.

'You look good yourself, Liu,' Yan said, inspecting the Lexus he had just got out of. 'And prosperous.'

'It's all investor's money, I'm afraid,' he quipped.

'How's that?'

'I started an IT firm. Now, I've to work my ass off to deliver the return on investment to my investors.'

'Ah . . . dreams do come true!' Yan said, feeling happy for her old friend.

'Hi Papa,' Ying turned and smiled at her father. 'So glad you're finally out. How was the drive with Liu?'

'Can't complain,' he replied. 'I'm just glad that there was someone to pick me up from prison.'

'C'mon, Papa! Did you really think we'll forget about you?'

'Thank you, girls,' he said gratefully.

Ying turned to everyone and said, 'Shall we?'

They began ascending the steps of a small hill towards the columbarium.

'This is not bad at all. Tranquil. I think your mom likes it here,' Li said with a mixture of melancholia and relief as he looked around. The girls had done a good job in settling Mei's post-mortem matters after she passed away two and a half years ago, one of which included picking a columbarium to keep their mother's ashes.

'My only regret was not being able to bid farewell to your mom before she passed,' he sighed.

'Mommy went peacefully, Papa. We were both there by her side,'
Yan said. 'I think it was best for her too.'

'Yeah, I suppose you're right.'

They climbed on in silence, enjoying the crisp air and the serenity
of the place.

'The letters I received from both of you while I was in prison,' Li
began again. 'They're the best things that happened to me. They helped
me see and understand . . . things.'

*Yes, Papa. How can we forget those letters? One letter a week—that was
what Ying had told me. They were Ying's therapist's idea. And Ying had forced
me to write to you too. I was sceptical at first—that I admit—because I knew
you would not take it well although it was liberating for both of us. Changed our
perspectives. But you were furious at first. Do you remember the names you had
called us? Ingrates? Rotten daughters? Patricides? How angry those letters sounded
when you decided to write us back. But Ying's therapists had explained to us that
it was part of the process, and she was right. You did calm down after a while and
realized how foolhardy your actions were. How I wept when you realized that you
had not one but two daughters whom you could love! And how I loved you when you
finally understood that I needed to leave you and live my life, lest I took the same
path as my mom.*

*And Papa, I want to tell you it's a life worth living. I have an education and
opportunities to dream and find myself. I understand self-care and forgiveness. In a
roundabout way, I should thank you for it because it was made possible with your
twenty-five thousand dollars.*

Li stopped climbing. He looked around as he spoke, not wanting
to meet Yan's eyes.

'All these years, I thought I was doing the right thing. And I've
been so blindsided by my obsession that I lost track of you, Yan.
I wish I could see it earlier—' He looked ashamed and guilt-ridden.

'It's a good day today, Papa,' Yan said quickly. 'Let's not dwell in
the past.'

'That's right, Papa. Whatever we wanted to say was said in those
letters. We've all done bad things to one another, but we've agreed that
all has been forgiven, remember?'

'You're right. You're right, no more words,' he said, failing to hide his emotions.

'By the way, when are you completing your university studies in Scotland, Yan?' Li asked, changing the topic.

'I'm only in my first year, Papa. I had to spend the first two years in private school learning English and catching up on the other subjects. I just completed my "A" levels last year,' said Yan.

'Which she passed with flying colours!' Ying teased. She liked to see Yan colouring up. Yan still wasn't used to accepting praises, despite the many she had got from her teachers and mentors at school.

'Is the money enough?' Li asked quietly. Much as he didn't want to bring it up, he had to ask. 'Most of it must be gone by now.'

'I've applied for scholarships, so I don't have to pay for tuition fees. And I have part-time jobs over there. I'm doing fine, Papa. Don't worry about me,' Yan said.

Li nodded.

'And Papa, I've not told you this, but I'll most likely not come back even after I've obtained my degree. I want to try to get a job and build my life there,' she added. She had reached this decision after a long struggle with herself. The old Yan wanted to return home and take care of her father, but the new Yan told herself it was time to let go.

Li felt a pang of sadness. He felt as if he was about to lose another daughter.

'No, no. It's amazing that you're getting yourself a good education. I should've done that for you years ago. You stay for as long as you wish. Don't worry about me. I'll be fine,' Li said, feigning a smile.

'Thanks Papa.'

'We don't need to be physically together to be a family. I understand that now,' he added.

'Hey, Ying's the one doing amazing things. She has enrolled in a Master's programme at Boston University and several of her short stories were recently published. She's the clever one,' Yan said, trying to lighten the mood.

'They are only for the school's publication. It's really nothing to shout about!' Ying rolled her eyes.

'You're both doing well,' Li said. 'I can't be any happier,'

They reached the top of the hill and entered the columbarium. From afar, Li spotted the picture of Mei placed in front of the urn, which was nestled in one of the many small cubicles that neatly lined the walls of the columbarium. They stood in front of the cubicle and like a rehearsed performance, bowed three times to the photograph in unison. Then, the girls busied themselves with cleaning the cubicle, dusting the urn and the picture frame, and putting fresh flowers in the vase.

Li picked up his wife's picture and looked at it for a long time.

'Do you see this, Mei? We're a family, at last,' he whispered.

He smiled a blissful smile.